IDENTITY THEFT

Laura Lee

"For he looks at himself and goes away and at once forgets what he was like."
                                            —James 1:24

Published by Elsewhere Press
Rochester Hills, MI

ISBN: 0-9657345-4-4

Acknowledgments

I owe a debt of gratitude to Kimery Campbell for her support. Without her championing of this project, this book would not have been published. I am grateful that so many members of my Birmingham Unitarian Church community supported its creation. Thank you to my early readers Sarika Patkotwar and Courtney Tetreault for their encouragement and feedback and to my U.K. liason Ruth Jones for help with American/British translation.

Thank you to my editor Shelly Caldwell, whose keen eye for detail much improved this manuscript. I am especially grateful for her ideas on formatting the e-mail messages and chat conversations in the text. Thank you to cover designer Mike Surber for his imaginative interpretation of the concept of "Identity Theft."

Many thanks to everyone who supported Identity Theft including (but not limited to) Judy Amir, Michele Bolton, Jodi Connors, Becky Engleson, Ivan Engleson, John Emmert, Barb Eschner, Jennifer Hunter, Kara Hunter, Dianne Ilkka, Barbara Kurko, Lawrence Larson, Carol Lee, Jennifer Lee, Carolyn Palmer, Kaaren Peters, Lynda Pringle, Sue Schier, Patricia Schwing, Helen Stewart, Fred Straky, Courtney Tetreault, Tracy Utech and Barbara Woolf.

The Tyranny of 800 Numbers

"This call may be monitored. ..."

When she saw the 800 number on the caller ID, Candi did not want to pick up the phone, but she had been through the routine long enough to know that the only way to stop them from harassing you was to talk to them. She had just come home from work and was still dressed in a green fitted blazer and matching slacks. The outfit had looked much better in the catalog on the size 2 model than on her size 12 frame. She plopped down on the couch, kicked off her uncomfortable high heel shoes, and waited to be connected to a human being.

"Hello, my name is Susan," said the caller.

"Your name is not Susan," Candi wanted to say. "How is the weather in Bangalore?" She didn't say that, though. She sat and waited for "Susan" to finish her script.

"I am calling in regards to your Capital One card. Your payment of $105 is five days late. Can you make that payment today to bring your account current?"

She wanted to say, "If I could, don't you think I would have?" There was really no point in saying anything like that. In harried moods, she had tried. It just made the call last longer.

"No," she said.

"When will you be able to make that payment?"

"April 5th," she said with a tone of certainty. She didn't know if she would be able to make the payment then, but the woman on the line didn't care about that. She just needed to plug a date into the computer. Once the right boxes were checked, Capital One would leave her alone for a while.

Candi understood that "Susan's" boss— the bank—didn't really care, either. They were thrilled her payment was late because it meant they could charge her late fees and jack up her rates. So everyone was happy. They just had to do this little bit of theater from time to time. Sometimes it amazed her to think they hired someone half a world away for this charade. Years of computer science and the space program had to happen in order for a woman in India to bully an office worker in suburban San Diego about a $100 payment that was five days late.

As she confirmed her address and phone number with the caller, Candi played with her shoulder-length brown hair. She half-consciously examined each strand, checking for split ends and light color. She had found a couple of grays that morning. She tried to convince herself they had actually been blonde hairs. Age 29 was far too early to start finding grays.

When Susan's computer form was filled out and everyone had played their roles, Candi unplugged the phone from the wall. She wasn't in the mood to act out that particular bit of kabuki again today.

She turned on the television and let it play in the background as she heated up her dinner—leftover Little Caesar's Pizza ($5 for a large). They key to reheating pizza without making the dough gummy is to put it in the oven and not the microwave. Candi set the oven to 450°, pulled out a baking sheet, covered it with a roll of aluminum foil and plopped two slices on top, but she tossed the tray into the oven before it had a chance to preheat.

Candi didn't have a kitchen, exactly; it was more of a food-making area. Her apartment consisted of three rooms. The front room, in which she was standing, was a combination living, dining, and kitchen space. The oven and refrigerator were in the back corner a few steps from the television and couch. Her bedroom was just behind the kitchenette through a doorway. If you needed the bathroom, you had to walk through the bedroom to get there. The bathroom, curiously, was almost as large as the living room.

The odd layout was the result of how it had been constructed. Hers was the only permanent building in the center of a trailer park. The single-story house had presumably belonged to the landlords at one point. They moved out and divided it into two apartments by boarding up two doorways (one in the living room, one in the bath) with plywood.

On the other side of the living-room plywood was a woman in her seventies who lived with her adult son, an Amway salesman who was always trying to convince Candi to take a spot beneath him in the sales pyramid. The old woman was almost deaf, so she kept the volume of the television on full. The plywood did little to absorb the sound waves. Even if Candi been somehow unable to hear every word of the programs, she would have been able to spot the comedies. The neighbor woman was easily amused and was constantly responding with a full-throated "Whoop-whoop-whoop!" The other quirk about Candi's place was that if she didn't keep the front door locked, people were always walking straight in without knocking. They assumed it was the rental office.

Candi had moved into this unglamorous space after losing her condo after the housing bubble burst. She had managed to sell it at a loss and get out from her underwater mortgage without suffering the indignity of foreclosure, but she had never quite recovered from it all.

As she waited for the oven to heat up, Candi took two beers out of the fridge. She drank one in a couple of gulps, as if downing a glass of water. The first beer was just to stop her from feeling like a raw nerve. It would be up to the second beer to make her relax.

On the television, a reporter was making a serious face in a cut-away from an interview with a transgender woman. The woman looked about as feminine as anyone else Candi saw on the street. "I was never comfortable in my body," she said. "I wasn't comfortable in the role society assigned me based on my gender."

Candi wondered in a vague way how she knew she was not transgender. She, too, often felt uncomfortable with the body she'd been given. It didn't quite represent what she believed she was on the inside. She also found herself uncomfortable much of the time in the role society assigned her based on her gender. Yet, she was quite clear for some reason that she was, in fact, a woman— she just wasn't all that good at it.

Candi picked up the remote control and flipped through the channels until she came to a cooking competition. The televised food made her hungry. She pulled the pizza out of the oven before it was completely warm. She put two pieces of the lukewarm pizza on a plate and sat down to eat in front of the TV. On the screen was a commercial for LifeLock, a company that protects its customers against identity theft. She wondered if they could perform their work in reverse. She woke up every day longing to have her credit history stolen. So far, no takers.

A pile of mail was on the sofa where she had dropped it as she came through the door. She ran her fingers over the pink envelope on top. It was a cancellation notice from her auto insurance company. Candi Tavris. At least they spelled the name right. Half the time some data entry person "corrected" the spelling of her last name to "Travis."

She had never much liked her name. As a kid, she'd wanted to be called Daphne after the character on Scooby-Doo. At that time her first name was spelled with the more standard "y." When she got to junior high school she had decided she wanted to sound more grown up. She asked her friends to start calling her "Candace." They did, but they did it in a sing-song tone to make fun of her pretension. So she gave up on being "Candace" and decided to give "Candy" a new spelling instead. As a grown woman, "Candi" struck her as a porn star name, up there with Bambi and Trixie. The tentacles of bureaucracy had her now, though. The computers knew her as Candi, and that's who she had to be.

Underneath the pink envelope Candi found a notice that she had been pre-approved for a Platinum Visa card— reserved exclusively for elite people like her.

She remembered when she was working her way through college as a waitress. There was a guy she liked who worked in the kitchen. He was sandy-haired, cute, funny. She had never been the one guys hit on—that was her younger sister Jackie's role—and his attentions actually made her look forward to clocking in at Applebee's. Then one day her potential new boyfriend told her, "If anyone calls looking for me, I'm not here." He was hiding from creditors, which could mean only one thing: He was a loser. When he finally got up the nerve to ask her out, she turned him down flat. She later learned that he had gone on to invent some video game; made a million dollars before the age of 30.

She had no idea how she had gotten to this place—in debt and living in the one house in a trailer park. That was not supposed to be her fate. As a teenager she had been the smart one, the responsible one. Jackie was popular and pretty, but Candi was serious, studious, and expected to excel. Jackie was voted best dressed and best smile in the school yearbook but Candi took home all of the academic awards and accolades.

She had done what she was supposed to. She went to college, got a degree, got a decent job. If she'd splashed out on shoes or purses, gone off on vacations, bought a big-screen TV, at least she'd have something to show for her debt. But for the life of her, she couldn't remember where the money had gone. Student loans, car payments, gas to get to her job. Somehow the powers that be had made going into debt seem like the responsible thing to do. "You have to build up your credit," they said. So she carried a revolving balance. Then she needed dental work, so she carried a little more. The car broke down and she put that on the card. Buying a condo, the banker had explained, was not going into debt—it was an investment. She could afford something just a bit out of her price range. It would pay off down the line because housing prices and her wages could only go up.

Meanwhile Jackie had dropped out of college in her sophomore year. She married an executive at Boeing and lived in a huge custom-built home. It was actually featured in a design magazine. With no children, Jackie's main occupation, from what Candi could tell, was shopping.

Candi worked in the packaging department of a technology company. She didn't actually pack things, she sat at a computer tracking inventory and placing orders to make sure there were the right number and kind of packages to contain all of the kinds of things they shipped. When people ask kids what they want to be when they grow up, they never answer something like that.

When the economy blew up, the aftershocks rocked her employer. "Downsizing." They hadn't actually used this word at the informational meeting where they lowered the boom. They brought in a cheerful human resources woman in a perfect suit. She reminded Candi of the models at the annual technology conventions.

"It's a challenging time, but an exciting one," Smiley Spokesmodel said. Candi imagined her gliding around on a circular platform modeling some virtual reality goggles. She used the word "competitiveness" the word "opportunity" the word "empowerment" and the word "change." Then she pulled out a chart with Corporate's concept of a new staff organization. "The Way Forward" was the header.

The chart did not include her position.

"This is just a proposal right now," Smiley Spokesmodel said. "This may not be what it looks like, but there will be changes."

Candi wondered whose job it had been to design the "Way Forward" chart and select the colors. Did a "transition expert" suggest that the turquoise would be calming? How much had she been paid? It was a simple design; only a few colors and lines to make it clear that she was no longer needed and all the work she'd done over the years for them meant nothing.

Candi imagined herself turning up the speed on the technology show platform, sending Smiley Spokesmodel flying into a bank of computer screens.

Overnight the mood at work was completely transformed. Someone came up with the expression BTM for "before the meeting." For example: "I had been working on a big proposal BTM but now I can't be bothered." From there ATM came naturally. For example: "I've been having a hard time sleeping ATM."

The first "exciting changes" happened a month later. One Friday at 3 p.m. a dozen people were handed letters outlining the details of their severance packages. They were told to clean out their desks as a couple of guys with "Security" t-shirts looked on. No one tried to punch the boss, trash the office, or make a scene. There was no shouting or crying. There was, instead, an appalling quiet as those who had been spared gazed on the blank faces of the condemned. None of them were yet able to process the emotional overload of how drastically their lives had changed.

Candi's co-worker Lydia made a show of faxing out resumes on the office copier. Lydia was in her mid-40s. She was full figured and had short hair—blonde, but with the tell-tale texture of dyed hair. She was gregarious and gossipy. She had no trouble speaking her mind.

"I am going to sit at my desk and update my résumé for an hour and then I'm going to fax five copies out on the office fax machine. Does anyone have a problem with that?"

No one tried to stop her. Soon most of the office had joined in the ritual in their own, more quiet, ways. Each fax was a small protest; symbolic, but useless. Candi felt like a giraffe on a battlefield. The hunters were coming. She had no place to hide.

She had written her letter of resignation—three times. In it she explained that she had too much pride to stay there and play their game, to serve them on their terms and to wait for them to determine her fate. She never delivered it. That was the worst part of being in debt. Pride was a luxury item now, out of her reach like caviar and champagne. She had to stay in that toxic environment as long as she possibly could to avoid going under completely.

*****

Candi turned the TV off and picked up a set of headphones: real ones, not those little iPod ear buds. (When she played music out loud it bothered the Whoop Whoop Whoop lady.) She plugged the headphone into the jack on her laptop and clicked on a playlist with the title "Work Antidote." It was full of her favorite songs, most of which were by the

80s pop star Blast. The music reminded her that there was something still alive inside her even if the world seemed intent on shutting it down. I am not my credit score. I am musical, I am sensual, I am alive.

I AM.

Through the headphones the sound was centered right behind her eyes, as if it emanated from her own mind. She took a deep breath and let the music fill up the space in her head where the worry was normally contained. Candi could not explain why Blast intrigued her so much. She was not the right age to be his fan. She hadn't grown up watching his videos on MTV, so she couldn't feel nostalgia for them. She had discovered his entire back catalog at once after Lydia posted one of his videos in her Facebook stream. (Candi was "friends" with most of the people she worked with.) Something about Blast sparked her imagination from the moment she laid eyes on him.

The fact that she had come a bit too late to experience him in his prime made him all the more special to her. It meant he belonged, in a sense, to her alone. She did not have to share him with a whole generation. He was like a perfectly polished gem that she had discovered by accident in a thrift shop.

Blast, she felt, was a man out of his own time too. He was lumped in with the "artists of the 80s" simply because that's when he happened to have had his greatest fame. The 80s synth-pop virus only affected a couple of his songs. His sound was all his own, and it was as contemporary as anything she heard streaming today. Most of the songs were not about love and heartbreak. They were a call to action, rallying the listeners to create a new society, a new world.

And, of course, Blast was sexy. On stage, when he moved, you couldn't take your eyes off him. He had flowing red hair, a square jaw, and high cheekbones made all the more prominent by the liberal application of stage makeup, dark eyeliner, war paint. His broad shoulders were accentuated by a slim waist. He clothed this body in tight leather slacks paired with colonial military jackets. He was tough, masculine, powerful;

and yet he didn't appear to take his "Blast" character all that seriously. In every video you could catch a self-depreciating grin—beautiful, wide. He smiled with his entire face.

Candi sat down in front of her computer and opened the folder with her collection of Blast pictures. His face had the calming effect of a drug. When she looked at him she forgot to think about Capital One, or how she was about to lose her job or how she managed to miss out on what she was supposed to be doing with her life.

Next she went to YouTube, hoping someone had uploaded something new, rescued another interview from a Betamax tape. When she didn't find any, she clicked on a familiar clip, a concert video from when Blast was young.

Her favorite part of this particular concert video clip was not his music at all. It was a single gesture in the pause between songs. As the audience cheered, he stopped and smiled to himself, taking it all in. His eyes fell to the floor. Then he raised his left hand and ran it through his hair. That was it. That was the moment: a simple, unconscious gesture. It was the real man shining through. She scrolled back and watched it over and over. She wanted to run her own fingers through that hair.

The motion made visible all the freckles on his arm, too. He was a redhead, so of course he had freckles, but with the stage makeup you never saw them. She wondered if he noticed the freckles when he was making tea and he picked up a mug, or was he as unconscious of his body as she was most of the time of her own? She wondered if the freckles covered his whole body or if there was somewhere that they stopped. If they did stop—where?

She clicked "replay" to watch the video again. In her mind, she moved Blast out of the video, off the stage, and right in front of her. When he saw her approaching, he slung his guitar to his side. He smiled that amazing smile and glanced at his feet, but only for a moment. His eyes met hers. She reached up and stroked his hair. Then she ran her hands along the coarse seam of his leather trousers until it came to rest in the warmth of his inner thigh.

Spider Under Glass

Ethan Penn's desk was right under the gold record. It hung a bit crooked, no matter how many times he tried to adjust it. He had some ideas about blue tack; it worked on his posters at home, but he never got around to bringing the stuff in. More annoying was the spider. At some point it had crawled under the glass and died. It had been there, preserved in the golden grooves since Ethan had gotten his job, about four months before. He looked at the dead bug every day. "Someone should get that out of there." But it was Blast's gold record, not Ethan's, and he was not going to be the one to take it apart and manage to break it somehow.

Ethan's desk wasn't actually a desk, for that matter. His computer screen sat on a door that was laid flat and balanced across a couple of two-drawer filing cabinets. He was the new guy, an add-on employee, and his job was simple. He did whatever no one else in the office wanted to be bothered with.

His immediate supervisor was the office manager, Brenda. She was a heavy-set woman in her early 40s. She wore her hair in a stylish black bob. She was a rocker and she dressed it, and yet she still managed to stay age-appropriate. So many middle-aged women made themselves look years older by trying to look too young. Brenda did the bulk of things; she answered the phones, handled bookings, dealt with all of the daily mini-crises that came with keeping a show on the road.

She'd been with Blast for 17 years—since he moved to America from London. She had a crush on him, which she seemed to believe was a well-kept secret. She was happily married, though, with a couple of kids, and clearly had no intention of rocking the boat. Another woman, Maggie, whose job was to line up free hotel rooms in exchange for advertising, told Ethan that Brenda once said she valued the unique role of being the one female friend Blast hadn't slept with.

Along with Brenda and Maggie, there was a used-car-salesman kind of guy who sold tour sponsorships, there was an accountant who came three times a week, a girl who came in about as often to handle on-line orders for concert merchandise, and a business lawyer who came in when called. Ethan did everything else.

He answered phones and routed calls to the right people. He ran things off on the photocopier. He mailed off promo kits to theaters that might like to book a gig. Sometimes the guys on the road needed someone to take care of something personal back home in L.A. and a lot of those tasks fell on him. "I ordered this thing and I am having it sent to the office, and when it comes I need you to send it to me at ..." Ethan had gotten pretty good at figuring out how to time deliveries so they caught up with people constantly on the move.

He opened fan mail and sent back the form letters and photos. "Blast gets so much fan mail he does not have time to respond personally, but he appreciates ..." It was time-consuming and only a bit more interesting than any other job stuffing envelopes. Most of the letters were predictable, "Your music means so much to me ... it got me through a hard time ..." Every once in a while a letter stood out, it was touching or personal or contained a request from a charity. He put those aside for the more senior staff to look at and follow up on. Then there were the strange ones: a woman who thought she was an alien and she and Blast came from the same planet, a guy who thought Blast was stealing songs out of his subconscious, a woman who sent a bunch of pictures she had made with Photoshop—the rock star's head on the bodies of hunted animals. He didn't answer those. They went into a special file, just in case.

The office was not set up to greet fans, but the address appeared various places and they occasionally showed up anyway. Ethan talked to them when they did. If they had come a long distance, as some had, he would give them a cup of coffee and chat with them for a while before sending them on their way. He liked the conversations because the fans looked at him like he was the luckiest guy in the world, not a stoner who still lived in his mom's basement.

"How did you get this job? You are so lucky."

He'd gotten the job through a friend, which was the way Blast filled most of his office positions—personal recommendation. Ethan spent a lot of time hanging out in bars with live music. He'd gotten friendly with a bass player whose best friend was the sound guy on Blast's current tour.

"So drop out of college and spend your time in bars, that's my career advice," he said. It always got a laugh.

The female fans sometimes flirted with him. He knew they were hoping to get in with him to meet Blast. He wasn't the type of guy that got swooned over. He was 22 years old, 6'2" and skinny, all arms and legs and knees and elbows. "Lanky" his mother called him. "Gawky" is what it meant. His nose was too big for his face and he had a mop of curly brown hair.

A lot of the visitors would follow up by asking how they could get a job. There was one guy who came in carrying a skateboard. When Ethan said they were all set for employees, he said "Can't you fire someone or something?"

The most common fan question was "Does Blast ever come in here?" and its variants "Is Blast here now?" "Do you know him?" "What is he like?" "What is it like working for him?" "Do you get weird fans in here?"

"What," he always wanted to say, "You mean besides you?"

There was one middle-aged woman who wanted to buy a Blast T-shirt. Ethan went into the back and got it for her. Then she wanted to know if Blast had worn the shirt. When he said he was pretty sure he hadn't, she suggested that they could make more money if they had Blast put on all the shirts before they sold them. She also thought they could make a ton of money by selling locks of rock star hair on ebay. This freaked Ethan out a little bit.

A lot of the time Ethan just sat around and surfed the internet, which was what he was doing when his friend Ale arrived. (Ale was his nickname, earned because he had fair skin and the kind of blond eyebrows that disappear: Pale Ale. His real name was Lloyd.) Ale made the international gesture for smoking a spliff (two fingers pinched in front of the lips then moved front and back) and then pointed out the door.

"Hey, I'm done for the day," Ethan called out to Brenda, "Taking off!"

"Bye, Ethan. See you tomorrow."

When Ethan got outside he found Ale in the parking lot, pacing around his Kia.

"Come on," Ale said, opening the door. "We're going to the park. Sasha's got a bonfire going."

"Who's Sasha?" Ethan said as he hopped in.

"Sasha. Come on, I told you about Sasha. The girl I met at the thing."

"Right."

"You've got to pay more attention to stuff, man."

"So you're really into this girl?"

"She's great. You'll see."

"Will there be other girls there?"

"Not until you find one. Seriously, this dry spell is really pathetic. You're the only one I know who can name drop that you work for a rock star and still not get laid."

"I work for a rock star, that's different from being a rock star, idiot."

"Working for a rock star is close enough. I run the one hour photo machine at the drug store. Spend all day looking at everyone else's vacations and birthdays. There is no way I should have more luck with women than you."

14

"When you can only afford to buy her half a Big Mac, I don't think that stuff matters much."

"Sex power," Ale said. "That's what rock stars have. Who is Blast? He's some dorky English guy. Strap on a guitar and rock 'n' roll. Use what you've got."

The friends had arrived at their destination; they followed a narrow trail back into a clearing. The bonfire was going full force, with sparks floating up toward the overhanging trees. Around the blaze were three plastic lawn chairs, two cases of cheap beer and a girl in a tube dress, squatting down to poke the logs with a stick. When she saw Ale, she stood up.

"Hi, Baby," she said.

Her long, straight, brown hair was decorated with a small braid woven with feathers. Ethan could tell she'd had a good head start on the pot.

"I'm Sasha," she said to Ethan. "It's short for Alexandria."

"How is Sasha short for Alexandria?" Ethan asked.

"It's a Russian thing," she said.

Ethan had no idea what that meant, but he nodded anyway.

"Come on," she said taking Ethan's hand. "I got some great stuff at a festival in Massachusetts from this guy who plays the didgeridoo."

Sasha liked to drive around the country and go to stuff like that. She made dresses out of hemp fabric and sold them for gas money.

She pulled a glass pipe, a lighter and a plastic bag full of herb out of a little leather handbag. "This is called 'paraphernalia' " she said, holding up the pipe. "I had to buy it in New York. It's illegal to sell in Massachusetts."

"I think the pot is illegal there too," Ale said.

"Here," she said, handing the lighter to Ale. "You do it; I don't want to set my nail polish on fire. It's flammable, you know."

"I think it's only flammable when it's wet," Ale said. "They use alcohol because it evaporates quickly. So when the polish hardens, it stops being flammable."

Ethan was surprised that Ale had given that much thought to how nail polish worked. Ale lit up, took a hit, and passed the pipe to Ethan. Ethan went over to one of the chairs and sat down before taking a drag. Ale and Sasha joined him in the other seats.

"You know in England they call it nail varnish," Sasha said. "I think they're right, don't you? When you varnish something it changes color. Polish is making something shinier. You don't polish your nails. You change their color."

"They also call cigarettes 'fags.' " Ethan said.

"Cigarettes are kind of homosexual," Ale said. He made a gesture that was a combination of smoking a cigarette and sucking a cock.

Ethan laughed.

"You're being gross," Sasha said.

Ale and Ethan looked at each other. Ethan could tell they were both thinking the same thing: "If dick jokes are out, what are we going to talk about?"

For all his bluster, Ale was just as intimidated by women as Ethan was, just as nervous about getting it wrong. Ale, though, would be curling up next to Sasha tonight. Ethan would be spraying air freshener, dropping Visine in his eyes and sneaking in so his mom wouldn't wake up and see him stoned.

They popped open beers and smoked and talked about the fire, the leaves, and the music at the festival. Through some thin trees Ethan could see a group of girls walking around their own campfire, poking it with sticks. He saw them mostly in silhouette; he caught a flutter of long hair, a feminine hand gesture, a tilt of the head. He could hear their distant laughter.

In his imagination he went over to them. "Can I join you?" They welcomed him like the bikini clad women in a beer commercial. They were overcome by his body spray or his soap and they crowded around him to muss his hair and pose. There are guys who would go over, strike up a conversation, and still be sitting and laughing with them three hours later. Ethan was not one of those guys. So he sat, hoping that the girls would get lonely and decide on their own that they wanted to join his group at their fire. It never happened.

Instead, he talked with his two friends until the sun went down. By then they were pretty well fried and they sat for a long time saying nothing, gazing at the flame, listening to the crackle and pop of moisture in the wood.

"Why is everyone so ambitious?" Ethan finally said. "I mean, why, you know what I mean?"

"Yeah, totally," Ale said.

"I mean, all you need … all you need …" Ethan said.

"They want you in the game," Ale said.

"In the game," Ethan added. "Like all you really need, you know what I'm saying? This stuff."

"That's completely right," Ale said. "I totally agree. I mean, why should you run around and …"

"It's a racket. A communist conspiracy," Ethan said.

"A capitalist conspiracy," Ale said.

Ethan was sure he had just discovered something really important but verbalizing it was too much effort, so he stopped talking.

"I've been thinking about that too," Sasha said, without looking at either of the guys. "It's not about money and power; rich and famous. We're all art." She was waving her hands in front of her face in a slow sweeping gesture. "God is an artist, and we're all his art. He sat down and sketched us and sculpted us. Art doesn't have to do anything. It just has to be."

"That is the deepest fucking thing I've ever heard," Ale said.

"He must have been in a Picasso mood when he sketched my face," Ethan said. No one laughed. At first Ethan was annoyed. Then he thought if they didn't laugh, maybe it wasn't a joke. Maybe all the ugly people were some kind of abstract masterpieces.

As if reading his mind Sasha said, "To God, it's all beautiful."

Ethan thought they had just stumbled onto the very meaning of existence. They held the key to something profound everyone else had lost.

Then he wondered if you could go to hell for wanting to bang your best friend's girl.

Laundry

Ollie was in a good mood when his day began. It was his first free day in three weeks of touring, and he didn't have to pack and check out of the hotel for another couple of days. This was the height of luxury. He was dressed in a pair of navy blue sweat pants—he'd slept in them—and a new t-shirt he had stolen out of the merch. The shirts cost about $1.20 each to make in Bangladesh, and they sold them for $30. It was a racket, but it was also the main thing that kept the tours profitable. The design featured a cartoon version of Ollie in his Blast persona. It was the only clean shirt he could find. He looked nothing like his alter ego at the moment, his face hidden a bit behind a pair of horn-rimmed glasses. He wore contacts on stage. It had been a while since he'd colored his shoulder-length red hair, so the roots were coming in grey. (Hats and bandanas disguised this when he performed.)

The television was on: a program about some guys in Texas who restore junk cars to their former glory and try to flip them to make a profit. Ollie glanced at it from time to time as he pulled stale garments out of his suitcase and sorted them into piles by color on the bed. No washing underwear in the sink today—this hotel had a guest laundry!

Once all of the clothes were stacked up, he grabbed a couple of plastic bags from a side pocket in his suitcase. He always kept a few plastic bags. You never knew when you were going to need them. They can serve as trash bags when those tiny hotel rubbish bins get full, you can use them to wrap up toiletries that leak and, of course, you can tote your laundry. When the clothes were bagged up, he threw a couple laundry detergent cubes into the bag with the darks. The detergent cubes were a great invention. Not only couldn't they leak during travel, you could move them around in the suitcase to help make things smell a bit more fresh. He also traveled with a small spray bottle with a mixture of water and vodka inside. The alcohol mixture could be sprayed on garments if they got a bit pungent. Worked wonders. He kept a couple of those round balls designed to deodorize gym shoes in there for extra assistance in the olfactory department. If the rock 'n' roll thing didn't work out, he figured he could always write a book called *How Not to Stink When You're on the Road.*

Ollie picked up the room key. He took a $5 bill from his wallet, which was lying next to his cellphone on the nightstand. He tucked the money into one of the plastic bags. Then he picked up the laundry and was about to head down to the front desk for change when a tinny version of the Beatles "Eleanor Rigby" started to play. When he had chosen that as his ringtone it seemed clever and ironic. Since then it had become increasingly depressing. He made a mental note to download a new one when he had the chance.

He was tempted not even to look at the phone. There is a level of fatigue that kicks in after a month on the road. You move from place to place, event to event like a wind-up toy. The momentum propels you. The most likely phone candidates were the office, one of his lawyers, or his soon-to-be ex-wife. Any of them would be a drain of his energy. Only one would take his refusal to answer the phone as a personal affront and further evidence of his bad nature. He stopped and glanced at the small screen. It was her.

"Hello, Mandy."

"Where are you?"

"Where am I? Let me think. Um, Phoenix. Yeah, Phoenix."

"What's the weather like?"

"I don't know. It's air-conditioned inside."

"So I have the date for Emma's choir concert."

Ollie went to the desk and flipped open the screen of his laptop. Typing with one hand, he brought up his calendar program. "Go on," he said.

"April 20."

"I'm in Cleveland."

"Of course you are."

Ollie rubbed his forehead. Were they really going to have this argument again? This same argument?

"It's my job. I have to make a living," he said.

"I know it is. Don't use that tone." She let out a heavy sigh.

"Don't use that sigh." There was a long pause. Ollie waited for Mandy to speak, but she said nothing.

"I don't feel good about missing it," he said. "It's hard on me already."

"Look; I know I'm wrong, OK?" she said. Her voice was still angry. It was always angry. "I know that it's not your fault and I don't have a right to get mad at you for the situation. I just … It's frustrating. She's been working on the solo … I'll make a video and send it to you, OK? It's fine. We're used to it."

Ollie could never figure out what she wanted from him. She was the one who'd wanted out, who said she didn't love him any more. She told him to pack his things and she changed the locks. She split the bank account. She hired a lawyer. He had begged her; cried. He would be willing to grovel even now if she hadn't made it abundantly clear that there was no use. "I don't want a life with you. Not any more." Now half her calls were about dividing up property and the other half were to complain that he was not involved enough. She wanted him to feel guilty for not being in the home she'd thrown him out of. It made his head spin.

"Why do you want to make me feel worse than I do?"

"I don't want to make you feel anything." There was that sigh again.

"Can I talk to her? Is she there?"

"She's at school. It's Wednesday."

"Right. Well, I have a day off."

"I'll have her call you tonight then; around eight?"

"Yeah."

"She misses you."

"I miss her, too."

"Well, OK."

"OK."

"Oh listen," Mandy said. "When you talk to her, she's going to try to steer the conversation to a car."

"She's had her driver's license for three months. She's angling for a car?"

"I know she has you wrapped around her finger. She'll use the guilt trip."

"I wonder where she gets that from." There was a silence. "Sorry," Ollie said. "What were you saying?"

"I told her if she wants a car she has to get a job and work for it. So I need you to back me up on that."

"No problem."

"No white- knight hero racing in."

"We're on the same team on this one," he said.

"Well, OK, then," Mandy said.

"OK."

"Go out and see something," she said. "You have a day off. Don't just sit around the hotel."

"I'm not," he said. "I'm doing laundry."

"Good for you," she said. "So I'll have her call later."

"Yeah. Bye."

"Bye."

He hung up the phone and put it back on the end table, then dropped down on the bed next to his laundry. ("Hanging up the phone" is a language fossil, from the days when telephones hung on walls.) After the call, not even the prospect of clean underwear was enough to lift his spirits.

Ollie had met Amanda Wheeler in December 1980. He was then a 20-year-old art student by day and a struggling musician by night. The band he'd formed with his friend Pete had regular Tuesday and Thursday gigs at the club around the corner. A few friends and admirers could be counted on to show up, but the band had not recorded anything or played anywhere but London.

Even then, when Ollie got on stage he had a beauty and charisma that drew women to him. Once he stepped off the stage, though, he could be counted on not to notice their advances. Ollie was what they call soft-spoken. Back then, before he was famous, people more often used expressions like "socially awkward" and "painfully shy."

He remembered the exact date when he met Mandy because he had just heard the news that his idol, John Lennon, had been murdered by an obsessed fan. He was walking down the street in a daze, trying to process the news and he nearly tripped over the legs of a tall girl who was sitting on the pavement. Her hair was bleached almost white. She wore a multi-layered, multi-colored skirt paired with torn fishnet stockings, and she was sobbing.

"John Lennon is dead," she said, revealing an American accent. "They killed him."

"They" was a funny word. One man had shot John Lennon. Who were they? The Americans? Society? The cruel world? All the people who didn't share the dream, who didn't imagine?

Ollie said nothing. He sat down beside her, and let her cry on his shoulder. When she had cried herself out, she looked up at him with eyeliner streaming down her face. (He would later try to copy that look for his stage makeup.) "I'm Mandy," she said.

They spent the rest of the day together. It was the first time that Ollie felt completely at ease with a woman he had just met. The conversation flowed without effort. It was as though they had known each other for years. He didn't want the day to end so he invited her to the club to watch him play. She said she could tell he was going to be a huge star one day. They spent the night together, and the next, and the next.

Mandy was from Connecticut. She had come to London to study fashion, but not at a university. She was from the kind of family that sends its kids off on an all-expense-paid adventure for a year between high school and college. So she had the leisure to scope out the underground music scene and sketch what the punks were wearing.

Ollie couldn't believe his luck that a girl like that could ever take an interest in someone from his background. He was born Oliver Alfred Thomas in South East London the bastard son of a barmaid and a construction worker. If his 19-year-old mother had had her way, Alfred would have been his first name. It was his maternal grandfather's name. There were so many Alfreds back in Oscar Wilde's day that after that generation no one wanted to saddle their sons with such a commonplace name any more. That's how the trendy becomes the quaint and old-fashioned. Ollie's father had not been interested in sticking around to be a dad, but he did put his foot down on naming his son Alf. It was his only family legacy. Ollie was raised to expect only one thing from life; that he would have to struggle and work hard.

Of his mother's four husbands, Ollie had liked the third best. He was a good-natured, alcoholic drifter who taught the boy to play guitar before disappearing into the night. When Ollie played the guitar he found a home, a space where he knew he belonged. At first he could not command his fingers to hold down the strings for the bar chords, but there was no question in his mind that he would master it. He had to. He was proud of the calluses that formed on his fingertips. He listened to the Beatles and tried to work out the chord progressions. This filled him with both elation and despair. The idea that he might have the power to do something as magical as making music propelled him. This was followed by the grief of knowing that "Strawberry Fields" and "Revolution" had already been written and that there was no way he could create anything that could possibly match them.

Mandy was the first girl he ever met who seemed to understand how much his calling meant to him. Ollie was immediately attracted to Mandy's American optimism and confidence. She exuded the belief that anything you dream is possible. She was absolutely convinced that Ollie would be a star and that together they would never be ordinary. Mandy came up with designs for stage costumes and dressed up the musicians like her own personal fashion dolls. She created posters and flyers. She started up conversations with kids at the club and talked up the band. She had an infectious energy, and her enthusiasm always rubbed off. She also took over the bookings and negotiated the band's pay, which was a great relief to Ollie. He was useless at it. He loved playing so much that he was afraid the club owners might not let him go on stage. His negotiations tended to go like this:

Club owner: How much do you guys charge? I normally pay 200.

Ollie: We'd like to get 100.

Club owner: OK, 100.

Ollie: But we could do it for 50.

Club owner: 50.

Ollie: We really just need drinks for the band.

Club owner: So if I give you a tab ...

Ollie: Just a beer, you know. That would be fine. A beer for each of us. We'd do it for free. We love to play.

Club owner: See you on Thursday, then.

It was Mandy who invented the persona of "Blast."

"You need to create a character," she said. "Like Bowie. You have a mask. You can be bigger than life that way."

25

She was right. Taking on the Blast persona freed him. Everything that he kept bottled up inside in his daily life exploded through Blast. On stage he channeled primitive energies, rebelliousness, joy, sex. It was captivating.

At first Pete balked at Mandy's interference, but he shut up when he saw the results. They were playing almost every night and the audiences were getting larger and larger. Pete started painting his face following Mandy's suggestions and adopted the name "Wing Dog." Unlike Ollie, Pete carried these affectations off the stage.

In the early days, Ollie and Mandy would stay up half the night drinking wine and talking. They had great sex, and he loved her body, but the real draw was her mind and her imagination.

His model of the perfect couple was John and Yoko. Ollie didn't care what anyone else said about it—Yoko Ono was crazy hot with her short skirts and her soft-spoken Japanese mannerisms. She covered her mouth when she laughed and yet she was ballsy as hell. She was the fire that drove the engine and the biggest rock star in the world went along for the ride. They made their own rules. Yoko sent John out to California for a "lost weekend" when he got restless, and she even chose a woman to be his mistress. That's when they weren't having bed-ins for peace. They were truly in love.

John and Yoko may have been as fucked up as anyone else, but if they were, Ollie didn't want to know it. He loved the photos of the two of them holding hands in Central Park, making music together in the Dakota, the Two Virgins cover. That was enough for him. It told him that a different kind of love was possible. If it had all been for show, he hoped no one would ever tell him. He and Mandy were going to be John and Yoko baking bread and making art.

When they were young, Mandy and Ollie talked a lot about this and how they would not be constrained by a life of prescribed domesticity and hypocritical rules about monogamy. "When we're in our sixties, we'll get matching tattoos!" The conversations were exiting and passionate, and he believed them.

Somewhere along the line, Mandy stopped wanting a life of artistic self-expression and sexual freedom. She stopped encouraging him to be true to his artistic vision, and started pushing him towards uninspiring sell-outs that would bring in fast money. She did a 180 on monogamy and started to grill him about his dalliances with other women. All of the conventional things they were never going to be—suddenly she embraced them and called him immature for not embracing them, too. Was she right that dreaming was the prerogative of the young and that conformity was the mark of a grown-up? Was that wisdom or defeat? That was the worst part of losing her. He wasn't sure any more.

She was the one who had changed, the one who strayed from the promises they made to each other. And yet when it came time to call the lawyers and file the papers, they would be judged by the social rules they had both agreed to ignore. In the eyes of the world, he was the bad guy. He was a child. He played around.

The irony was, for all of her talk about his sex and rock 'n' roll lifestyle, Mandy was always more sexual than he was. On the road he had access to groupies when he wanted, and he did from time to time, but not nearly as much as people imagine. (Touring wears you out.) It was fun. He liked it. Who doesn't respond to the joy of discovering a new person, getting to that moment of mutual consent for the first time? As far as he was concerned, it had nothing to do with his marriage and what he had thought was an enduring emotional commitment. Sex with the strangers and sex with his wife were entirely different things. If they were honest with themselves, he was quite convinced that most people would want to have both if they could—the hunt and the nest.

More often than not, he would have been happy just to lie in bed with Mandy and talk for hours. Invariably though she would stop the conversation because she wanted sex. For her, sex was a thermometer of some kind. It was the proof that he desired her and loved her. She seemed to need the affirmation more than the pleasure. He didn't need sex to prove they were lovers. She was the one obsessed with it.

Ollie could not think about all of this any more. He took off his glasses and set them on the end table. He rolled onto his side and pushed the plastic laundry bags away. He felt heavy. He could not imagine anything besides lying in bed that would not be too much effort. He closed his eyes.

He opened them again when he heard the chorus of "Eleanor Rigby." He fumbled for his smart phone, and when he finally got his hand on it and looked at the screen he saw that it was 4:30 p.m. He'd slept through the whole day.

It was a Los Angeles number, one of his office extensions.

"Hey, it's Ethan," said the voice on the other end of the line. ("On the line" is a language fossil, from the days when telephonic communication was conducted over cables.)

"Hi," Ollie said, rubbing his eyes.

"So um, Eric Hollander called," Ethan said. Hollander was Ollie's divorce lawyer. "He says the papers are ready and he wants to know where to send them so you'll get them."

Ollie let the finality of the word "papers" sink in.

"Hello?" said Ethan.

"Yeah, sorry. I just woke up."

"Sleep in until the afternoon, that's the rock star life, eh?" Ethan said. Ollie did not laugh, so Ethan pressed on, sounding a little embarrassed. "Do you want me to have him overnight it to you at the hotel there or should we do it to the theater?"

"No the … here, the hotel. That's fine. We got, what? Two days here?"

Ethan went on to discuss more business, television interviews or some such, but Ollie didn't really hear any of it. When the call was finished, he turned off the TV and went to take a shower. As the hot water rolled over him he tried to bring back the joy he'd felt that morning at having nothing but laundry on his to-do list. It didn't work, but the shower made him feel a bit more human.

After the shower, he sat down at the desk and checked his e-mail. He deleted the spam and left the business-related messages unopened. There was nothing left. So he logged into the official Blast website. They'd mostly set it up as a way to sell merch. Of course, in order to get fans to check in regularly and see if there was a new t-shirt on sale, he needed to provide "content." Generally this consisted of cheery posts about what city he was in and how great the audience was there. He used an app that allowed him to update the Blast web page, the Blast Facebook page and Twitter at the same time.

"I'm in Phoenix," he typed into the status bar. Then he sat staring at the screen trying to figure out what to say about it. "It's the desert," he thought. "Everything is dead here."

He deleted the status and clicked over to the Blast Facebook page to see what fans were posting. He scrolled down the page, glancing at the breathless praise.

"Blast's show in Albuquerque rocked!"

"It did not," he said to the screen. He had been a zombie, dazed, absent, off his game. Albuquerque had been a nightmare. Being praised for a mediocre performance was depressing. Could they not tell the difference? Did they think that was the best he could do?

He clicked back to the official website and navigated to the fan forums. He wanted to see if any of the people at that show had been more discerning. The threads were sorted with the most active discussion at the top. He expected a thread about Albuquerque, his last gig, to be up there. Instead, the topic of the day was Blast's divorce. There were messages about the beauty of his ass, how he still "had it" at his advanced age, and massive speculation about which fan had the best shot with him now that he was going to be single.

He closed the web browser and fired off an e-mail message to Ethan.

"I need you to take over the social media for a while.; too much going on here." He included a list of the necessary passwords.

"Right, my laundry," he said out loud to nobody.

Candi's Bad Date

"A.J. Jones."

The pit of Candi's stomach reacted to the name on her caller I.D. It heaved with revulsion. The body reacts to the idea of sex with someone you don't find attractive the way it might react to the smell of spoiled food. She had read somewhere that the disgust reaction was a natural defense against being poisoned.

A.J. was not a repulsive man. He was kind, nice. The memory of her time with him repulsed her anyway. Logic told her that this was entirely unfair to him, but logic did not rule when it came to these things. Attraction was an animal instinct. It was there or it was not.

She'd met him in the waiting area of the instant oil change place. As she sat drinking a stale coffee and browsing a worn copy of Car and Driver magazine, the guy next to her started up a conversation. They hit it off well enough, but he wasn't her "type." Her fantasy man had broad shoulders and a slim waist like Blast. This guy had slouching shoulders and a thick waist. He was only a few years older than her, but his hair was already thinning. Some women like that. He did have those big Italian eyes like Sylvester Stallone, kind of tilted and sad looking. It might be a face, she thought, that she could grow to like. Jackie was always telling Candi that she was still single because she was too picky. "There are a lot of great men out there but you don't even pay attention."

Her relationships with men had been disappointing: There was the guy who would buy her ice cream and then make snide comments about her weight. There was the one who told her he'd really wanted to date her sister, but she was OK too. There was the one who was so jealous and insecure that he put her down constantly and made her life hell. Then there was the one who dumped her to go out with a girl who was literally a fashion model—she was right there in the department store catalog with the letter B by her hip. After they had broken up, Candi saw the guy with his new girlfriend at a party. The girl glanced at her, looked her up and down, whispered in the guy's ear and then laughed. That moment had come to symbolize her whole romantic life. One after the other, men had made her feel like she was the second choice, good enough if no one better came along, but not quite up to their standards.

Most of Candi's high school and college friends were married now, and she couldn't help but feel that she had been left behind. She was not sure why she felt this way. She had never been one of those girls who had her wedding gown picked out in 6th grade. But it was beyond question that there was an age at which people get married, she was past it, and that made her different. As much as she liked to pretend it didn't matter, it did. So when A.J. asked for her number she gave it to him. A pleasant, plain-looking man was a rational choice, she told herself. She was too old to be picky.

The dinner had been pleasant. He was trying hard to impress. (Why do guys always recite their résumés to you on first dates like you're interviewing them for a job?) She wasn't attracted, so she didn't care if she impressed him or not. He must have read this as confidence or interest. To be fair, he could be forgiven for reading interest (rather than boredom) into the fact that she had accepted his dinner invitation in the first place.

Candi tried to be interested. He had a good sense of humor and a good job and he said the right things. He didn't like one-night stands. He wanted to meet someone special. He wanted a serious relationship. He even said he liked long walks on the beach. (She was skeptical about that one.) She could see that other women would find him attractive, but she couldn't summon any lust herself.

She was so out of practice with the whole dating thing that when they got back to her apartment and he asked, "Can I come in for coffee?" she didn't realize he was asking for sex. She started for the kitchen area to brew the coffee, but he stopped her with an arm around her waist. Next thing she knew, his mouth was on hers, his shirt was open, his fly

32

undone. He had a hairy chest, wiry, not smooth as she preferred. She was put off by his pot-belly. He didn't feel right in her arms at all. Too bulky. Too foreign. When she saw him standing naked and fully erect in front of her she was repulsed. She was not cruel enough to tell him, of course. It seemed easier to do it and get it over with than to persuade him that she'd changed her mind.

She lay down on her sofa and let him pull down her nylons and panties. She kept her eyes shut tight and tried to imagine it was Blast's tongue lapping between her legs. A.J. climbed on top of her, and was about to enter her when she realized he did not have a condom. She certainly hadn't prepared with one. It was her opportunity to call it off.

"You should go," she said. "You should go."

He finally did. But he hadn't stopped calling. She knew she was wrong to let him hope, but how could she say it? It was too awful. What is the diplomatic way to say "I don't find you attractive—even though I almost had sex with you." She was a coward. He would figure it out eventually.

Was it really too much to ask to want the kind of love they make movies about and sing songs about on the radio? Was to too much to wish to be swept off her feet, to feel passion and to give herself with lusty abandon? Was that really reserved for other people—people more beautiful or charming?

She turned away from the telephone and back to the television screen. She was playing her DVD of Blast's 1982 tour of Japan. It was a down-tempo moment in the concert; Blast seated on a stool playing his guitar. She could hear the rest of the band was also playing, but they were not shown. The director had opted for a tight close-up and occasional pans to the audience all glowing with their lighters above their heads. The song was "Mutual Consent," not one of Candi's favorite tracks, and one Blast himself had dropped from subsequent tours. Even so, the intimate recording made it one of her favorite parts of the concert.

Candi especially enjoyed the way he cocked his eyebrow and lifted his shoulder as if to both apologize and shrug off the need for any apology as he sang about how beautiful a night with a stranger could be. It wasn't a stagey moment, didn't seem rehearsed and she felt as though, if she looked at it closely enough, she could see through the mask and know something of the real man.

Of course Candi understood that this was an illusion. She could not know a person by seeing his face on TV. She had no expectation that she would ever meet him and she had no plan to try. If their paths ever were to cross she would get nothing from him but an autograph. Yet she had to indulge her fascination for him, to imagine being with him, making love to him, being known by him. It meant that she had not stopped believing that she was worthy of something magical, sexy and glamorous. The fire was still burning inside her, and so far the world had not managed to put it out.

That's when she noticed the toilet was still running. She got up, walked to the bathroom, and shook the handle. The constantly-running toilet was an annoyance, but Candi didn't want to bother the landlord in case she was laid off and had to beg him for mercy on the rent.

Candi returned to the living room, and with the concert still playing on the television, she opened her laptop and navigated to the official Blast web page. She read the latest blog post about the band's show in Phoenix then she navigated to the fan forum. She liked to glance at the forum from time to time and see how the fans interacted with one another. There were a few people who posted all the time. They had clear personalities and many of them seemed to know each other in person from meetings at various shows. They had their own catch-phrases and in-jokes. There was never enough news to satisfy their need for a Blast fix and so they would make things up. They polled each other on their favorite Blast songs, favorite concert moments, favorite costumes. They talked about what movie roles he would be great for, speculated on what movie stars he ought to date. Some of them wrote fan fiction and uploaded Blast-inspired art. Candi was a lurker; she observed without participating. There was something a bit naughty and voyeuristic about this, like peeking through the windows into someone else's party.

On a normal day there would be several active topics vying for the top position in the forum. Now one topic had sucked the energy from every other conversation. The number of responses was easily double that of any other thread. She clicked on it.

"This is an interesting place," was all it said. It was signed "Blast."

The "reply to" address was the rock star's. It was the same address that appeared all over the site, and when Blast updated his blog. Blast had decided to interact directly with his fans. There was an electricity in the thread as the fans posted comments and questions, trying to grab Blast's attention.

"I saw you in Boston last year. You signed an autograph for me. I was the one with the red hat, do you remember me?"

"No," said Blast.

"No." That was all he said, but the poster (whose screen name referenced the title of Blast's first album) went into a swoon. "Blast talked to me!!!!!!!! I can die now!!!!!!" she had typed along with an ASCII cartoon that vaguely depicted someone fainting.

Even the guy Candi had dubbed Tom "I Know Blast Personally" Reed got in on the act, posting question after question.

After that Blast did another amazing thing. He stayed. He responded to questions and joked with fans. It was amazing. You dream your favorite star will be as interested in you as you are in him, but you never expect it. And yet here he was. The reality of Blast changed everything.

That night Candi lay in her bed unable to sleep. She could not stop thinking about Blast. His experiment with posting in the forums might not last forever. She had to write something that he would see. She wanted to convey everything to him, what his music meant to her, how important he was in her life. She needed to sum it up in a paragraph. One shot. What could she say?

She got out of bed and went back to the computer. She went to the forum and clicked reply under Blast's first message. A text box appeared. She stared at it, and stared at it. She stood up and paced. She sat back down and put her fingers on the keys.

"I'm Candi," she wrote, then deleted it. "I love your music." No, that was no good. Everyone loved his music, that's why they were there.

"Blast, I have never written a fan letter before, but I just had to …." Delete. Delete. Delete.

Everything she wrote was coming out as a cliché, embarrassing, cheesy, flat, or pointless. What did she need him to know? What was the truest thing she could say?

"Blast, when I saw you here I couldn't let the opportunity to talk to you go by. I don't know what to say because you don't know me, but you have meant so much to me. When I can't deal with the stress of my everyday life I play your music at full blast. I blast Blast! It makes it better."

There was an option to attach a graphic file to her post. She clicked on the paperclip and searched for the picture of the costume she had worn the previous Halloween. She'd dressed as Blast in his "Lamplight Explosion" period. The costume featured a shiny nineteenth-century vest in a velvet purple with a long matching cape and a top hat. The original must have been expensive, and she had searched through thrift shops for months to come up with pieces for her approximation. Should she include the image or did it make her seem silly? She decided to attach it.

She was happy with her message, but she wasn't sure there was anything in it that might lure him into responding. She needed him to acknowledge her existence. She needed to ask a direct question of some kind. "What music do you blast when you feel that way?" She hesitated for a moment before hitting "post."

She felt elated and also nervous. She hoped he would read her post but she also feared it. Being known was a risk. As long as he was unaware of her he couldn't think badly of her. She reassured herself with the thought that if he did read her post and hate it he would forget her very quickly.

That night she dreamed of Blast. The dream was warm and sexual and also surreal. For some reason they were on a cruise ship that travelled on train tracks. This was perfectly normal in the dream. She would have to look up ship and train in a dream symbol guide to see what it was supposed to mean.

She got up, put on a pot of coffee and then poured herself a bowl of cereal. When she went back to get her coffee, she realized she had forgotten to pour the water in the back. There were only three steps to making coffee. Coffee, water, turn it on. It was amazing how often she managed to miss out one of them. She poured the water in and waited again for the coffee to brew. As she did, she decided to turn on her computer and let it boot. That only took a couple of minutes.

The coffee pot was now only about a quarter full. She grabbed her mug and poured the coffee anyway. The water splashed down on the heating element with a hissing sound. The computer was fully up to speed now and Candi clicked on her bookmark for the Blast fan forum. She did not think that Blast would have answered in the few hours that she was sleeping, but she had to check anyway. She scrolled down to her post and saw that there was a reply. When she read it she was so shocked that she took a large gulp of her coffee. It burned her throat going down.

"Wow, you're cute." Blast had written. "I like John Lennon."

Half Cloudy Thursday

Three of the bulbs were missing on the dressing room mirror at the OGE Energy Theater. It wouldn't have been a problem, but they were all on one side. It cast an odd shadow across Ollie's face as he tried to put on his stage makeup. He ran his finger along the grey line and then under his eyes. The shadow seemed to complement the dark circles. He decided to trace its contours with liquid eyeliner. He turned his face to the left and to the right and examined the result. There was a thin line between looking cool and looking like the biggest prat on the face of the earth. He suspected he might just have crossed it. He often straddled that line.

Max, the drummer, was going on and on about dry wall or some such thing. He'd been talking about renovations for a month now. It all started when his wife bought a new faucet for the kitchen sink. The faucet wasn't compatible with the size of the twenty-year-old pipe. So they replaced the whole sink. Then they discovered they didn't make sinks any more that fit the size of the hole in their counter. So they had to replace that. Next thing you know they were redoing the floor and a month later they'd torn out two walls and were redoing the ceiling.

"So we want to do a drop ceiling," Max said. "But if you don't get it lined up just right you end up with leaky insulation and all your money goes out the roof."

Max called himself a "drummer-songwriter." When they tell cautionary tales to young musicians, they warn them about drugs, drink, crazed fans but no one says you might be bored to death by a tedious drummer.

"Did you know carbon monoxide can seep through drywall?"

This was only slightly better than the conversation of the evening before when Max and the guitar player Graham, who both had young children, got into a debate over who was the better host of Blues Clues. (Such a pointless conversation; clearly it is Steve.)

The bass player, Joey, meanwhile was bent over a thick textbook. Joey was the son of one of the original band members from the early club days. He was getting his degree in mathematics at the University of London and had taken a semester off to tour with the band.

"Why are you studying?" Max asked him. "You're on break."

"It's fun," Joey said, hardly glancing up.

"That's fun?"

"Yeah."

"If you're going to be in a rock band, you have to get better hobbies," Max said. "It's one of the rules: sex, drugs, and rock 'n' roll."

"Leave him alone," said Graham, the guitar player. "He's bettering himself."

Ollie put together a new band for each tour. This had more to do with necessity and availability than any desire for novelty or artistic control. Graham was the only member who had been with him for a while. His involvement with Blast dated back to the "great shake up of 83" when all of the original band members quit.

For years Ollie, "Wing Dog" Pete, and the original band members had struggled together, traveling in a broken-down van and playing every hole-in-the-wall that would have them. By 1982 their hard work seemed to be paying off. Blast, which was both Ollie's stage name and the name of the band, was in high demand. They consistently filled clubs and they even had to turn some gigs down. Their loyal fan base and Ollie's cheekbones caught the attention of an A&R man for a major label.

"I love your look, and you have the stage presence," he said. "But I don't know if you have a single. Make me a demo, and if I hear a hit, I'm ready to sign you."

That night the band celebrated their hard-won victory with a few too many free club beers. It turned out, however, that their celebrating was premature. After listening to a demo of their most popular songs, the label was still not convinced that they could do anything sufficiently commercial. They liked the charisma and the package, but they wanted to completely alter the band's sound.

"Something more poppy." "Give us a hook." "You know, a dance-y song." "A love song. 'I love you baby"; that kind of thing."

What did they need artists for if they wanted every song to be exactly the same? Why not just hire a bunch of pretty boys and have them do the material they wanted? That's when the nightmare idea hit them all at once—that was exactly what they thought they were doing.

Ollie had read somewhere that when John Lennon wrote a song that he felt was not quite up to his standard he would say, "Give it to Ringo." It had become a catchphrase in the band. After a couple hours drinking vodka and feeling alternately angry at the monumental idiots and sorry for themselves for needing to please them, Wing Dog hit on an idea. He said, "We should write the most bloody awful give-it-to-Ringo song ever done. We should just take every crass, commercial, unoriginal idea and put them into one hideous song."

It was brilliant. They would record a "fuck you" demo and deliver it to the label as a going away present. It would be the most vapid, cliché-ridden song ever written. Then they could tell the story on stage and play the song as a joke and the fans would love them for it. They started brainstorming obnoxious ideas. Their spirits lifted immediately. This was going to be fun.

Their masterpiece had to be bad in a particular way: commercial, sell-out, of the moment. Ollie sat down with a spiral notebook and jotted ideas as the band members tossed out all of their musical pet peeves, the cheesiest elements of every horrible bubble-gum track they knew.

First of all, it would need a nonsense chorus for the kiddies to sing along to. Nothing as challenging as sha-na-na-na, sha-na-na-na-na; get a job. Something like ooh—ooh—ooh—ooh.

> *I love you—ooh—ooh—ooh—ooh*
> *Violets blue—ooh—ooh—ooh—ooh*

Awful! It was perfect.

Maybe it should have a dance to go with it, someone suggested, a name of a new dance right in the song. Ollie came up with the idea of putting the name Blast right in the song.

> *I love you—ooh—ooh—ooh—ooh*
> *Violets blue—ooh—ooh—ooh-ooh*
> *Come and see—eee—eee—eee—eee*
> *Do the Blast with mee—eee—eee—eee*

Dreadful.

> *Eee—eee—-eee—eee—Blast with me!*
> *Blast with me!*

It was perfect. Ambiguously sexual. It had a beat. Both clichéd and meaningless, and they could go on and on about this great new dance, "The Blast," which would, of course, be heavily promoted with a glitzy music video. Blast does the Blast! Ollie nearly wet his pants from laughing.

"Come on, it needs more, it needs more," said Andy the drummer, barely able to catch his breath.

Ollie reasoned that the main thing he could do to make a song radio-friendly was to give a DJ something clever to say when he saw the title. Fortunately, DJs are not the most intellectual lot. They believe that playing a song like "Monday Monday" on a Monday is clever. If he wrote a day-of-the-week song, he would explain to the label folks, there would be at least one day of the week it would have to get airplay. He thought long and hard about all of the days-of-the-week songs he knew, and decided that the best days of the week for the aspiring radio star were

Wednesday and Thursday. There were millions of songs for Friday and Saturday. Monday and Tuesday were covered in the 60s with "Monday Monday," "Ruby Tuesday" and "Tuesday Afternoon." But when was the last time anyone found themselves humming a catchy Thursday song? Never happened.

> *I love you—ooh—ooh—ooh—ooh*
> *Violets blue—ooh—ooh—ooh—ooh*
> *It's Thursdeee—eee—eee—eee—eee*
> *Do the Blast with me—eee—eee—eee—eee*

The mispronunciation of Thursday to make it rhyme was a happy accident.

What else did DJs talk about? The weather : "The rain is coming down in sheets." "Drive carefully." "Here's Supertramp with 'It's Raining Again.' " There were lots of rain songs. There were even a few dozen good sunshine songs. What was lacking was a good "partly cloudy" song.

> *I love you-ooh—ooh—ooh-ooh*
> *Violets blue—ooh—ooh—ooh—ooh*
> *It's Thursdeee—eee—eee—eee—eee*
> *Half Cloudeee—eeee—eee—eee—eee*
> *Come and see—eee—eee—eee—eee*
> *Do the Blast with me—eee—eee—eee—eee*
> *Blast with me!*
> *Blast with me!*

Then Wing Dog stumbled on the piéce de résistance: DJs have big egos. They should put a reference to DJs right in the song. "I mean, why do you think David Bowie's DJ got all that play?

> *"I am a DJ, I am what I play.*
> *Can't turn around or,*
> *can't turn around, or—oooh. "*

Not all that articulate for a DJ." They would one-up Bowie—they'd throw in a reference to VJs. So awesome, so tubular, so totally 80s. They could kiss up to the folks at MTV.

Ollie filled up the verses with shite about:

> *VJs spinning lies,*
> *making me lonely,*
> *dreaming of your eyes.*
> *Teens like us,*
> *we feel love too.*
> *They'll never understand*
> *anything that we do.*

When Ollie was quite sure he'd written the worst lyrics humanly possible, Wing Dog sat down at the synthesizer to record a demo. He programmed the tinniest, most soulless drum machine groove he could find in the synthesizer's pre-sets. Then he added mechanical squeaks and wails, à la Thomas Dolby's "She Blinded Me with Science," to make it all technological, futuristic and Flock of Seagulls.

Ollie sang at an uncomfortably high pitch, trying to channel pre-teen Donny Osmond singing "Puppy Love." On top of that he added hand claps—there had to be hand claps—and some Michael Jackson-style oohs and aahs.

It was stunning achievement in crass, commercial awfulness. They were all delighted. They listened to it over and over, laughing from the deepest parts of their bellies, with tears rolling down their cheeks. They imagined the executives starting at them wide-eyed.

The next day Ollie and Wing Dog brought their recording to the tone-deaf hit maker and sat back waiting for him to laugh, but something horrible happened. The A&R guy loved it. He loved every clichéd, over-the-top thing about it. He loved the hand claps. He loved that it sang about teenage love. He loved the beat, and the squeaks, and the reference to VJs. "That's your hit. Write more like that. I knew you could do it!"

Then he called a marketer to come into the office and listen. The marketer was so excited that she called other people into the room to hear the hit. One person rattled off names of choreographers who could create the "Blast" dance. Another suggested video directors. A third was talking about what the sleeve would look like and how to tie it all together.

Ollie and Pete were shell-shocked. They never found the moment to say, "But it's a terrible song. It was a joke. You were supposed to hate it." They were swept along as the label folks did their job of making the song a hit and Blast a rock star.

"Half Cloudy Thursday (Do the Blast with Me)" went straight to number 2 and became the only top-five hit of his career. (He had two more top tens and four top twenties before his record label decided his style was passé.) He would have to perform that song at the end of every concert for the rest of his friggin' life.

Ollie was not thrilled by the turn of events, but he was pragmatic. He knew that a musician is not handed a gift-wrapped opportunity to top the charts every day. He had worked too hard not to take it. Rock stardom meant he could pay his bills and be a musician at the same time. He would not have to take a job driving a truck or laying brick. He would not be playing to tiny clubs when he was 40. He could be a man and support a family instead of always struggling and getting by. Compromise once or twice and earn yourself a career, the right to make a living playing the guitar. That one hideous song would give him a huge audience who would be open to hear the stuff he wanted to write. To him the choice between an audience of thirty club kids vs. 30,000 was not difficult.

Wing Dog called this "selling out." He was bitter about the whole situation and constantly expressed it.

His father owned a chain of dry-cleaning shops. It was easier for him to talk about being true to his art. He always had something to eat. He started to grouse behind Ollie's back to the other guys, presenting Blast as the problem, the one man keeping them from having real success. Ollie found speeches about authenticity from a guy calling himself Wing Dog on and off stage to be ridiculous. What was it he thought they could say as underground darlings that they couldn't say as pop stars? The band members were all willing, Ollie noticed, to cash the record label's checks.

What he found more hurtful than Wing Dog's grousing was how the club fans turned against him. In the early days there had been so few of them that he knew them all by name and thought of them as friends. It wasn't that they hated "Half Cloudy Thursday," which was entirely justified. They lost interest in Blast because he was no longer obscure. He was of no use to them as a marker of outsider cool. The fame-induced change in their relationship was experienced as a mutual and inevitable betrayal.

Ollie liked being famous. You're not meant to, of course. You're meant to go after it and then put it down when you get it. What's not to like, though, about people treating you as if you were extraordinary and giving you opportunities you'd never get as Mr. Unknown? It had its downsides, but overall there was more good than bad as long as you didn't take any of it too seriously.

The initial promotional push was endless, exhausting, and surreal. There were television studios, cameras in your face, rock journalists with notebooks. It was like being a car going down the assembly line. The fame factory does its work and you roll past. From the conveyor you can see everything around you: sometimes screaming girls throwing themselves at your car; sometimes groupies offering themselves up on a platter; sometimes agents, marketers, musicians, people who think knowing you can make them money. You roll along and they spray you with the gloss and the paint, and then you get to the end of the conveyor and you stand blinking as you realize you're still the exact same person you were at the start of your journey. As long as you keep moving, you don't have to make sense of it. So you try not to stop. No one got enough sleep. When they do the rockumentaries they underestimate the value of that—sleep. Long tours end in exhaustion; almost a trance state.

By the time they were presented with their gold record, the members of the band were dazed, burnt out, divided, and bitter. Wing Dog staged his revolt. With recording executives looking on and cameras clicking away he dropped the framed disc, said "Give it to Ringo" and walked away. Later that day the other three members quit. They went on to record an album together without Ollie. It somehow managed to be edgy and experimental and also completely uninteresting. It disappeared without a trace. The last Ollie heard, Wing Dog, now back to being plain old

Pete, had taken over his father's dry-cleaning business. He had no music career, but he had his pride.

Having received his gold record and been ousted by his band on the same day, Ollie lay punch-drunk on the sofa buried in Mandy's arms. "Was I wrong?" he asked her. "Is any of this an experience worth having?"

"Hey," she said, running her fingers through his hair. "You have a gold record. Do you believe that? You did it. You remember when we sat in that drafty flat with the shared kitchen and we dreamed about this day? You made it happen. We're here. Those guys were holding you back. You're a rock star with a gold record. You can do anything you want to. I can't wait to see what you do next."

Then she stood up and picked up the gold record, which had been sitting on the table in front of them.

"You know what I want to do?" she asked.

"What?"

"I want to see if we can play this thing." She flipped the frame over on the table and started to peel back the metal tabs that held the matte in place. "Come on," she said. When she had taken everything apart, she handed the disc to Ollie. "Give it a try."

Ollie got up from the couch, walked over to the stereo and put his prize on the spindle. He placed the needle in the gilded groove in the middle of a track. It started to play.

Mandy clapped her hands, "I knew it would work!"

They listened to the swell of a synthesizer. The sound was familiar, but it was not his album. It was a breathy chorus: "Ha-ha-ha-ha-ha."

"Oh my God," Mandy said. "It's Spandau Ballet." She sang along.

Ollie and Mandy had always hated that song. They sang along and laughed until tears were running down their cheeks.

"I know this much is true."

They collapsed under the weight of their laughter, and the giggles and howling soon gave way to kisses and caresses. They made love on the floor as the stylus clicked in the golden inner groove. The insanity of the day, of the year, drifted away. After that all either one of them had to do to make the other laugh was to sing a chorus.

> *Ha-ha-ha-ha-ha.*
> *I know this much is true.*

Mandy could always do that for him, make the madness go away. Now he wondered how she could expect him to cope with the madness of divorce without her. He'd thought he had a good marriage. It wasn't like other people's, but he thought that was what made it work.

"It must be hard being apart so much," people always said.

It was never hard for him. In fact, he'd thought it was the key to their success. Ollie was an introvert. Solitude suited his temperament. The time apart kept things fresh and gave them time to have lives of their own. They had something to share when they came back together. It was ideal for him. He'd believed she was happy too. How many years had she been unhappy? Did it start when Emma was born? Before? He hadn't thought enough about it back then. He could think of almost nothing else now.

Ollie tried for the thirtieth time that day to put Mandy out of his mind. He made a conscious effort to tune back into the room around him.

"The thing is, I don't really like crown moulding," Max was saying.

"Where are we?" Ollie asked. (In another context such a question would be taken as a sign of delirium. On the road it was common.)

"Kentucky," Joey said without looking up.

"Birthplace of the cheeseburger," Max said.

48

"Is that true?" Ollie asked. "No one thought of putting a slice of cheese on ground beef before someone in Kentucky?"

"Someone had to be first," Max said.

Rock 'n' roll.

Friend Me

Outside of work Candi had few friends. When you're poor and your friends are poor it's fine. You hang out and whoever has money that day buys the pizza or beer. That's how it worked in college. But when you're poor and your friends have good jobs it is always a problem. If friends wanted to socialize with Candi, they would invite her to restaurants or movies or concerts. Candi couldn't afford it.

If she told the truth, it put her friend in an awkward position. There were only a few options. The friend could change her plans, offer to treat Candi, or do what she really wanted to do and leave Candi behind. It was OK once or twice, but eventually Candi found it easier to say that she was busy and avoid the unpleasantness. Her friends started to believe that Candi had little interest in them.

These days she kept up with her high school and college pals mostly by clicking "like" on news of their promotions and pictures of their babies. The two people she seemed to interact with the most online were a girl who had bullied her in high school and some guy she had met one time three years ago at a party. She did not remember his face (he had chosen a cartoon ninja for his Facebook photo) and he could be counted on to post emotionally tone-deaf responses to whatever status she posted. (He tended to click "like" whenever she wrote that she was feeling stressed out or overwhelmed. Perhaps he did not have a firm grasp of what the word "like" meant.)

For the past few weeks, however, she had not been lonely for a moment. Her e-mail inbox was intoxicating beyond anything she could ever have imagined. Nothing in her world had more potential to transform her. Working hard could not, education could not, self-help books could not, dating men she met in oil-change places could not.

She had been corresponding with Blast. What began as a fan-celebrity relationship had evolved into a fun flirtation and friendship. They were on a first-name basis; he'd told her to call him Ollie. She knew why she was drawn to the screen, but what amazed her was that the rock star seemed drawn to her too. He wrote to her every day, often several times a day. She was starting to form a new image of herself, not as a powerless, indebted office worker, but as a sexy, fascinating, risk taker.

Between e-mail messages, Candi liked to fantasize that he was with her. She sometimes spoke out loud to the Ollie she imagined at her side. She observed her own life as if through his eyes. At the moment she was lying on her couch watching the commentary track of a DVD with her head propped against the pillow that she was pretending was his chest. She had a big bowl of microwave popcorn, which she was sharing with her absent love.

In real life, she understood, Ollie would never be caught dead watching a chick flick. He certainly would not stick around for the director's commentary. This was her fantasy, though, and so for the moment he would indulge her. Movies like this had always been a guilty pleasure for Candi. They were formulaic and fluffy, an insult to her intelligence, and yet who could resist the idea that we live in a world were perfect romance is possible? You run away from life, trade homes with another woman in an exotic faraway city, and no sooner have you unpacked than someone who looks like Jude Law knocks on your door and wants to make love to you. And wouldn't you know, it turns out that he is secretly a family man and totally the marrying kind. Candi suspected that these kinds of movies did to her brain what a diet of Twinkies would do to her body, and yet she couldn't get enough of them.

In the commentary track, the film's writer and director was explaining her costuming choices. It was important, she said, that Jude Law's character was wearing a tie when he knocked on that door. Otherwise, she believed, audiences would not relate to Cameron Diaz's character. They would think she was a slut. Good girls only have anonymous sex with boys in white collar jobs.

"I feel so manipulated," Candi said out loud to the invisible Ollie. She did not know what Ollie's response would be, but it would probably be funny. Ollie had a great sense of humor.

In spite of all sense of caution and common sense, Candi was starting to think of the rock star as her closest friend. It made her believe, as she had not since childhood, that movies like The Holiday might be documentaries. She had never felt so alive.

Nor had she ever felt so vulnerable. At any time Ollie could throw up a protective wall that would shut her out entirely. If she said the wrong thing, it would all go away. Each message was fraught. Every lull or pause, even a message that seemed a bit less playful than normal, was a harbinger of what seemed the inevitable moment when the window would close and she would go back to watching him from afar.

She checked the clock. Ollie's concert would be wrapping up soon. Candi turned the DVD off and fired up her computer, ready to pounce the moment a message appeared.

Color With a U

After he'd dropped out of college, Ethan had moved back into his teenage bedroom. He still slept in the twin bed, although he'd upgraded the racecar sheets. It was in the basement, which afforded him some privacy, and the equipment he'd bought for his dorm room, — the mini-fridge (full of beer) and the television—made it seem like an apartment; as much of an apartment as it could be in his mom's house.

When he was a teenager, Ethan had hidden out in this room, then decorated with Nine Inch Nails and Green Day posters. After he'd gone off to college, his mother had repainted the room a somewhat feminine shade of light blue. Back then he wanted to avoid any parental intrusion into what he thought was his oh-so-grown-up life. Now it was the shame of being a complete stereotype of a loser that made him want to hide away.

He could hear the upstairs television through the ceiling. His mother's favorite program was "Two and a Half Men." She watched the Charlie Sheen reruns before everyone knew Charlie was crazy. Ethan couldn't stand the show. Each joke about the younger brother being a mooch for living with a relative was like a punch to the gut. It wasn't just that show. You never knew, when you watched a sitcom, when a joke about an immature mooch would rear its head. That's why he preferred to watch CSI. They were too busy dissecting corpses using 3D hologram machines to make cheap jokes that kick guys when they're down.

Ethan was sitting in bed watching CSI with his laptop balanced on his lap. It occurred to him that most people don't actually use laptops on the top of their laps. He thought this was a clever observation and he made a mental note to tell Ale when he showed up.

With the exception of the sit-coms, Ethan liked television. On TV people were always saying clever things to each other, or doing extraordinary things. Completely unexpected events happened to the characters in every episode. If real life was like that maybe you'd get bored with it all.

55

"Oh, another serial killer stalking my co-workers: is it Thursday already?"

Ethan kept checking the Blast e-mail account. It was fairly active with middle-aged fans posing questions and sending compliments. He answered them in a standard way.

"Thank you for your interest in a new album. Stay tuned for a few advanced tracks which we'll be making available online in the coming weeks."

They were not the reason he checked the account so frequently. He was hoping to hear from his favorite pen pal, a young woman named Candi. She stood out right away because of the picture she'd posted of herself. She had dark hair, big eyes, a button nose and a playful smile. She looked like the personification of joy. Ethan wanted to keep her talking to him as long as he could. When he got impatient for her replies, he clicked on a file where he had saved all of their messages. He started reading from the beginning. The first two messages had been posted to the Blast forum, after that, they had continued corresponding through e-mail.

To: Blast <blastproductions>
From: Candi Tavris <PackagingGal>

Blast, when I saw you here I couldn't let the opportunity to talk to you go by. I don't know what to say because you don't know me, but you have meant so much to me. When I can't deal with the stress of my everyday life I play your music at full blast. I blast Blast! It makes it better. What music do you blast when you feel that way?

To: Candi Tavris <PackagingGal>
From: Blast <blastproductions>

Wow. You're cute. I like John Lennon.

(Anyone who knew Blast at all knew the answer to that one.)

To: Blast <blastproductions>
From: Candi Tavris <PackagingGal>

Thanks. You're not so bad yourself.

I like the Beatles too.

I have so much admiration for people who write music. How can you possibly come up with a melody and a song?

Ethan had to stop for a moment and give some thought to that one. When he tried to imagine what it would be like, it occurred to him that writing a song was probably a lot like what he was doing with his e-mails. Both lying and song writing were part of the same creative urge to bring something into existence that never was before. Now Ethan had a chance to share his creation with another person, to let her catch a glimpse his dream world. It was liberating. He had never thought of himself as creative before, but now he knew he was a special kind of artist, a teller of lies.

To: Candi Tavris <PackagingGal>
From: Blast <blastproductions>

I thought I would write to you directly. Playing a song for someone is like sharing a dream you had the night before. If she sings along, it's like you've found a way for your subconscious to speak to hers.

After that, the correspondence took an unexpected turn.

To: Blast <blastproductions>
From: Candi Tavris <PackagingGal>

Wow, that was an amazing answer. I feel that way too when I listen to your music. It's like something speaks to me at an almost unconscious level. I hope that doesn't sound too weird. Is it strange to have fans telling you how wonderful you are all the time?

To: Candi Tavris <PackagingGal>
From: Blast <blastproductions>

It's a nice little ego stroke. It's nice to be appreciated and to know that people like what you do.

To: Blast <blastproductions>
From: Candi Tavris <PackagingGal>

I'm happy to be of service. (Stroking you)

To: Candi Tavris <PackagingGal>
From: Blast <blastproductions>

So, this stroking you speak of—is it metaphorical?

There was a knock at Ethan's door. Ethan jumped and nearly dropped his laptop on the floor. He was startled and disoriented, not by the fear of being caught, but by the sense of being dragged back to another life that he'd forgotten belonged to him. Ale walked in without waiting for Ethan to respond to the knock.

"It stinks in here, man," Ale said. "It's like stale pot and dirty socks. Can't you open a window or something?"

"It's a basement. Do you see any windows?"

Ale threw the baggie of pot down on the bed. It was nearly empty.

"Is that all we've got?" Ethan asked.

"Who's 'we,' white man?" Ale said. "When is the last time you bought? Like never."

"I buy."

"Seriously, do you remember the last time you bought?"

"No, not really."

"Yeah, that's what I'm talking about. It's your turn next time."

"Yeah, yeah." Ethan took some rolling papers out of his end table and started rolling a joint. He was good at it and proud of his skill. "Joint rolling and lying," he thought to himself. His two talents.

"How much does the rock star pay you?" Ale asked, sitting down on the foot of the bed.

"Not enough."

"Dude, you don't pay rent. How can you not afford to spring for pot? Where are your priorities?"

"I said I'll get the next one," Ethan said. He lit the joint, took a drag and handed it to Ale.

"You've got to have a moral center," Ale said. He took a drag. "Get right with Jesus."

"Shut up," Ethan said. "I said I'd do it. You keep going on about stuff."

"So you know what Sasha said to me yesterday?" Ale asked. "She said, they always talk about how women want stability and men want variety, right? But then you look at something like Playboy."

"She looks at Playboy?"

"I guess so, I don't know. Let me finish my story. So she says, 'if men want so much variety, how come all the women in those magazines look the same?' "

"So is Sasha like, bisexual?"

"You're entirely missing the point of my story. Forget the Playboy part."

"I thought the Playboy part was the point of the story."

"Yeah, but not the way you're looking at it."

"So what is the point?"

The joint was very small now and Ale was pinching it with his fingernails. "Huh?"

"What's the point?"

"What were we talking about?"

"Playboy."

"Oh yeah."

The conversation trailed off at that point. Ale and Ethan finished the joint and stared at the ceiling. It was a dropped ceiling with rectangular panels. They were white with little pinpricks in them. Ethan wondered if that was for decoration, to let gasses through or if it was part of the manufacturing process. He wondered why he had never thought about the pin pricks on the ceiling before. The panels at the end of the room, near the door and the wall were not full rectangles. They were squares and it reminded him of some modern geometric art. There was art everywhere if you took the time to look for it. That is what made pot so great.

"You know, I use my laptop on my lap," Ethan said to Ale.

Ale gave him a blank stare. He had no sense of humor. Just then the laptop chimed indicating that there was a new e-mail. Ethan had a Pavlovian reaction to the sound. He immediately grabbed his computer, ready to flirt with Candi. He wanted to pretend Ale was not in the room, but Ale stubbornly continued to be there. If Ethan was going to answer Candi, which he desperately wanted to do, he was going to have to let Ale in on his secret. He explained to his friend how Blast had asked him to update the social media on his behalf. So it was his job to write about concerts he'd never played and to respond to fans as if Blast was aware that they had written. At least, that was how Ethan understood his mandate.

"Most of the fans are, like, my mom's age," he told Ale, "but there's this one girl I've been writing to kind of regularly."

"As Blast?"

"Yeah, look here's her picture."

It was a tremendous effort for Ale to move from his spot to look at the computer screen. When he did take a look at Candi he said, "Nice."

"She's been totally into it," Ethan said, pointing at the screen. "It's been getting kind of hot."

He opened one of the steamiest parts of their correspondence and let Ale read it off the computer screen.

To: Blast <blastproductions>
From: Candi Tavris <PackagingGal>
I was so nervous at first writing to you, but it turns out you're not scary at all.

To: Candi Tavris <PackagingGal>
From: Blast <blastproductions>
Only thing scary about me is the freckles! My friends call me Ollie.

To: Blast <blastproductions>
From: Candi Tavris <PackagingGal>

Ollie, I love your freckles.
Makes you wonder how far they go ... ;)

To: Candi Tavris <PackagingGal>
From: Blast <blastproductions>

Makes me wonder the same about you :) The freckles go all the way.

To: Blast <blastproductions>
From: Candi Tavris <PackagingGal>

Why Ollie, what exactly are you wondering about me?

To: Candi Tavris <PackagingGal>
From: Blast <blastproductions>

Are we flirting? I was just wondering what flavor of candy you are?

To: Blast <blastproductions>
From: Candi Tavris <PackagingGal>

Something sweet, but not too sugary ...I'm a fan of hard candy. I eat it very slowly, it's important not to rush. Some people are impatient, but I prefer to suck on it a long time. Nothing like a good candy stick going past your lips. Very nice. Anything else you wanted to know?

Ale's eyes grew huge. "Whoa!" he said. "She wants to do that stuff to Blast?"

"Yeah."

"Ewww," Ale said. He raised his hands to chest level and shook them back and forth. "How old is he?"

"Fifty-something."

"Ewww," Ale said again. "Why do all the attractive young women want to sleep with old geezers?"

"I think rock star trumps geezerdom," Ethan said with a shrug.

"Still," Ale said. He got up to get a beer from the mini-fridge. "You'd think after a thirty-year run of rock stardom the old guys would step aside and give the rest of us a chance."

"Would you?" Ethan asked, throwing a pillow at Ale.

"You have a point there," he said. Then he pointed at the computer. "You're writing this from Blast's e-mail account?"

"Yeah. I'm supposed to check the fan mail and stuff."

"But what if he reads it?"

"Oh, I delete it after I get it. And I clear out the sent box."

"What if he checks it? Doesn't he have a password?"

"Yeah."

"What if he logs on before you do, and there's one of her messages. Like she hit reply and there is all of the stuff you wrote."

"I never thought of that."

"You have a pot-addled brain."

"Like you don't?"

"Here's what you have to do. Set up, like, a free e-mail account. Then you tell her this is your personal, private e-mail for people, you know, that you want to have sex with. Stars have personal e-mails and public ones, don't they?"

"Yeah, Blast's got his own private one."

"Yeah, so, set up a new account and tell her you want to keep talking through your private account."

Ethan logged onto a free e-mail site and started filling in the form to create an account. "What should I call it? Ollie Thomas? His real e-mail is olliethomas286."

"Don't use his real one," Ale said. "Duh. Go with something that reminds her that he's a rock star. Rockstar101."

"He wouldn't call himself 'rock star,' " Ethan said, shaking his head. "Only someone who's not a rock star would call himself rock star."

Ethan decided to name the account "ollieblast."

Ale was now gazing at the screen over Ethan's shoulder. "Yeah, that's good," he said.

Ethan started to type his first "ollieblast" message.

> "Hi Candi, this is Ollie. This is my personal e-mail account for friends. I didn't want your messages to get lost in the shuffle. You've got a great sense of humor. Play on!"

Ale looked at Ethan's message. "Look at this," he said. "You're never going to make her think you're Blast with this. That's not how British people talk. First off, he'd spell humor with a u."

"OK, Prince Charles, you try it." Ethan said shoving the keyboard in Ale's direction.

"I will," Ale said, pushing Ethan out of his way. He glanced up at the ceiling for a moment then started typing.

> "'Ello, luv. This is Ollie. I'd like to write using my personal account. How have you been faring this fortnight?"

"Seriously? 'Ello, luv?" Ethan said. "He's British; he's not a Dickens character."

"What's wrong with that? Doesn't he drop Hs and stuff?"

Ethan tried to remember how Blast spoke. Did he say "Send my mail to the 'otel"? Ethan didn't think so.

"He doesn't talk like that," he said. "Anyway, even if he did, he knows how to spell." He nudged Ale aside. "Give me the computer."

Ethan began to type.

"Use the word 'knackered,' " Ale said.

"What's that?"

"It's British, it means tired."

"Are you sure?"

"I saw it in a movie once. Put 'I just got back from the show and I'm knackered."

Ethan followed Ale's lead:

"I just got back from the show in ..."

He stopped typing and clicked over to another tab in his browser. It had Blast's tour schedule on it. "South Dakota. You know anything about South Dakota?"

"The capital is Pierre."

"Not like that you moron," Ethan said. "I'm in South Dakota, average rainfall ..."

"Doesn't he just stay in the hotels and theaters anyway?"

"I only get to see the hotel and theater," Ethan typed.

"Theater should be spelled 're'," Ale said, pointing to the message on the screen.

Ethan hit the backspace key and replaced the "er" with "re."

"I'm knackered," Ethan typed. "But, I was thinking of you."

"Oh, that's good," Ale said.

"What else?" Ethan asked.

"That's enough," Ale said. "Just send."

Ethan hit send.

"Well, what now?" Ale said.

"We wait, it's not like she's going to be sitting there waiting for our …" Ethan's thought was interrupted by a beep. He already had a reply:

"Want to Skype?" it said.

"Skype," Ethan said. "Shit, I hadn't thought of that. What do we do?"

"Duh. Tell her you dosn't have Skype," Ale said. "That's easy enough." Ale took control of the keyboard

"Sorry, luv; I haven't got Skype," he wrote and immediately pressed "send."

"Will you stop with the 'luv' stuff?" Ethan said.

In a few seconds there was a new message:

"I like how you call me 'luv.'" it said.

Ale stuck out his tongue at Ethan.

Then a new message:

"Do you want to chat?"

Ale and Ethan looked at each other in a panic. They weren't sure they could think fast enough to chat with her. They sat staring at the screen. After a couple more messages, they had settled on a chat client that couldn't be connected to any of the real Blast social media and they began to speak in real time.

OLLIEBLAST: Hello luv.

CANDI136: :)

CANDI36: I heard one of your songs in the grocery store today.

OLLIEBLAST: Which one?

CANDI36: Blast with Me.

"That song sucks," Ale said. He gave Ethan a little punch on the shoulder. "Tell her that song sucks."

"I'm Blast, remember? I can't tell her my song sucks."

"It sucks eggs."

CANDI36: It's not really my favorite. I like "Explosive Simplicity."

"See, she doesn't like it either," Ale said.

"Give me something I can actually say. Come on."

"Ask her to tell you more about the candy thing."

Ethan typed.

OLLIEBLAST: I like that one, too.

"Lame!" Ale said, "You're going to put her to sleep."

CANDI36: I like "Sins of the Flesh" too.

OLLIEBLAST: I like them too. Oh, you meant the song.

CANDI36: LOL. You know I read that the average American hears 5 hours of music a day.

OLLIEBLAST: In a row?

CANDI36: LOL. It's like the stuff in stores and the stuff they play on elevators.

"Lift!" Ale shouted.

"Huh?"

"They call it a lift. In England. For elevator."

OLLIEBLAST: I don't think they really play music in the lift.

"There you go," Ale said. He went to get a couple more beers out of the mini-fridge. "Put luv at the end of that."

"No."

CANDI36: They play it in the frozen food aisle.

OLLIEBLAST: And it took six takes to get the bass right.

CANDI36: On Blast with Me?

OLLIEBLAST: Musicians agonize over every note so it can play in the background.

CANDI36: Sounds like a metaphor for life.

OLLIEBLAST: What isn't?

CANDI36: Good question. It was fun to hear the song and think "I know him."

OLLIEBLAST: What do you think would happen if we really got to know each other?

CANDI36: LOL. OK. You want me to talk dirty?

OLLIEBLAST: Yes, please.

"Cor blimey!" Ale said in a terrible mock-British accent. "I 'ope she uses bad words. That's 'ot."

"Will you be quiet?"

CANDI36: I love how politely you ask.

OLLIEBLAST: Well?

CANDI36: I think I need more foreplay before I can do that.

OLLIEBLAST: I thought you wanted to stroke my ego.

CANDI36: Yes, I'd like to stroke you, but I need to get warmed up.

OLLIEBLAST: You'd be warming me up.

CANDI36: True.

There was a lull.

"Say something!" Ale said.

"What should I say?"

"I don't know, but use the word 'willie'; that's what they say over there."

"I'm not whipping out my willie yet."

After that moment, coming close to the cybersex threshold, Candi and Ethan demurred. Candi didn't seem quite ready go to for it, and Ethan didn't know what to say to get her going, especially with Ale there critiquing everything he wrote, but they kept chatting for another hour. Candi was flirtatious and suggestive but mostly talked about music. When she finally logged off Ale said, "That was a blast. You have to find some more fans like that."

As Long As You Both Shall Live

The Marriott in South Dakota had a strange quirk. Someone had had the brilliant idea of installing motion sensitive lighting so that when the guest walked in, the lights came on automatically. Or they would if the motion sensor were installed near the door. You had to drag your bags half way into the room before the lights started to blaze. This also meant that any time you stood up in the night to go to the toilet the lights would all come on. It was a good thing, Ollie thought, that he wasn't sharing the room with anyone. The room did have a comfortable reclining chair. It was one of those small pleasures of touring, a comfortable chair here, a nice view there, special soap or shampoo in the bathroom.

Ollie switched on the television. There had been another one of those mass shootings. A guy went barmy and shot a dozen people in the office building where he worked. To Ollie it meant that regardless of what channels the hotel subscribed to, there would be something interesting to watch on TV. He flipped through the channels until he found CNN and then threw the remote into the center of the bed. He listened to the report as he opened his suitcase and pulled out a small bottle of vodka and the manila envelope that held his final divorce papers. He'd been carrying them around for about a week, and hadn't found time to look at them until now.

The television coverage of real-life mass shootings was like genre fiction, a cookie-cutter mystery, except that in this case you know who done it, but you keep flipping pages to find out why. This story followed the same basic formula as other mass shootings; only a few characters and details were switched. There were the politicians praying for the families, the candlelight vigils, the photos of people in tears surrounded by police in bullet-proof vests, there was the slow unwinding of the killer's biography that revealed everything but his motives. There was the debate about guns and mental health, destined to go nowhere. "Heroes" who jumped in front of bullets and newsmen drawing optimism from the fact that people came together to help the victims.

Ollie set the divorce papers and the vodka on the end table beside the comfortable chair, and then went to the bathroom to find a plastic-wrapped cup. On the way back to the chair, he unwrapped the cup and threw the wrapper in the small hotel rubbish bin. (Why did hotels always have such small bins?) Then he picked up the two cans of Coca Cola he'd bought from the vending machine on the second floor. They were still cold.

On the TV screen was the last tweet of one of the victims. She was looking forward to going to a concert with a friend that weekend. She'd just bought the tickets. She didn't know that would be her last public utterance. Her first, really, for a national audience.

"I shouldn't know this woman's name," Ollie thought.

He sat down in the recliner, poured a couple of shots worth of the vodka into the plastic cup, then popped open one of the cans of Coke and filled the cup the rest of the way. He took a large swig of the mixture, then opened the manila envelope, removed the papers, and rested them on his leg.

"Dissolution of Marriage"

"Dissolution." He pictured a drop of blue food coloring dissipating in a glass of water, slowly losing cohesion until the color was entirely invisible. It wasn't the right image, or the right word.

"Wrenching Apart of Marriage," he thought. "Sledgehammering of Marriage." "Explosion of Marriage."

It wasn't that either. What was it they said in the ceremony? "What God has joined together, let no man put asunder."

He was being put asunder.

On the TV one of the shooting survivors was being interviewed. He'd hid behind a filing cabinet and watched a female coworker get slaughtered. He couldn't have helped her. They'd both have been mowed down. Even so, Ollie was sure survival guilt would be the main feature of this man's future.

The victim called the gunman "a coward."

"Yes," Ollie said out loud to the television. "Cowardice was his problem. If only he'd been the type of person to take risks."

In America it was all about winners and losers. This sick fuck had to prove he was a man; wasn't that part of the problem?

Mass shootings were entirely American, like McDonald's and strip malls. They were America's shadow self—the antithesis of its outward optimism. The shootings were made up of all the same material of American life, self-help and Hollywood, posturing and imperialism. They loved superlatives, the Americans.

"The most deadly shooting at an office complex since ..."

It was a land of people schooled in self-promotion, who stuck brand names on every building, who fundamentally assume that being known has a dollar value. They are spectacular and public in everything, even going mad. America's madmen go off in a cinematic way.

Then again, all of that was far too reasonable. We're unable to uncover the motive of the serial killer, Ollie thought, because our minds are too rational to comprehend the simple fact that the cooking-foil people told him to do it.

Ollie flipped through his dissolution papers; scanning, not reading. He didn't need to read them. The lawyers had gone back and forth over every word so many times that he almost had it memorized. He only needed to glance through to be sure they hadn't thrown in some last-minute surprise language about the custody of his left nut before he took the pages to the notary to sign. There were phrases that were burned into his brain. Mandy was "the moving party." Ollie was the "non-moving party." Initially he'd thought this was a mistake, as he'd been the one to move out of the house.

His lawyer explained that it meant it was Mandy's divorce. She was making the motion, taking the action. Ollie found the expression "non-moving party" to be unintentionally poetic. Mandy was leaving him because he had not changed, and because she had. She had moved away from him. He'd even started to write a song with "Non-Moving Party" as the working title. He hadn't gotten far. The concept was strong in his head, and yet he couldn't seem to sit down and work it out, write it down, or record a demo.

"Custody of the minor child"

The language was so cold and inhuman. It talked about property and ignored everything that mattered. Who had the right to feel wronged? Who got to keep the torch burning?

He remembered the night she'd said the words: "I want a divorce."

He had pulled out the biggest suitcase he could find and hurled things into it.

"You want me to go? I'll go!"

It wasn't until he got to the hotel that he had any idea what he'd packed: A bunch of VHS tapes, a "World's Greatest Dad" statue, a metronome and no socks.

There were moments early on when it almost seemed as if they might get back together. Once the lawyers got involved there was no hope of that. Lawyers are only good at one thing, taking sides. He honestly couldn't blame it all on the legal profession, though. He'd been petulant and fought for custody of the dog, Paradiddle, even though he was on the road eight months a year and knew there was no way he could care for him.

"Emma is attached to the dog," Mandy said, bringing him to his senses.

On their now-meaningless wedding anniversary, he'd taken the leather jacket she'd customized and given him for their third (the third is the leather anniversary, apparently) and left it on her front porch to make her feel guilty. When he asked for it back, she said she had donated it to Goodwill.

Ollie did not feel what he had expected when faced with the final papers to sign. He felt no sense of finality or loss—only annoyance at the intrusion. Who were these bureaucrats who assumed they had the right to declare two people married or unmarried? What stake did they have in the whole thing? Who kept track of everyone's couplings and un-couplings and filed them in alphabetical order? Whoever they were, Ollie hated them.

Putting ink on the page wouldn't make them divorced. His marriage had dissolved long ago, before he was even aware of it, before Mandy even spoke those words. Why should he have to document the fact for a bunch of office clerks? What business was it of theirs that he had failed?

There were no surprises in the documents, so he put them back in the envelope and threw it on the bed. He would find a notary the next day. There was nothing more to do. He poured some more vodka into his cup without adding any more cola. He took another sip and enjoyed the slight burn at the back of his throat. He did feel lighter. The process was over. He was free of it.

"Maybe I should go home to England," he thought. "They have no machine guns and they live on a manageable scale." Moving to America and settling in Los Angeles had been Mandy's idea. He had never felt at home there. It was nothing but a smog-laden showcase of traffic congestion as far as he was concerned. Even the year-round summer temperatures seemed unnatural. He didn't have to plan his life around Mandy any more, not around their marriage, not around their divorce.

On the screen was a picture of the woman who'd been killed in the room with the filing cabinets as her co-worker looked on. They'd taken the image from her Facebook profile, no doubt. They'd carefully selected a picture to tug at the heart strings. She was in her mid-thirties, and the photo showed her and her husband, smiling, as a little boy in a baseball cap, their son, sat on the ground at their feet and ate an ice cream cone.

"'Till death us do part," Ollie thought. He took another swig of his drink. "'Till death us do part."

Celebrity Gossip

In the movies, when people get fired, they are always given a brown cardboard box with handles and a lid. This is so ubiquitous that when Candi googled "getting-fired box" a stock picture of that type of container came up right at the top. She wondered if television offices had a special layoff supply closet where they kept them. When Janice from the next cubicle was sacked she tucked her personals into her purse and carried a few things in the crook of her elbow. Many of her co-workers had already taken their personal effects home so they could avoid the spectacle when their time came.

After the initial shock of the reorganization had worn off, people in the office settled into a death-row calm that was almost enjoyable; the camaraderie of fellow passengers on a sinking ship. No one was too busy to complain or gossip. You walked down the hall and saw people playing solitaire, surfing the web, making personal calls. "What are they going to do, fire me?"

Candi spent most of her workday looking up old interviews Blast had done and mining them for clues as to how he felt about life and love. (Especially love.) She was disappointed at how little he discussed his personal life. The reporters rarely asked him about anything besides the music. Movie stars were always being asked about their relationships and personalities. Maybe when you present yourself as a character called "Blast" reporters respond in kind, interviewing the character rather than the man.

In a second browser tab she pulled up a page listing Chinese suppliers. She could click to that tab if anyone came up behind her. In a third tab, she had the web interface to her e-mail account. Clicking the "get mail" icon sent a little spike of dopamine through her brain. Typically she would look up Blast interviews, read a paragraph or two, then navigate to her e-mail. She checked so frequently that often there were no messages at all. When the "logging into server" message was replaced by a black bar she could hardly bear the 10 seconds of anticipation. As the bar lengthened to show the download progress she imagined something being physically pulled from a shelf in the ethers.

"Limited Time Offer!"

"On the Road to Debt Free Living!"

"Notice of ebay policy updates."

There was something meditative in the process of deleting the spam and clicking "check mail" again. Then when she had almost given up there it would be, a message from Blast's personal account. When she saw the address she could feel it in her chest, a small pain. Was it her heart skipping a beat?

> To: Candi Tavris <PackagingGal>
> From: Oliver Thomas <ollieblast>
>
> What do you think would happen if we met? Be advised: Anything you write here could be held against you.

Candi sat biting the nail of her index finger. She needed a response that was clever and suggestive. Everything that came to her head was overt and un-clever.

Candi turned and looked across the room to one of the cubicles on the other side. Lydia had her back to Candi. She and Candi had bonded in their mutual appreciation for Blast. Lydia had been enamored with the rock star when she was in high school and he reminded her of her youth. When Candi's e-mail flirtation began she had to tell someone. Lydia seemed the most likely candidate. Because she loved Blast, Candi suspected she would understand something that others could not: the magic of it all.

She was afraid that in the light of day the online flirtation might cease to be a mysterious and sacred adventure. It would sound like ordinary run-of-the-mill cybersex, identical to the words on a million screens. To share the secret with anyone who was immune to Blast's charms was to risk destroying a delicate, meaningful fantasy.

As a rule, Candi would never forward personal e-mails. She considered it unethical. Yet in this case, she felt she had to make an exception. She needed confirmation that she was not deluding herself, that what she perceived to be flirtation—even invitation—from the person she most admired was really there, it existed in the message and not only in her head. Candi was awash in hope and doubt. It couldn't possibly be true. It couldn't last. It couldn't possibly progress. But what if it could? What if it was? What if it did?

She needed a more objective eye, someone who could keep her from getting whiplash as she spun back and forth between crippling self-doubt and boundless elation. Thus all her scruples about private e-mails were relaxed.

Lydia was hunched with her chin on her fist, head tilted away from the screen. With her other hand she was clicking her mouse.

Candi hit "forward" and sent the rock star's message to her. After a moment, Lydia's posture changed. Her back straightened, and her shoulders tilted back. Then she leaned into the computer and started to type.

A few moments later, a reply from Lydia appeared in Candi's inbox.

"OMG—OMG, girl! He wants you to up the game."

Candi had started to compose her reply to Lydia when she felt a hand on her shoulder.

"Come on," said Lydia. "We're going to lunch."

"It's 10:30," Candi said.

"What are they going to do ..."

"Yeah, OK."

The lunchroom had a sink and counter, a microwave oven and a full-sized refrigerator full of Tupperware boxes with labels like "Ellen's

Lunch: DO NOT EAT." It also housed the office copier and the coffee machine, so Candi and Lydia were constantly having to lower their voices or stop talking as co-workers walked through.

As she waited for the microwave to heat her TV dinner, Lydia spotted a glossy corporate newsletter on the counter. These messages had littered the office ever since The Meeting. The fliers and posters all featured photographs of smiling, interracial models dressed in professional attire looking excited about the future of the organization.

"It's like being a cow and having to look at endless ads about how great the burgers are going to taste," Lydia said as she dumped the flier into the recycling bin. Candi laughed.

The timer went off and Lydia pulled her TV dinner out of the microwave. When she started to peel back the cardboard lid, a puff of steam was released, burning her fingers. She dropped the container on the table. Fortunately, it landed upright.

"So here's what I think you should do," she said before sucking on her index finger. "You need to take a sexy selfie and send it to him. Nude; at least topless."

"I can't do that," Candi said as she removed her BLT From its plastic bag.

"What have you got to lose?"

"I don't know; self-respect?"

"The rules are different when it comes to rock stars," Lydia said.

"Are they? I don't think they are."

"Sure you do," Lydia said. "Or you wouldn't be talking so dirty with him. Don't feel bad about it. If I wasn't married and Blast was coming on to me, you can bet I'd be right there. I have to live vicariously through you. Let me tell you something. Don't pass this around, but I wish I'd been more of a slut when I was younger."

Candi laughed.

"Seriously," Lydia said. "It's my biggest regret. When I was in my 20s I was so serious, and I thought I was ugly. I worried about my reputation, what people thought about me. Now I look back at pictures of myself then and how beautiful I was. I never knew. That was the sexiest I was ever going to be and I wasted it feeling insecure and ugly. You're supposed to do wild and crazy things when you're young. At some point that moment is past and you're supposed to be a grownup. I missed it, but this is your moment."

"I don't want to come across like some kind of groupie," Candi said.

"That's just the old double standard," Lydia said. "Men don't have to worry about being sluts or groupies. Grown men look at girlie magazines, don't they? Why is it that the only time a girl can openly lust over a man is for, like three years, when she's in school and he's a rock star?"

"Yeah, that's kind of true."

"I don't think women give up their celebrity crushes because they grow out of them. I think you get to an age where the stigma of being too much of a fan outweighs all the pleasure you get from openly lusting. I think you should stage your own mini-revolution and go after what you want."

"I don't want to scare Ollie off," Candi said. Just then Bob, from accounting, came in to use the copier. He chuckled.

"What are you laughing at?" Lydia asked.

"Ollie," he said. Then in a mocking tone: "I know Blast so well I call him Ollie."

"How long were you standing there listening?" Lydia asked.

"Nude selfie."

"Shit," Candi said. "Don't tell anyone, OK?"

Bob just laughed, picked up his copies, and walked out.

"Don't mind him," Lydia said. "He's just jealous."

79

"I don't know," Candi said. "Maybe he's right. What is wrong with me that I need some rock star's approval?"

"Just because something makes you feel vulnerable doesn't mean it's a character flaw. When you appreciate someone you want them to appreciate you, too. I mean, what if you didn't? I think you'd be a psychopath."

"You really think I should do it?"

"Send him a selfie and say you want one of him. You want to see him naked don't you?"

"If I get a picture, I'm not sharing it with you."

"Aw, come on."

"He trusts me. That's one thing I know. He's taking a risk talking to a fan like that, giving me his personal e-mail. He trusts me, and I'm not going to betray that."

"Do you trust him?"

"Yeah, I do."

"Then up your game."

Meet Me After Midnight

Ethan could see that Candi was online, and he was impatient to chat with her. Unfortunately, Blast would not be off-stage yet. Candi followed Blast's schedule closely. If he started talking to her when he was supposed to be doing an encore, she would know.

To kill the time until they could chat again, Ethan watched interview clips of Blast on YouTube. He was trying to get a feel for the way he spoke, his word choices and cadence. He kept a little notebook at his side where he could write down British expressions Blast used. It was disappointing because even though Blast spoke with what Ethan assumed was a cockney accent, he rarely used different words or expressions. There was nothing that translated into text. Ethan wished there was a way to spell out Ollie's glottal stops. When he got tired of watching Blast, Ethan started watching Russell Brand. His accent was similar, but he was more entertaining.

The concert would be over by now, but Blast couldn't make his appearance two seconds after curtain. Ethan tried to imagine what the band would be doing. They would just be finishing the encore. They'd go back stage and take a shower, if there was one, or wash up in the sink if there wasn't. From what he'd been able to gather it took the guys a good half hour to get out of the theater. Then there were backstage fans and the bus ride to the hotel.

Ethan paced. Since he had been talking to Candi, nothing else seemed to matter. She was all he could think about. She made him feel dizzy and alive and defenseless and bulletproof at the same time. His relationship with Candi made him a superhero with a secret identity. When he walked down the street he looked like the gawky nobody he was, but by turning on his computer he could go into a phone booth and become Superman. Candi was his Lois Lane.

Usually when he was dating a girl he spent most of his time trying to figure out what women wanted. With Candi he didn't have to. She told him exactly what she wanted so he didn't have to waste all that energy trying to impress her. He wasn't afraid that anything he said would turn the girl off. That meant, in a weird way, he could be more himself when he played the part of Blast.

The more she expressed desire and admiration, though, the more he saw the gulf between the character he was creating and who he really was. The more unworthy he felt, the more out of his league she seemed. The more she was out of his league, the more he wanted to win her. It was a constant cycle of desire, frustration, excitement, and self-punishment.

Ethan sighed and checked the time again. He knew that there was no way Blast would be back at his hotel yet, but he couldn't wait a second longer. He opened his chat client knowing that Candi would be waiting for him.

OLLIEBLAST: How are you tonight, luv?

CANDI36: Frustrated and depressed. Or was that a rhetorical question?

OLLIEBLAST: What's the matter, luv?

CANDI36: You make me feel so much better when you call me luv. :)

OLLIEBLAST: I live to serve.

CANDI36: It's the layoffs I told you about. It's toxic at work. It's draining me.

OLLIEBLAST: I'm sorry, luv.

CANDI36: Now you're laying the "luvs" on a bit thick. :)

OLLIEBLAST: Sorry, luv. :)

CANDI36: I'm so glad I can talk to you. Everyone is going through the same thing at work, so you can't really get sympathy.

OLLIEBLAST: I'm sympathetic.

CANDI36: Can I get a "poor baby?"

OLLIEBLAST: Poor baby. :)

CANDI36: The stupid thing is I never really liked the job anyway. But I wanted people to think I was good at it.

OLLIEBLAST: I don't know what to say. I'm not good with words.

CANDI36: Only music?

OLLIEBLAST: Yeah, I always knew I wanted to play music. It's what I live for.

CANDI36: I wish I had something like that. I admire that.

"I do too," thought Ethan.

CANDI36: I follow your tour schedule along. I look at the map. I imagine each place. It's like running away. I live through you.

OLLIEBLAST: Where am I now?

CANDI36: LOL

OLLIEBLAST: No, seriously, where am I now, I don't remember?

He'd heard Blast and the guys say things like that when they were on the road. He thought she'd like it.

CANDI36: You're in Mississippi.

OLLIEBLAST: That's right. The people here all speak with accents.

CANDI36: Oh, no wait, I'm on the wrong month. You're in Maryland.

OLLIEBLAST: I meant American accents. You all have accents to me.

Ethan was always making mistakes like that—forgetting where he was, forgetting he was British, forgetting the lyrics to his own songs, forgetting the details of his biography. What he discovered, to his surprise, was that when he did mess up, he didn't need to cover because Candi was happy to jump in with her own explanations.

CANDI36: You must get so tired on tour. You don't know which way is up or down.

OLLIEBLAST: Bloody well right, luv.

CANDI36: I'm looking at a picture of you. Do you remember it? It's black and white, and you're wearing this smoky eye makeup, and you're rubbing one eye.

OLLIEBLAST: I don't remember.

CANDI36: It was with the article in Creem.

OLLIEBLAST: It must be old.

CANDI36: It's sexy.

OLLIEBLAST: I only have the one picture of you.

CANDI36: I'll send you some more if you want.

OLLIEBLAST: Yes, please.

CANDI36: LOL. Is it weird that I know so much about you and you know so little about me?

Ethan laughed at this. He had to stop for a moment to consider how to reply.

OLLIEBLAST: You don't really know me.

CANDI36: I know, but I've read all the interviews, watched the videos on YouTube.

OLLIEBLAST: The interviews aren't very revealing are they?

CANDI36: But they're there. There are no interviews or videos of me on YouTube.

OLLIEBLAST: You could make one. That's why they call it "You Tube."

CANDI36: No one would watch it.

OLLIEBLAST: I would. :) There's a lot you don't know. Believe me.

CANDI36: Tell me something. Something people don't know about you.

Ethan tried to think of something he knew about Blast that most people didn't know. He'd already told her his friends called him Ollie. He'd told her what the office looked like. He'd told her about the spider in the gold record. He'd told her that Blast was shy in person. He'd made up all kinds of sexual fantasies for Blast. What other private details did he have to share? He knew Blast took his coffee with cream and sugar and that he more often drank tea, also with milk and sugar. That didn't seem like the kind of thing she wanted to know. He knew that Blast liked to read thick books about history. As Ethan didn't, this didn't seem like a promising line of conversation.

OLLIEBLAST: I can't think of anything.

CANDI36: You just said there's a lot I don't know. I won't tell anyone. It's between you and me.

Ethan decided the only way to keep the conversation flowing was to stop trying to say what he thought Blast would, and to just answer her questions. What don't people know about me?

OLLIEBLAST: OK. I feel like there are two versions of me. There's the one that people think I am, the one everyone wants me to be, and then there is who I really am.

CANDI36: I think everyone feels kind of like that.

OLLIEBLAST: Do you ever have that feeling that you just wish you didn't have to be yourself all the time? Like you kind of suck at being yourself?

CANDI36: I know what you mean. LOL. At work, I feel that way all the time. Sometimes I wish I could wipe the slate clean and start over and get things right. Not be in debt.

OLLIEBLAST: Like someone is out there keeping a permanent record and once it's written down you can't change.

CANDI36: It takes on a life of its own. They blame you if you don't resemble what the papers say you are supposed to be.

OLLIEBLAST: If people decide you're a loser, you're a loser.

CANDI36: No one thinks you're a loser.

OLLIEBLAST: You just think that because you don't know me.

CANDI36: You really think you're a loser?

OLLIEBLAST: People are disappointed because I'm not what they expect me to be.

He wanted to tell her how his mother had mapped out his whole future for him. How he was supposed to go to college and get a degree and get a good job. How he hated academics and didn't relate to the other students with their ambitions and dreams. How going to college would mean a job that didn't suit him, but not going meant backbreaking work and a job that paid nothing. He wanted to tell her how overwhelmed he was that what he did now would determine the direction of his entire life. He was a failure, but he'd failed at something he'd never even chosen.

Was he really supposed to feel bad about that? "I'm not really a loser," he wanted to say. "It's just the only thing I know how to be right now. I slid into it. It fits me." He couldn't say any of that without giving himself away.

> CANDI36: There must be a lot of expectations.
>
> OLLIEBLAST: I like being Blast, I get to put on a character and be someone sexy. But I'm not Blast.
>
> CANDI36: I guess that's why I love the character so much. It's the energy you put out. All that energy of life without compromises or consequences. I know that's not how life really works, but it should be.
>
> OLLIEBLAST: Who I am in reality doesn't matter that much.
>
> CANDI36: I'd like to know, Ollie.

The name "Ollie" produced a small pang of guilt.

> OLLIEBLAST: Tell me who you are first. When you're not being who they think you are at work.
>
> CANDI36: It's like all my life I was scared of what I really want. So I go for something that is close to what I want but not the real thing. Half the time it's like I have a life that's based on what my favorite TV programs are. No one's A&E Biography says: "She went to work and on Thursdays she watched Project Runway."
>
> OLLIEBALST: What are your favorite [backspace ....] favourite programmes?
>
> CANDI36: It seems pathetic to list them now.
>
> OLLIEBLAST: I like CSI and Breaking Bad.
>
> CANDI36: CSI is too gross for me.
>
> OLLIEBLAST: Yeah, I can see that. It's like cartoon gross though.
>
> CANDI36: I'm pretty sure it's gross-gross. The other thing that annoys me is that all of the lab rats look like supermodels.
>
> OLLIEBLAST: Have you noticed how people on TV shows who look like supermodels can never get a date?
>
> CANDI36: Yeah, what's that all about?
>
> OLLIEBLAST: What do you watch?

CANDI36: I like the competition shows. American Idol, Iron Chef, Project Runway.

OLLIEBLAST: Only weird people don't have a TV.

CANDI36: But don't you wonder if that's all there is to life, being entertained?

OLLIEBLAST: Hey! I'm an entertainer!

CANDI36: You're an artist.

OLLIEBLAST: What's the difference?

CANDI36: I know it when I see it.

OLLIEBLAST: Why do you say Blast is [backspace ....] I am an artist?

CANDI36: Because you make me believe the world can be different.

OLLIEBLAST: That's escapism. It's entertainment, isn't it?

CANDI36: No. Entertainment is predictable and formulaic. It doesn't make you question your assumptions.

OLLIEBLAST: My music does that?

CANDI36: It does for me.

OLLIEBLAST: Let's pretend you and I are king of the world.

CANDI36: King and Queen.

OLLIEBLAST: Lord High Commanders.

CANDI36: OK.

OLLIEBLAST: What would you do?

CANDI36: I'd make sure no one had a boring job.

OLLIEBLAST: What about all the boring things that need to be done?

CANDI36: We get rid of all the bureaucracy so all the paperwork goes. That's probably 80% of the boring jobs gone right there.

OLLIEBLAST: If there were no bureaucracy people would have to take responsibility for what they did instead of saying "It says on my screen. ..." No one would go for it.

CANDI36: I never thought of that. "It's not me it's the rules."

OLLIEBLAST: Most people don't want to make decisions. They want someone to tell them they're right.

CANDI36: You're right. LOL. When I watch you, you know what I think about?

OLLIEBLAST: Sex?

CANDI36: That too. ;) I was going to say I think about the days when people had nobility and honor. They fought for honor. How do you have nobility today?

OLLIEBLAST: You could become a soldier.

CANDI36: Yeah, but when politicians talk about "heroes" I don't believe they mean it.

OLLIEBLAST: What do you think they mean?

CANDI36: Vote for me.

OLLIEBLAST: LOL.

CANDI36: I think that's why I was drawn to you in the videos. People are hungry for nobility, not just to be entertained.

OLLIEBLAST: I'm noble and an artist. You'll make me get a big head.

CANDI36: That's what happens when someone strokes your ego.

OLLIEBLAST: !

CANDI36: Did I ever tell you I like your tattoo?

OLLIEBLAST: That's a change of subject.

CANDI36: No, it works in my head. :) Was thinking it looks kind of tribal.

Ethan could not remember what kind of tattoo Blast had, and he hoped Candi would not ask him anything too specific about it.

OLLIEBLAST: Yes, it's kind of tribal.

CANDI36: That's the nobility I was talking about. See? It's connected.

OLLIEBLAST: Why is it noble?

CANDI36: People used to get tattoos to show what tribe they were in. Now they get them for self-expression. Narcissism. Did I spell that right?

OLLIEBLAST: Don't ask me!

CANDI36: Maybe they're looking for a tribe. Advertising "this is me" are you one of my kind? You know what I mean?

OLLIEBLAST: Have you seen the guy who tattooed his whole face to look like a skull?

CANDI36: Oh yeah. That's a desperate cry for attention.

OLLIEBLAST: Are you always this deep?

CANDI36: You bring it out in me.

OLLIEBLAST: No, it's you. I'm like Dumbo's feather or Dorothy's red shoes.

CANDI36: You bring a lot of things out in me.

OLLIEBLAST: Should I ask you what you're wearing?

CANDI36: A blue satin nightgown, it's clinging to me because I just got out of the shower and I'm still wet.

OLLIEBLAST: Are you making that up?

CANDI36: Does it matter?

OLLIEBLAST: No. :) Tell me about the shower.

CANDI36: It was hot.

OLLIEBLAST: Hot and wet.

CANDI36: You should have been there.

OLLIEBLAST: Soapy skin feels nice. :)

CANDI36: If I think about you tonight when I'm in the shower will you think about me in yours?

OLLIEBLAST: Yeah.

CANDI36: I'm going to picture you, with the steam all around you. Your eyes are closed, you're running your hands through your hair and the shampoo is running down your body. Over your tattoo. Can you picture me like that too?

OLLIEBLAST: You have a tattoo?

CANDI36: No. :) I meant in the shower.

OLLIEBLAST: I'm picturing it already.

CANDI36: Ollie, can I ask you something?

OLLIEBLAST: Yes.

There was a long pause.

OLLIEBLAST: Still there?

CANDI36: Yeah.

Ethan waited. Finally she wrote:

CANDI36: The stuff we talk about—do you mean it?

OLLIEBLAST: Yeah.

CANDI36: I mean it too.

CANDI36: So this is real?

Ethan stared at the words on the screen for a moment.

OLLIEBLAST: Yes, this is real.

*****

The next day Candi changed her relationship status on Facebook to "It's complicated."

Nude Selfie

It was late evening. Candi had finished her dinner of boxed macaroni and cheese mixed with ground beef and left the dishes, unwashed, in the sink. She was lying on her couch with her arms above her head, crooked over the arm rest. Her phone was on the coffee table beside her. She was listening to the latest Blast CD, her favorite. The song was called "Authenticity."

> *What if you woke up*
> *to find you had died?*
> *What would become*
> *of your lingering pride?*

Candi imagined Blast's flowing red hair, his large child-like eyes, the freckles on his arm. After a few moments she got up, closed the curtains, and made sure the front door was locked. She didn't want any strangers walking in tonight.

Candi unbuttoned her blouse, slid it off her shoulders, and hung it over the back of the sofa. Then she unhooked her bra and let it fall. She ran the fingers of her left hand over her breast as she looked down at her body. Next she unfastened her slacks, unzipped them and slid them down. Although she was alone in her house, she had the sense of being watched as she removed her panties. She was not one of those people who walked around naked. She never even walked the few feet from her bathroom to the bedroom without putting on a robe.

Nervous and excited, she walked to the bathroom and stood in front of the full-length mirror. She almost expected to see an airbrushed model looking back at her from the glass. She was disappointed. She grabbed the little round paunch on her belly, squeezed it and sighed. Then she stood up straighter, rolled her shoulders back and sucked in her gut. Now the image was not so bad. She ran her hands down her thighs. Then she turned to the side. Oops. She would definitely not be photographing herself from the side, but with the right angles she might be able to create the illusion that she was sexy.

She walked back to the living room and lay down on the couch with her arms above her head. She was imagining Kate Winslet in Titanic. She tried to pose her legs; one bent, one straight. Then she picked up the phone, and changed the camera direction from back to front so she could see her own image. It was not good. Lying on her back flattened her breasts. If her breasts were all flat, what was the point?

So she flipped over and slid down to the other end of the couch. She leaned over the arm with her breasts hanging. She held the camera in front of her at arm's length. It was hard to breathe in this position so she snapped the picture quickly. She sat with her legs crossed and looked at the image. More awkward and goofy than sexy. She clicked on the trashcan icon and erased it.

"Why am I doing this?" She thought.

Then she got up and went back to the bathroom, taking the phone with her. She stood before the mirror and struck her earlier pose: shoulders tilted back, gut sucked in, one leg slightly in front of the other. Then she changed the camera direction from front to back and held it at her waist so she could see the full image from the mirror in the screen. She took a picture. It was not too bad, so she kept going. She took six more before she found one that pleased her.

She stood wiggling her fingers, staring at the image of her nude self. She did not have to send it. She could change her mind, delete the pictures, and no one would ever know. She tapped on the image and brought up the "share" icon. "Before I can change my mind," she thought as she pushed it and typed in Ollie's personal e-mail address. "I want you to hold it against me. Now I want one of you," she wrote in the body of the e-mail. She clicked send. The message was gone.

*****

92

The next morning Candi got up and raced to the computer. She stood, tapping her foot as she waited for it to boot and the e-mail program to launch. She sat down, and her left leg bounced in the chair. It seemed as though it took forever for the messages to download from the server. She felt a tightness in her chest when she realized Ollie had not replied.

That day at work, Candi was unable to concentrate. People spoke to her and it barely registered. "Uh-huh." She didn't even bother concealing her e-mail program with the Chinese supplier tab. She couldn't. That would prevent her from clicking the "check mail" button every 30 seconds. From time to time there would be a false alarm, a black bar indicating that something was downloading.

"Free Kindle Ap for Smartphones"

By 4 P.M. her stomach was in knots, her hands were shaking, her cheeks were flushed, and she thought she might be running a fever. She was sure she'd made a horrible mistake.

On the drive home from work she turned off the radio. The music was too loud for her sensitive nervous system and when the cheery announcers spoke, she couldn't understand them. They might as well have been speaking in Icelandic.

Candi was not the type of girl who sent out nude photos to men. Why had she made an exception for Ollie? Because he was a star? If someone had told Candi about some girl who'd sent a nude picture to a star she would have said that girl was pathetic, a slut selling herself short. A fantasy liaison with a public figure rarely turned out well for the woman. Ask Monica Lewinsky.

Had anything really changed since the nineteenth-century novels when the woman who was bold enough to pursue her passion risked social destruction? Now they don't jump in front of trains like Ana Karenina, they aren't branded with a scarlet letter. No, they end up as a punchline in a bawdy joke on a TV talk show.

She had known all of this when she sent the picture, but she also knew that if she hadn't taken a shot, she would always have wondered "What if?"

That evening she heated up a frozen dinner, but threw most of it away. Her stomach was clenched and it was uncomfortable to eat. She made a vow to herself that she would not write Ollie again before he answered her. And she paced. And she paced. ...

Airbrushed

Holy shit! There were breasts in his inbox.

Ethan's day had been average up to that point. He'd run to the post office to mail some paint and fabric swatches from Max's wife. He'd run off a bunch of promo mailers. He'd added a couple of media events to the online calendar. He had just found a moment to check the secret "ollieblast" account and BOOM!

He looked behind him to make sure no one was looking. He clicked the "x" in the corner to close the image file. He logged out of his account and closed the browser.

He tried to go back to work, but he couldn't get the image out of his mind. He took out his cell phone and logged back into the secret account. A cell phone was much easier to keep on his lap, away from prying eyes.

Candi's breasts were medium; neither small and pointy nor the silicone balloons he was used to seeing in internet porn. They were kind of perfect. She stood with her right leg tilted a bit to conceal most of her pubic patch, but it was visible enough that he could tell she kept it neatly trimmed into something between a full bush and a landing strip.

When he'd become accustomed to seeing those parts, he took in her body as a whole. She was not at all fat, but a bit rounded in the hips and belly. This excited him to no end because it meant she was no packaged fantasy model, she was a real woman who had undressed for him. He had seduced her and she had made herself available for his eyes only. She stood with head high and shoulders straight, but there was a blush in her cheeks and her smile was not an expression of rehearsed seductiveness. It seemed to plead, "Here I am, please don't reject me."

Ethan was not a virgin, but his fumblings in the dark had been few and far between. He'd never experienced anything like this—a woman offering

95

herself up freely, expressing pure, unconditional desire. He put the cell phone away and slid his chair further under his desk so no one could see his body's response.

He glanced up at the gold record. That's when it hit him—Candi had not undressed for him but for Blast. Ethan looked at his computer screen. He typed Candi's name into a search engine and clicked on various results. He could not focus on the letters on the screen. His pulse was racing; his head felt as if it had a white noise machine in the center.

For the first time since he started the game, he realized there could be real consequences. He had gone too far to tell her the truth, and yet lying to her was becoming cruel. He was starting to think he might be in love with Candi. He couldn't bear the thought of letting it all come crashing down.

On his lunch break, Ethan dashed out of the office. He made a panicked call to Ale. He walked down the street as he spoke. The motion did little to dispel his anxiety.

"You have to tell her," Ale said.

"I can't," Ethan said. "She'll hate me."

"You kind of deserve it," Ale said.

"I know, but I really like this girl. You don't know—we chat, it's not just sex talk and me pretending to be Blast. We can talk about anything."

"Yeah, like, except who you really are."

"You have to help me. I think I'm in love with her. I can't tell her now. I just have to keep playing a little longer until I figure out how to tell her so she doesn't hate me."

"I sympathize, dude, but honestly, I think the ship's sailed on that one. You need to find a girl who's actually, like, in the same zip code. Who actually knows your name. I've heard the best relationships are between people who know each other's names."

Ethan got to the corner and paced in a tight circle.

"I know it sounds stupid. But I really know her. And she knows me. It's better than the real world. It's mind to mind. You can't get closer than that. This is an emergency. I need you to come over tonight and help me figure out what to do. She wants a picture, and I'm not Blast."

"Do you listen to yourself when you talk?"

"I need to know what to do."

"I told you what to do."

"I mean what else to do."

"Yeah, OK, man. I'll come by. But for the record ..."

"You're on the record. You're on the record. See you tonight."

* * * * *

That night Ale arrived with, appropriately enough, a six pack of pale ale.

"OK," Ethan said, popping open a bottle. "I think I've figured out what to do. I can take a picture of my junk without my face in it."

"In your underwear?"

"No, you know, naked," he made a vague gesture below the belt. "My junk."

Ale rolled his eyes and shook his head.

"What?" Ethan asked.

"You don't understand women at all."

"Oh, you've been with Sasha three months and suddenly you're the expert on women?"

Ale took a swig of his beer and wiped his mouth with the back of his hand. "I know more than you, man. You can't just send a picture of your cock. That's way too aggressive. You'll freak her out."

"She started it. She sent me a picture. How can she get freaked out?"

"OK. One more time. She wants a picture of Blast."

"How can she get freaked out if she asked me to send a picture?"

"She didn't say 'send me a close up of your cock' did she? She wants to see your face."

"I can't show her my face, idiot. It's not my face."

Ale shook his head again. His expression said that Ethan was a lost cause. "It won't work anyway," he said. "Think about it."

"What?"

"Think about what the guy looks like."

"What?"

"He's a redhead."

"Shit," Ethan said, rubbing his temple. "I didn't think of that. So ..." He looked down at his fly. "I could shave."

"No man, it itches like hell."

"How do you know?"

"I just do. Remember when I was going with Paula? We were bored. It doesn't matter. I'm just saying ... Anyway, Blast is British."

"So?"

"Those guys aren't circumcised."

"Seriously?"

"The socialist health service over there doesn't pay to snip the babies."

"Well, I can't change that." Ethan took another sip of his beer and then let the bottle rest on his leg. "I bet Candi doesn't know that."

Ale leaned in to Ethan emphasizing every word. "She lies in bed every night jilling off to Blast's poster. She's given some thought to what it looks like."

"Gross. Don't tell me that," Ethan said. It all seemed hopeless.

"I can't believe I'm about to say this," Ale said.

"What?"

"You have Photoshop, right?"

"Yes!" Ethan jumped up so quickly he almost spilled his beer. He opened his laptop and fired up his photo editing program. He ran his finger along the track pad. "So we just need to find a picture of Blast." He typed Blast into an image search engine. After scrolling through a couple of screens of explosions, Ale suggested he try Blast + musician. Ethan found a page of images of the rock star. "How about this one?" Ethan said. "He's got no shirt on."

"He's wearing stage make up," Ale said.

Ethan scrolled through a few more screens and finally came to a promising image of Blast sitting for an interview. He had his glasses off, his hair pulled back and he was facing the camera. He downloaded it to his desktop. "So we have a face. We just need to find …"

He typed the words "red uncircumcised" into the search engine.

He expected to find the perfect image immediately. Instead he was presented with a bunch of strange medical questions. "I am uncircumcised and the tip of my penis is raw and red." Ewww.

"Seriously," Ale said. "You have to be the only person in America who can't find porn on the internet."

"You try it," Ethan said.

Ale typed "gay porn redhead" into the search bar. Then he gave an "I told you so" shrug. "Please tell me this wasn't some elaborate hoax to get us to watch gay porn together. Like you're not thinking we're going to end up making out on the bed or something because you're cute and all but …"

"Shut up."

After a bit of uncomfortable perusing of men in leather chaps and every manner of butt shot they finally found just the right body, red-haired, uncircumcised and with a similar skin tone to Blast.

Ethan used the lasso tool to circle Blast's head. He copied it and then pasted it on the porn guy's body. The head was way too small. So Ethan started again. He reduced the size of porn guy and then pasted Blast's head again. This time the head was too big. He went back and forth like that about six times before the image looked vaguely human. Unfortunately, Blast's head was facing forward and the guy's body was a little bit turned. Ethan went back online to find another picture of his boss. He re-sized, cut and pasted. This one was a little bit better, but the skin tones didn't match.

"Try grayscale," Ale said.

"What was the point of the whole redhead thing if I'm doing grayscale?"

"OK," Ale said. "Try to get them to match, then."

Ethan's overly enthusiastic use of the smudge tool made it look like a kid had finger painted all over the naked guy's neck. Undo. As he was working on erasing the individual pixels of the background behind Blast's head, Ale finished the beer and fell asleep on Ethan's bed.

Ethan's right hand was aching, so he wiggled and stretched it. Then he looked away from the computer and covered his eyes. Under the darkness of his palm, he rolled his eyes to relieve some of the strain. Before returning to his art project, he decided to check his own e-mail. Next, out of habit, he checked the private "Blast" account. There was a message from Candi.

To: Oliver Thomas <ollieblast>
From: Candi Tavris <PackagingGal>

My e-mail program says you got my message, but you haven't responded. Normally I would have heard from you by now. Was it too much? This isn't a thing I usually do. Please send some response because I'm going a little bit crazy.

Ethan had been so focused on how he would respond to her photo request, he hadn't thought about how it must have felt for her—waiting for him to answer.

To: Candi Tavris <PackagingGal>
From: Oliver Thomas <ollieblast>

I'm sorry. Don't be embarrassed. It wasn't too much. I loved it. I have been busy. I should have answered sooner. I wasn't where I could write this morning.

He had barely sent his message when a reply came.

To: Oliver Thomas <ollieblast>
From: Candi Tavris <PackagingGal>

Can we chat?

Ethan looked at his art project, sighed and then opened his chat client. It showed that Candi was online, waiting for him.

OLLIEBLAST: I didn't mean to leave you hanging.

CANDI36: I thought maybe I scared you off.

OLLIEBLAST: No way. I've been working on a picture for you.

CANDI36: Working on?

Yeah, Ethan thought. What do I mean "working on"?

OLLIEBLAST: I'm airbrushing.

CANDI36: I don't care about that.

Ethan looked at his Frankenstein porno image. He suddenly thought it might be too sexy. Blast was middle aged and a little bit thick in the middle. The porn star was muscular and had a six pack. Ethan made a mental note to use the smudge tool to tone that down.

CANDI36: You still there?

OLLIEBLAST: Bob's your uncle.

CANDI36: What?

Ethan had no idea. He thought it sounded British.

> CANDI36: You're acting kind of weird today. Did I make you uncomfortable?
>
> OLLIEBLAST: No. It was great. I loved it.
>
> CANDI36: You don't need to send anything you don't want to.

Ethan thought about using this as an out, giving up on the whole Photoshop idea. But she had made a bold move, and he didn't want to leave her out there on her own. He wanted things to move forward.

> OLLIEBLAST: I want to but I want it to look good. Let me tease you a little bit longer.
>
> CANDI36: You've been teasing me for a long time.
>
> OLLIEBLAST: It's a lot of buildup. I don't want to release the tension too soon.

Falling back into innuendo was the easiest thing to do.

> CANDI36: Premature portraiture?
>
> OLLIEBLAST: Yes, that's it. I should have answered you when I got your message this morning. I'm sorry.

Ethan had a flash of inspiration. Blast had uploaded three new songs that morning. He would not only get Candi to forgive him for not being online, he would make her happy that he wasn't. It was genius.

> OLLIEBLAST: Have you listened to the new songs yet?
>
> CANDI36: No, are they online?
>
> OLLIEBLAST: Uploaded them today. That's why I was busy.
>
> CANDI36: I'll have to check them out.
>
> OLLIEBLAST: Listen to "Meet Me After Midnight."
>
> CANDI36: Is that your favorite?
>
> OLLIEBLAST: It's about fantasy. I know you have a lot of ideas about me, and fantasies.
>
> CANDI36: I do.
>
> OLLIEBLAST: And I have my fantasies.

CANDI36: You do?

OLLIEBLAST: Listen to it, and see if you have any idea where the inspiration came from.

CANDI36: Is it about me?

OLLIEBLAST: It's about having the image of a woman stuck in your head. Wanting to be with her, but being apart.

CANDI36: Who is the woman?

OLLIEBLAST: Listen to the song.

CANDI36: You want to be with this mystery woman?

OLLIEBLAST: The more you know, the harder it is to keep the fantasy that comes from not knowing. You know?

CANDI36: LOL. The mystery is part of the fun, but reality could be more fun. No?

OLLIEBLAST: That's my question. Are you in love with the fantasy or ...

He couldn't finish the thought.

CANDI36: Or with you?

OLLIEBLAST: What do you think?

CANDI36: Let's keep playing and find out.

OLLIEBLAST: I'm going to send you a picture tomorrow. I really need to fix it up.

CANDI36: You're so funny. You're a rock star and you're worried about disappointing me.

OLLIEBLAST: I am worried about that. If you do end up disappointed some day, just remember that I do like you. I don't want you to get hurt. I think you deserve a chance to live your fantasy for a while. I've messed up a lot of things, but I'm trying to do something good.

CANDI36: Just be yourself. You won't disappoint me.

OLLIEBLAST: I hope not.

Reports of My Death ...

Ollie had suffered a crash after the initial rush of fame. All of the television analysis about why rock stars self destruct is wrong, though. It's not because they have too much access to parties and drugs, or that they surround themselves with yes-men and users. Those are really just symptoms. And it's not because stars are self-centered gits who crave adoration and attention and can't stand it when it's gone.

For many years before "Half Cloudy Thursday," Ollie had dreamed of being on stage, being cheered, being on the covers of magazines, on MTV, having hits. Those dreams sustained him, they comforted him when he was down; they gave him something to shoot for, a reason to get out of bed in the morning. Suddenly he had achieved all he imagined and more. He'd even been presented to Her Majesty the Queen. What is left to dream about when you've achieved everything you wanted? Who are you if you are not a man who dreams? What did any of it mean anyway? When he dreamed of fame, he always imagined it would be coupled with admiration for his best work. If his biggest hit was his worst song, how could he know for sure when he was succeeding as an artist? How do you measure it? Did anything he did matter?

The only thing that prevented Ollie from having an existential crisis at the height of his fame was that he didn't have the time. He'd been far too busy. His depression corresponded with the dip in his fame, but it was not cause and effect. The pause in his celebrity happened to be the first time he was able to catch his breath and ponder it all. It was a cliché, of course, a rite of passage. Post-fame rock stars go to ashrams or convert to Catholicism or they get busy self-destructing with alcohol or drugs. John Lennon had his "lost weekend." Ollie had followed Kurt Cobain's example. He tried to take his own life.

He had made the album he'd always wanted to make. He'd put his heart and soul into it. But the label had lost interest, moved on to the next boy band, and did nothing to promote it. They seemed almost annoyed that he was bothering them with another record. It didn't even crack the top 50. The biggest twist of the knife was that Duran Duran was making a comeback at just this moment—with a song with a lyric about a rainy Thursday, no less.

Ollie was left alone to wonder who had become rich off his hit singles. He was by no means poor, but he had not come out of it with the wealth he'd assumed rock stars made. He was sure that boatloads of money had been made in his heyday—by someone else.

It seemed clear that he had to take a break from music and go on to something else. The moment he had that thought, however, he became suicidal. He had to make music or he might as well not exist. He could not help but write songs and record, even if no one ever bought them again. He felt as though he was cursed, damned to a living hell on Earth.

As it happened, he and Mandy were also going through a rough patch. They'd had a fight about some tabloid picture of Ollie with a television actress he hadn't even slept with. The fight was silly when it came down to it, a symptom more than a cause. Ollie had come to realize that there was a downside to all that American optimism. Not only did Mandy believe that anything could be made better, she believed it had to be made better. That applied not only to Ollie's career, which was impossible to improve then through any level of positive thinking, but also to their marriage. She was always reading books to find out if they were communicating properly. (He always seemed to fail those tests.) She consulted magazines to know if they were having enough sex and if it was the right kind. For fun, she took fill-in-the-blank quizzes to measure how happy she was, and they seemed to make her miserable. So she went back to America to spend some "time apart" to "get her head together." He was left alone with his black thoughts.

It felt as though his blood had suddenly become three times thicker than usual. His body was heavy. He would lie in bed until dinnertime, then think about how he had to get up but then he wouldn't. Eating was too much effort. It got to the point where even hating himself was too much effort. Depression was an absolute absence, as if his soul had been shut off and his body was trying to go on like an underpowered machine.

He had always imagined that when he became famous he would gain lots of friends. He had made a few acquaintances through his work, but he had lost friends, too. If he was quiet and hid behind a book (these days it was often a tablet computer) people no longer assumed he was shy. They assumed he was snubbing them.

"He's too good for us now that he's a star."

He never thought he was "too good." Quite the opposite, in fact. He was anxious, afraid of rejection, and worn out by social interaction, as he always had been.

He felt keenly the limits of friendship. It was not that he had no real friends or family. He knew there were people who loved him and who would do anything they could to help him. He simply could not communicate what he was going through. Even if they had felt similar emotions they couldn't touch those places. They didn't have the power to reach in to his soul and soothe it. Asking them to try seemed cruel.

So he put on the Beatles' White Album and swallowed a handful of prescription sleeping pills with a bottle of beer. As "Dear Prudence" swirled around him he imagined fans holding candles, like John Lennon's mourners in Central Park. He thought about the radio station announcing his death and playing his music. Then it dawned on him what song they would play. "The pop singer Blast, born Oliver Thomas, is dead by an apparent suicide at age 33. The singer was best known for his hit 'Half Cloudy Thursday ...'"

He gasped. If he were to die right then, the worst song ever written would be the first line of his obituary. "Blast, who wrote a crap song then killed himself ..." This caused him such panic that he called down to the porter and asked him to get an ambulance straight away.

The hospital treated him with a stomach pump. The doctors called it "gastric lavage." This sounded to Ollie like something you might pay for at a spa rather than what it was—shoving a plastic tube down his throat and sucking out the pills and vomit. Then they loaded him up with antidepressants. The fog began to lift and as it did it became harder and harder to re-create the mindset that had brought him to this place. Knowing that he could have died meant that he had chosen to live. Until then he had lived by default. If life was a conscious choice then he would have to re-order things so he would never face that particular abyss again.

When Mandy heard what had happened, she rushed back from America to be at his side. She was upset and worried, which was to be expected, but she was also angry.

"What were you thinking?"

"I was messed up," he said.

"Were you thinking 'I'll show them'?"

"Maybe."

"Screw them," she said. "Who are they? They aren't invested in your life. I am. I'm the only they. Did you want to show me?"

"No," he said. "Honestly, no. I ..." He shook his head. He couldn't explain.

"That's not good enough!" she shouted. She leaned forward and pinched the bridge of her nose with her fingers. Then she took a deep breath and continued in a more even tone. "You keep everything bottled up inside. I have to listen to your song lyrics to know what you're thinking. Everything you do is for those people out there, this audience, them, and they can't love you. They're never going to love you. But I do. And I'm here. And if you try to kill yourself again—I'll kill you."

The whole sorry incident brought them closer together. Mandy would later say that it was probably the best thing that happened to their marriage, "in a weird way." It made her feel needed again. That was her theory. He had a theory of his own. Maybe his rock-bottom moment satisfied her need for constant growth and improvement. The marriage didn't seem great when compared to an imaginary ideal. It looked much better when contrasted with death by suicide.

Somehow the news of his pathetic attempt at self-slaughter reached the press. A week later, he and Mandy were watching a chat program and a comedian Ollie had always enjoyed went on a rant about over-privileged performers who think it's trendy to suffer from depression. The comedian didn't name names, but it was clear that Ollie was the target. "This poor millionaire rock star is depressed. The coal miners with black lung must be reading that and saying, 'Poor bloke, I wish there was something I could do for him.'"

It is a strange thing about England: they love the underdog. Once the underdog gets to the top, they want to do him the favor of knocking him down so he can be a beloved underdog again. They are so dedicated to this that it takes them a while before they catch on that the person they put on the pedestal fell off some time ago. Mandy was outraged by the incident, and against Ollie's objections, she wrote letters to the comedian, the television station, the newspapers. Her pleas only increased the comedian's outspoken criticism of Ollie's audacious depression.

Mandy had had enough of England. She wanted to go home. They had some contacts in Los Angeles, so that is where they settled. Not long after, Emma was born, and with her came a new vision of the future, a reason for Ollie to keep going. Now he knew exactly why he had to keep making music. It was to pay for diapers, dance lessons, orthodontia and a college fund.

Genetics is a capricious thing. If a brain surgeon and a super model have a baby chances are nine times out of ten the kid will end up with the mind of a super model and the face of a surgeon. Emma, on the other hand, had been blessed with an almost ideal collection of traits. Ollie might not have wished his red hair and freckles on his progeny, but he was pleased that from the moment she was able to sing "Twinkle Twinkle Little Star" she seemed to share his appreciation and aptitude for music. He taught her to play piano and bought her a child-sized pink guitar.

His one regret was that he had missed so much of her childhood by being on the road. He had missed her first steps. He learned about her loose tooth and her first visit from the tooth fairy by phone. Mandy taught Emma to ride a bicycle while he was on tour in Japan.

He was proud of the young woman Emma had become. She was outgoing and optimistic like her mother; not introverted and insecure like him. She had her mother's bone structure, and her father's drive. At 16, she already had her entire future planned. She wanted to go to UCLA and major in film studies. She wanted to be the next Kathryn Bigelow and win an Oscar for best director. Her mother would design the Oscar gown. All of that was a long way off, of course. But if the first line of his obituary were to read, "Oliver Thomas, father of Emma Thomas, the Oscar winning director" he could die happy. (Preferably at an advanced age and peacefully in his sleep.)

The Purpose of Bay Leaves

Early in the evening Candi was sitting at her computer. Her eyes felt as though they were square. She'd been staring at screens all day. First at work and now at home, as she scanned online job postings. In the good old days you could send the same résumé off to different potential employers. You had them printed up in bulk. Now that everyone had a computer, each résumé was expected to be specific to the job. Not only that, every company had its own web form. One wanted her to input exact dates of employment. One wanted a long description of her responsibilities. Another would hardly let her say anything, making her come across as fairly unimpressive. One wanted a functional resume, another chronological. Some of them would time out while she was composing her answers. It was tedious and draining. The worst part was that no matter how much she tweaked the document she couldn't help but feel that summing herself up in this way diminished her. It reduced her life to a series of uninspiring titles and provided no evidence of all she knew she was capable of doing. "Logistics agent, packaging department." Was that all she was? Soon she would not even be that.

All of the articles she read on how to prepare your job search, how to describe yourself in a résumé, and what kind of personality to project were worded in encouraging and cheery ways, and yet they made her feel depressed. "Who do I need to pretend to be in order to get employed?"

She read that narcissists did better in job interviews than normal people because they are so good at self-promotion. "I love working with people." "I consider myself to be a leader." "My biggest drawback? I guess I would say that I am sometimes too much of a perfectionist. I always want to do an excellent job and I push myself very hard." Candi rubbed her aching eyes.

Ollie would not be online for a few more hours. So she decided to take a break and check her Twitter feed. Someone had retweeted an article

111

from the Dallas Morning News that suggested you could "cast aside job uncertainty with witchcraft." Candi couldn't help but click the link.

The paper interviewed a psychic, astrologer, and Wiccan high priestess whose great innovation was to translate ingredients like "eye of newt" into everyday items you might have in the average kitchen.

"You don't necessarily have to believe in magic for it to work," the psychic said, "but you have to believe in yourself and want it to work."

Candi thought, "Why not?" She didn't believe in witchcraft, but she wanted to cast aside job uncertainty. She'd tried everything else. It couldn't hurt to cast a spell to remove her "financial curse." She began by doing what anyone in the twenty-first century does when trying to remove an evil hex. She typed "curses" into Google.

Dozens of pages instantly appeared, offering solutions to her special problem. She clicked on one at random. A page with neon green text greeted her (apparently those who practice spells have a web-design challenge).

For this spell, she would need eight candles, a heavy-duty safety pin, a bag of charcoal, and a tarot deck. She would need to perform the spell during a full moon at midnight. It involved digging a hole twelve inches deep and wide, using a ceremonial knife to carve a magic word into one of the candles along with the name and birth date of the person who had hexed her.

She didn't get very far before she realized that this spell would take a lot more time and effort than she was willing to invest. First of all, it was not a full moon. When you discover you are hexed, you don't want to wait around for the next full moon to put things right.

Then there was the whole matter of gathering up ceremonial candles, tarot cards, and charcoal. She was hoping for a spell that involved more common household items like a glue stick and a TV remote control. Besides that, this spell was supposed to turn the bad luck back on the person who had originally cursed her. That didn't seem very polite, so she continued on her quest for a magical cure.

She finally found it on a UK psychic site. Amidst discussions by professional psychics of whether curses are real or just a scam she found a recipe for a "cleansing bath spell." The psychic who had posted it was confident it was authentic. Soaking in a tub was on par with her level of commitment to the Wiccan cause.

The spell's ingredients were pretty simple: three bay leaves, one lemon, flour and three handfuls of sea salt. Candi didn't actually have a lemon or sea salt handy, but she did substitutions all the time when baking cookies, she was sure it worked the same with spells. She took out a bottle of lemon juice and her shaker of table salt.

The web site explained that bay leaves open your psychic channels. Candi had always wondered just what bay leaves did. When recipes called for them, they told you to put them in, and then take them right back out. Candi had never eaten anything and said, "Mmm. You used bay leaves didn't you?" So now she knew—it was there to ward off evil during cooking time.

She filled the tub with warm water, squirted in some of the lemon, shook a bit of salt in, tossed in the flour and the three bay leaves and then got in and soaked by the light of a candle. The candle wasn't in the instructions; it was her personal touch. She figured you should take your cleansing spell bath by candlelight. She didn't actually believe the spell would do anything, but there was some small part of her that hoped, and the warm water was relaxing.

After a long soak, she got out of the tub and wiped the flour scum off her body with a towel. Then she realized she had to clean her tub. As she was up to her elbows in green cleanser the phone rang. As she ran to get the phone, her wet feet slipped out from under her. She landed on the bedroom floor with a thump. That would leave a bruise. She raised herself up on her elbow and looked at the phone. It was an 800 number. So much for witchcraft. Still lying on the floor she picked up the receiver and put it to her ear.

"Hello?"

"This call may be monitored …"

Candi sighed.

"Hello Miss Travis, how are you today?" said an overly cheery male voice.

"I was much better before you called," she thought. "And my name is Tavris not Travis." She answered, "Fine."

"That's good to hear," said the cheery harasser. He was probably a college student. He sounded too articulate to be a prisoner, but then you never knew these days. Maybe he was in for white collar crime or drugs. Probably not credit card fraud or they wouldn't give him access to people's account numbers, would they?

"The reason I am calling is that your Master Card payment is five days past due in the amount of $130," he said. "Can I put a payment through for you today?"

"No," she said.

Did they really expect everyone to stop living and devote every moment of their lives to paying them? They probably did, actually. They didn't care about her life or health or sanity at all. She wasn't real to them. She was a profit center, a series of digits. It is shocking, when you grow up, to realize how many people there are in the world who care nothing about your life at all.

"I'd like to help you avoid any negative impact on your credit," said the caller.

"It's a bit late for that," she said.

That is when it hit her. Ruining her credit was the only thing they had to threaten her with. They had already done it. Why was she killing herself, feeling constantly stressed, anxious, depressed? They had no more leverage.

"Do you know when you'll be able to make that payment?"

"When I'm good and ready," she said and hung up the phone.

She felt powerful. She didn't have to feel guilty because they told her she was supposed to. Maybe the magic bath had worked after all. She decided that when her direct deposit came in she was going to buy tickets to Ollie's upcoming concert and she would not allow herself to feel anxious about it. It was not wasteful; it was an investment in her future, her real life. If all went as she hoped, these would be the last days of her life as the old Candi. Nothing was more important. This was her "Goodbye to Sandra Dee" moment. No creditor was going to stand between her and a happy ending.

The next day after work she stopped at the ATM. When she drove up to the machine she noticed that the car in front of her had driven off leaving the receipt hanging. She pulled the receipt from the machine and relished the naughtiness of looking at someone else's bank balance. The previous patron had transferred $100 from savings to checking to bring the account to a positive balance——of 41¢.

She was so delighted that she laughed out loud. Other people's account balances looked like hers too. She almost wanted to take the slip of paper home and frame it. Someone out there was trying to make us all hide in shame, she thought, because if we didn't we might find out that there are no Joneses to keep up with. Then the jig would be up.

She pulled up at the department store humming Blast's "Explosive Simplicity." She wanted to buy just the right outfit for her first in-person meeting with Ollie. It had to be sexy, but respectable. It was the fashion equivalent of walking a tight rope. You're "sexually liberated" if you have the budget to dress like Samantha on "Sex in the City." If you like sex and you dress poorly you're a cheap slut.

She tried on five outfits before she settled on a floaty black skirt that ended just above the knee and a tastefully low-cut white blouse that crossed in the front and was held shut by a single button. It was a blouse she could wear to work without causing any comment, but the lone button meant she (or Ollie) could open it with a single motion. She imagined that scenario on a continuous loop as she rolled her cart to the lingerie department. She tried to remember the last time she'd bought a matching set of bra and panties. It was back when she was dating Chad. So it had been at least four years.

Candi selected a white lace bra—front closure— with matching panties, garter belt, and stockings. She'd never worn a garter belt before, but she wanted to be the kind of woman who did. Before she put the ensemble in her cart, she looked at the price tag. She was shocked when she realized that the underwear was more expensive than the outerwear. She almost put it back, but then she reminded herself of the stranger's bank receipt and her vow to be human for one day. She was going to be sexy for Ollie. Nothing else mattered.

(When they do those makeover shows on TV, they always assume the woman "let herself go." They assume she is suffering from a tragic case of low self-esteem. They never consider the possibility that the subject of their makeover didn't "let herself go," she just couldn't afford the $500 in clothes they buy her with the studio budget.)

Candi's total came to $128, almost exactly what she owed to Master Card. It was fate. Candi felt a nervous twinge as the sales clerk ran her card. She tried to decide what to take off if the transaction was declined.

"Thank you very much," the clerk said and handed Candi her receipt. "Come back soon."

She walked out of the store with a bounce in her step. She was a real person—a person who goes shopping and buys things and walks out with bags. She went to the salon next door and had her hair cut and styled with layers and highlights. Then, just for good measure, she decided to buy her dinner at Whole Foods, a supermarket that was far out of her price range. Her sister Jackie bought all of her organic fruits there for her top-of-the-line juicer. "The bottled juices lose all the vitamins—and don't get me started on the concentrate."

Candi wandered through the store with its wheat-grass fragrance, feeling as though the vegan police might arrive at any moment and finger her as an imposter. She seemed to pass just fine as the kind of person who only buys organic, free range, gluten-free waffles. At the salad bar she stocked up on three flavors of marinated tofu cubes. She was having so much fun that it wasn't until she got home that she remembered that she didn't like tofu. She threw it in the garbage and made macaroni and cheese from the box instead.

In the privacy of her own bedroom she decided to model her new lingerie. As she rolled the stocking up her leg and hooked it onto the garter she felt seductive and alluring. She ran her hands over the smooth stocking. When she stood in front of the full-length mirror the image she'd had of herself in her mind vanished. She looked nothing like a Victoria's Secret model. It was just her—pot belly and cellulite—but with lace on top. She was crestfallen. She sucked in her gut, and tried to stand at different angles. By standing as tall as she could, holding her breath, and putting one leg a bit in front of the other (the pose she'd mastered for her selfie) she managed to get to where she didn't entirely hate what she saw. In just over two weeks, Candi had learned Ollie's tour route would take him to San Diego. She wondered how much weight she could lose in that time.

Call Me Cyrano

Ethan was in his underwear, sitting on his bed. This was not unusual. What was unusual was that on his lap, instead of his computer, he had a book. It was not even a science-fiction paperback; it was a real, heavy, hard-cover book without a dust jacket. His mother had nearly fallen out of her chair when he said he was going to the library. Maybe she thought he was going to go back to college.

Ethan had started to think a lot about Cyrano De Bergerac. It was one of the books he was supposed to read in his world lit class in college, but he had never got around to it. Everyone knew the story, though. A French guy with a huge nose is in love with a woman named Roxanne. She has the hots for a handsome guy who doesn't know how to form a sentence. So Cyrano writes the love letters on behalf of the handsome guy. He seduces Roxanne in another man's name. He sort of remembered there being a balcony scene and swords.

Ethan was now Cyrano. He was writing the words that were making his Roxanne swoon. The problem was that he couldn't remember how the Cyrano story ended. He thought the play might have a few clues as to how he could get out of the mess he'd made for himself. The thing is, Ethan wasn't much of a reader. He had to keep drawing his attention back to the page. He wondered how it would go over if he were to tell Candi she was "a peach divine smiling in a nest of strawberries." Then his mind wandered. He dropped the book on the floor and was about to pick up his laptop when his phone rang.

"Hey," Ethan said.

"What are you doing?" Ale asked.

"Reading a book."

"If you don't want to come out just say so, don't make something up."

"I was reading a book," Ethan said.

"Come over," Ale said. "Sasha and her friend are coming over. We're going to play strip poker. You have to come, her friend is cute."

"What's her name?"

"Keziah."

"Is she black?"

"No, she's not black. I mean, Sasha didn't say she was black."

"You think she's going to say, 'I'm coming over with my black friend?'"

"What difference does it make? She's a girl and they want to play strip poker."

"You're so full of shit," Ethan said. "You said she was cute and you haven't even seen her. You don't even know if she's black or white."

"Come over and find out then. All you do is stare at the computer and chat with that Blast groupie."

"She's not a groupie," Ethan said.

"Whatever," Ale said.

"She's not a groupie. Don't say that."

"You have a chance here to meet a real person."

"Candi is a real person," Ethan said. "You don't know anything about it. We talk about all kinds of stuff. I know everything about her."

"You know what you remind me of?" Ale asked. "Did you ever see that movie where the guy thought he was dating one of those blow-up sex dolls?"

"What kind of movies do you watch, man?"

"No, OK, this is better. You know what you're like? That Star Trek movie. You know, the one where they killed off Captain Kirk? I think that was the one. There was this space cloud—ribbon, —and if you got stuck in it you lived your perfect fantasy, like Piccard had this French family, but it wasn't real. So Captain Kirk and Captain Piccard had to destroy the vortex to return the world to normal. It had that Clockwork Orange guy in it. Remember?"

"How come both of your examples of how I have to live in reality come from movies? You know those aren't real, right?"

Ale let out a deep sigh. "Are you coming over or what?"

"No, man. Sorry."

"It's not healthy," Ale said.

"Yes, Mom," Ethan said, and hung up. He looked at the book on the floor, rubbed his head, and then picked up his laptop. He remembered that Steve Martin had done a comedy version of Cyrano with Daryl Hannah as the love interest. It only took him a couple of minutes to find a site where he could stream the whole thing for free.

Ethan loved the movie. He liked the part where Darryl Hannah gets locked out of her house naked. More important, he identified with Steve Martin's insecurity. The only time his Cyrano could express his deepest emotions was when he was pretending to be someone else. The best part was that even though Cyrano was playing kind of a con on Roxanne you're supposed to root for him. Everyone is supposed to want Daryl Hannah to end up with big-nosed Steve, not the thick, handsome guy he's pretending to be. It is almost like it's Roxanne's fault for being shallow enough to want the guy with the good nose. (Cyrano is not to be blamed for wanting the beautiful Roxanne instead of the plain woman his nose could attract, of course.)

Ethan watched the last scene four times in a row. At first, Roxanne is angry that the Cyrano character has duped her. But a few hours later she is outside Cyrano's house calling up to him where he is sitting lonely on the roof. She says she realizes that she was not in love with the handsome guy. "It was how he made me feel. He made me feel romantic ... But it wasn't him. It was you." And then the music swells and they kiss and live happily ever after. With each viewing, Ethan became more reassured that Candi would forgive him when she learned the truth. She would realize she was in love with him, not the rock star.

(Had Ethan done his homework in college, he would have known that the happy ending was a Hollywood invention. In the original Roxanne marries Christian, not Cyrano, and shortly thereafter becomes a widow. Cyrano takes his secret to the grave.)

After Roxanne, Ethan started looking up and streaming all sorts of romantic comedies. There were tons of stories where one character deceives another on the road to falling in love. The movies started to blend one into another. They started with a case of mistaken identity. Sometimes one character set out to deceive another, sometimes it just happens and the character goes along with it and can't find the right moment to tell the truth. Either way, because of the lie, two people who would never have spent time together meet and they fall in love. Then there is a crisis and the lie is revealed. They seem like they are going to break up but then one of two things happen—either the guy who did the deceiving makes a big show—he chases her down, makes a speech outside her window or something or, as in Roxanne, the deceived party thinks things over and realizes that she loves the essence of the man, not the outward package. In the end, the couples were always ready to forgive and they lived happily ever after.

Romantic comedies were not documentaries but they were female fantasy, Ethan reasoned. So watching them was an education in what women wanted. The more he watched, the more it seemed as though women, deep in their hearts, want someone to seduce them with bald-faced lies. As long as he could give a convincing enough speech when he explained that he did it all for love, everything should work out fine.

Preparation

The woman in the spandex leotard was speaking in a rhythmic staccato: "Pump it out right here. Again. Here we go right here. March it out, right left again. Pump it up. Step side to side."

Candi was stepping left and right and punching the air in front of her. She wasn't sure what her core was, but it was going to be flat if it killed her.

The freakishly fit woman in the fat-burning cardio DVD was giving peppy encouragement.

"You're doing a great job!"

"Yeah, right." Candi puffed back.

"Doesn't that feel good?"

"No."

Candi did her workout with the curtains closed and the lights off in case a shadow of her clumsy, jumping form might be visible to someone outside. She had the vague sense that the models in the video were laughing at her.

Her sister Jackie was naturally slim no matter what she ate. Candi had inherited a less forgiving metabolism. As she got close to puberty, her parents started to whisper about when the baby fat was going to disappear. She was taken to a doctor who talked to her mother about the problem of Candi's body as if she was not even in the room. Candi's parents taught her to count calories and looked at her with disapproval whenever she ate something sweet. Jackie had no dietary limits. Candi was sent off to aerobic dance classes while Jackie stayed home and played with her friends. It all seemed like punishment for a deep moral failing. The result was that Candi associated working out with shame and humiliation. It was something to be done in secret in the dark.

"Step it up that's right now. Don't forget to breathe."

123

"Does anyone really forget to breathe?" Candi wondered. She was in no danger of forgetting, she was more likely to hyperventilate.

"I give up," Candi told the television. She picked up the remote and turned the DVD off and fell down on the floor to catch her breath. This was the fourth time she'd done this workout this week, and it was only Thursday. She was entitled to give it a rest.

Candi lay there marveling at her life. She and Jackie had carved out their own distinctive roles in the family. Jackie got to be prom queen and she was expected to fall in love with the handsome prince and have a dream wedding. Candi graduated third in her class. She was slated for career success. Although she would never admit such a thing out loud, Candi was convinced that as a woman being "the smart one" was the less desirable role.

Now the poles were shifting. Candi might not have lived up to expectations where her career was concerned, but she and a rock star were about to become lovers. She was sure of that. But what kind? She'd been operating under the assumption that her flirtation with Ollie meant she was special. She was attractive enough to pique the interest of the most eligible man.

But what if she wasn't? Maybe he flirted with lots of his fans through e-mail. Maybe he got them worked up and had different bed partners in each of his tour cities. If that was the case, she wouldn't be special at all. She would be a slut who threw herself at a famous guy. Was she unique and intriguing enough to stand out, or was she more like the women who crawl out from under rocks in political scandals—the recipients of the powerful man's crotch photos and dirty texts? She did not know how to ask Ollie, but it was imperative that she find out.

Candi got up and went to take a shower. As the bathroom filled with steam, and she watched the soap lather running over her body she thought about her suggestive correspondence with Ollie.

"Soapy skin feels nice."

She wanted him with every fiber of her being. It was a physical ache that started in her sex organs and filled her whole body. It was tangible and undeniable. Since she started flirting with Ollie, she had never felt more alive. In one sense it was like sleepwalking. All of the stresses of her day-to-day life were still there but she was numb to them. But when you sleep, you dream. The dream world that had been opened up to her was much more beautiful than the world she had been forced to inhabit before. She knew what being alive smelled like. She could feel her soul, liquid and juicy. She was not willing to let her soul dry out again. No, she could not let this feeling go.

If she wasn't willing to give it up, she knew better than to ask him what it all meant. You should never ask a question if there is only one answer you can accept. She needed to make love to Ollie. She didn't care if it was once or a million times. She wasn't willing to stop the game if she didn't hear what she wanted. So she resolved to keep her doubts to herself and enjoy it for whatever it was.

By the time she put on her pajamas and sat down at the computer screen, however, her resolve was gone. Her slut-fear didn't correspond to any of her own rational thoughts or emotional desires. It was an invading concept, imposed on her from somewhere outside. Yet it overpowered everything. Being a "groupie" or a "slut" meant that you were worthless. The world could do whatever it liked to you. You could be mocked, written off, abused, and no one would come to your defense. The terror had all the natural force of the fear of falling or fire. It was driven by the instinct for survival. These two great life forces, eros and fear, did battle inside her. She had to know that she was more than just a groupie.

She sat, biting the nail of her index finger, staring at her computer screen as she tried to decide how to bring this all up to Ollie without it being "a thing."

To: Oliver Thomas <OllieBlast>
From: Candi Tavris <PackagingGal>

I can't stop thinking about you coming to San Diego. I have been thinking about how we've gotten to know each other. I hope you know I don't just want to be with you because you're a star. I don't think of you that way any more.

*****

Candi got up, made herself a cup of tea and paced. When she sat back down and checked her e-mail she had a reply. Ollie must have answered on his phone backstage. Even though the e-mails flew back and forth they never switched over to chat.

To: Candi Tavris <PackagingGal>
From: Oliver Thomas <OllieBlast>

You know that when you say you want to sleep with a guy he doesn't usually care why, right? :-)

Candi grimaced. He was deflecting.

To: Oliver Thomas <OllieBlast>
From: Candi Tavris <PackagingGal>

I'm being serious.

To: Candi Tavris <PackagingGal>
From: Oliver Thomas <OllieBlast>

OK. Thanks.

Thanks? Candi wanted to reach through the computer and shake him. Did he really not know what she was getting at? Or did he know exactly? Maybe her worst fears were true.

To: Oliver Thomas <OllieBlast>
From: Candi Tavris <PackagingGal>

This is important to me.

To: Candi Tavris <PackagingGal>
From: Oliver Thomas <OllieBlast>

I don't know what you want me to say.

To: Oliver Thomas <OllieBlast>
From: Candi Tavris <PackagingGal>

What I'm saying is it's important to me that I'm not just a fan to you.

To: Candi Tavris <PackagingGal>
From: Oliver Thomas <OllieBlast>

Don't worry about that.

To: Oliver Thomas <OllieBlast>
From: Candi Tavris <PackagingGal>

You're being a jerk.

To: Candi Tavris <PackagingGal>
From: Oliver Thomas <OllieBlast>

Why? What did I do?

To: Oliver Thomas <OllieBlast>
From: Candi Tavris <PackagingGal>

You're not answering me.

To: Candi Tavris <PackagingGal>
From: Oliver Thomas <OllieBlast>

Being a fan is really admiring someone, right? Why would I think less of you if you feel that way about me?

To: Oliver Thomas <OllieBlast>
From: Candi Tavris <PackagingGal>

I get what you're saying.

To: Candi Tavris <PackagingGal>
From: Oliver Thomas <OllieBlast>

You're like a rock star to me. Did you know that?

To: Oliver Thomas <OllieBlast>
From: Candi Tavris <PackagingGal>

Really?

To: Candi Tavris <PackagingGal>
From: Oliver Thomas <OllieBlast>

Yeah. I look at your picture and I imagine what it would be like to be with you. You're this unattainable celebrity. I wish I could wear a t-shirt with your name on it so everyone would know what a fan I am. You're not the kind of girl who would ever look at me in real life. If you saw me on the street you'd walk right by. The only reason we met is that you're a fan of Blast. If it weren't for that you wouldn't know I exist. So I don't know what is wrong with being a fan. If you talk to me, and you're a fan of the guy in the e-mails, then it's amazing.

To: Oliver Thomas <OllieBlast>
From: Candi Tavris <PackagingGal>

It's amazing to me too.

To: Candi Tavris <PackagingGal>
From: Oliver Thomas <OllieBlast>

Am I still a jerk?

To: Oliver Thomas <OllieBlast>
From: Candi Tavris <PackagingGal>

LOL. No.

To: Candi Tavris <PackagingGal>
From: Oliver Thomas <OllieBlast>

Don't worry about what I think of you.

Preparation H

Ollie's hemorrhoids were acting up again. Fortunately, there was a chain pharmacy right across the street from the La Quinta (Graham said La Quinta was Spanish for Super 8). Chain stores produce a feeling of comfort and stability when you're on the road. It doesn't matter what city you're in. You walk into a CVS and you will know, instinctively, which well-lit aisles to walk down to find your brand of choice. The store seemed a bit more crowded than he was used to. "It must be a weekend," he thought, but he couldn't remember for sure.

Without thinking, he walked straight through the cosmetics aisle, turned right, passed two aisles then turned right again. As he expected, he was in the aisle with the products related to digestion and all its embarrassing machinations. The hemorrhoidal remedies were generally toward the end of the aisle below eye level. American stores had such a mind-boggling array of brands with subtle and pointless distinctions. "Super strength," "with aloe," "specially formulated to relieve itching," "compare to the active ingredient in Preparation H." There were gels and suppositories, different types of applicators. Ollie preferred the gel to the suppositories, and the semi-clear Vaseline-y kind to the white fish-scented kind made with shark oil. Beyond that he couldn't be arsed. He picked one of the store brand knock-offs and made his way to the checkout.

There were a couple of people in front of him, so he passed the time glancing at the headlines on the impulse purchase magazines. A Kardashian was breaking up with someone who US Magazine assumed he would know on a first name basis. Jennifer Anniston had a secret. Another young movie star, who he'd never heard of, had the words "Gay Lover Bombshell" under his picture on the cover of The Enquirer. People, it seems, buy pictures of Hollywood's best- and worst-dressed on impulse. They must not be as quick to part with $4 for Newsweek or National Geographic.

He had reached the front of the line and put his purchase on the counter. The clerk appeared to be around 40. She was attractive, with shoulder-length brown hair and big, dark brown eyes. She looked at him with a slight squint of the left eye, as if she was trying to place him. Then she stood up a bit taller and gave a broad, genuine smile. (Not the "Have a nice day" smile she'd given the previous customers.)

"Hey," she said. "Aren't you Blast? You're doing a show at the Pepsi Theater right?"

"Yeah," he said softly, trying not to draw attention to himself. He was thinking about the hemorrhoid cream on the counter between them.

"Wow," she said. "That is so cool. I love that song, you know, the one about the weather."

"Thanks," he said, thinking about the hemorrhoid cream on the counter between them.

"Hey, Jane," she said, calling out to a girl at the next register. "Look who it is, it's Blast. She's a huge fan."

Now Jane was looking at him, as were the customers in both of the lines. Ollie was focused on the hemorrhoid cream on the counter. He had an impulse to pick up a magazine and a few candy bars to cover it up but he stood frozen, smiling.

"Listen," said the clerk, "Can I get your autograph? Wait, let me find my purse."

"Yes," Ollie said. He could feel the blood rushing to his cheeks. "But, if you don't mind, could you ring me up first?"

Finally she looked down at the hemorrhoid cream on the counter between them. He watched, with horror, as what he was buying registered on her face. The recognition lasted only a moment before it was replaced with the "Have a nice day" smile. She ran the package over the scanner and dropped the product into a plastic bag. "That will be $4.99," she said in a tone of overcompensating cheerfulness. "Do you have a CVS card?"

"Yeah," he said, reaching into his wallet. He handed her his card and a $5 bill.

"That's so cool," said Jane, who was watching the transaction over the first clerk's shoulder. "Blast has a CVS card!"

She would probably go home and blog about selling hemorrhoid cream to a rock star.

He signed the back of a register receipt for each of the clerks and posed for cell phone pictures with a few of the customers, all the time distracted by the nearly translucent bag sitting on the counter with his hemorrhoid cream inside. As soon as he sensed a break, he grabbed the bag, waved at the crowd and left. A few customers stood in the parking lot and watched him walk all the way back to the hotel.

As Ollie walked into the lobby, he pulled his key card out of the back pocket of his jeans. He'd forgotten to take the little paper envelope along with it, so there was no indication of his room number. It was on the second floor, he thought, something like 212, or had that been his room the night before? He went to the check in desk.

"Excuse me," he said.

The harried young woman behind the desk did not recognize him. She had burgundy hair and band-aids on her ear lobes. The management must have thought that preferable to ear stretchers underneath. She looked to Ollie to be about Emma's age, but she was probably in her early to mid-twenties. (It was getting harder for him to tell the difference these days.) She lifted a finger in a "just a minute" gesture and picked up the ringing telephone. She cradled the telephone on her shoulder and started clicking away at the computer in front of her.

"For how many nights?"

An Asian-American woman with a self-assured (pushy) stance and a loud voice came up beside Ollie and thwacked a television remote control on the counter.

"This doesn't work," she said. Ollie might as well not have been there. The clerk raised the "just a minute" finger again.

It was one of the paradoxes of Ollie's character. When it came to his career he was ambitious, sometimes to the point of obsession. When it came to things like this, saying "Excuse me, I was here first," he was entirely meek.

As a boy, he'd suffered from a stutter. It wasn't until he was eleven years old, with the help of a school speech therapist, that he had been able to mostly cure his verbal tics. Even now, when he was under extreme stress, he occasionally stammered. The negotiations with Mandy and the lawyers had been full of hesitations and pauses. The worst part of it was watching her impatience. When they were in love, she had found it endearing.

It was easy enough to come to the conclusion that his drive for musical success was over-compensation for being an outsider in his youth. Maybe there was some truth to it. Part of his attraction to music had been that he never stuttered when he sang. As a teenaged member of a garage band, he could avoid having to socialize yet still be a part of all the parties. Music was always welcome. He got applause, people remembered he'd been part of the good time, and no one even noticed if he didn't talk to anyone all night.

But what did any of that prove? Who didn't have a story to tell about his awkward teen years? You could find something in just about anyone's life, point to it, and say "this trauma gave him his drive." Being more comfortable in front of an audience than with individuals was just another personality quirk.

The Asian woman had become impatient with the clerk. She was tapping the remote control on the counter. Without looking away from her screen, the clerk reached under the counter, pulled out a new remote, and handed it to the customer. The woman took it and walked away without saying "thank you."

The clerk hung up the phone. "Hi," she said. "How can I ..."

The phone rang again. She picked it up.

"Isn't there some sort of rule about first come, first served?" Ollie wanted to ask. Because he was himself, he did not.

"Six to ten A.M.," she said. "You're welcome."

When she hung up the phone he spoke quickly; he didn't want to be derailed again.

"I don't remember my room number," he said.

"What is your name?"

"Oliver Thomas," he said.

She clicked on the keyboard. "Oliver Thomas," she said. "Oh, I'm sorry. There's a note here not to give that room number to anybody. I guess Oliver Thomas is some kind of celebrity."

"A musician," Ollie said. "I'm Oliver Thomas."

"A lot of the people who play at the Pepsi stay here," she said.

"Right," he said. "That's what we're doing. We're on a four-month tour and we stay in so many hotels, I can't remember my room number."

"I think someone named Blast is playing tonight," she said. "He's like an 80s guy or something."

"Right. That's me," he said. "The 80s guy."

"Really?" she said. "So is 'Oliver Thomas' one of those fake names celebrities use so no one will know where they're staying?"

"It's my real name," he said. "Did you think Blast was a real name?"

"Whatever," she said.

"I don't mean to be a bother," he said. "But I'm having a bit of a bad day, and if you wouldn't mind helping me ..."

"The thing is, I just can't give out the number because you say that's who you are. What if you were, like, some kind of stalker?"

"Yes, that is quite vigilant of you," he said. He took his wallet from his pocket and pulled out his driver's license. "Look. Oliver Thomas. Could you tell me my room number, please?"

She looked at the license, and then glanced at the screen.

"212."

Ollie returned to his room, put his drug store purchase to its intended use, and then fell onto the bed. He lay there looking at the non-descript floral painting on the opposite wall. He'd always been a bit fascinated by hotel art. People usually put art in their rooms to reflect some aspect of the personalities they wanted to project. The interior of a hotel reflects everybody and nobody. What type of art do you pick for people who don't live there, who are just passing through? It was art specially selected to avoid offending anyone. Therefore it was art selected because it would not be interesting enough to anyone to cause any distraction. The art of the dull.

He'd read an article once about these young artists who checked into hotels, took the framed pictures down and painted original art behind them then put the frame back up so that it was a secret treasure to be discovered. For a while after he read about it, he would run his fingers around the edges of hotel paintings to see if one was in his room. He stopped when he realized he wasn't discovering any hidden treasures, just learning a lot about the level of the housekeeping—something he preferred not to know.

Ollie covered his eyes with the crook of his elbow. He thought about what a strange place it was he inhabited, where one minute his celebrity intruded on his privacy and the next he couldn't even get a hotel clerk to believe he was himself. Once you've been a rock star with a certain level of fame you never become entirely un-famous, you just become less famous. Intermittently famous. He suddenly longed for genuine human contact. He picked up his phone and dialed Emma's cell phone number.

"Hey, Dad," she said.

"Do you have time to talk? Are you driving? You're not driving?"

"Dad, I'm not driving." She laughed. He imagined her rolling her eyes. "I was just watching TV. What's up?"

"Max is thinking about linoleum tile for the kitchen floor," he said. Emma laughed. "I forgot my room number and I just spent an hour in the lobby trying to convince a 12 year-old clerk to give it to me."

"I'm sure she wasn't 12, and I bet you didn't stand for an hour," Emma said.

"It's hyperbole," Ollie said.

"So you're going to be home for a while this week."

"A little while, about a month, then we take off again to Europe. How is the job going?"

"Oh that," Emma said. "I don't like it. I think I'm going to quit. There have to be better things to do than fast food."

"Will you be able to save for your car?"

"I don't know," Emma said. "I might not need one."

"I thought you had your heart set on it."

"Yeah," she said. "But nobody drives in New York, so ..."

"New York?"

"Yeah." There was a long pause. "She didn't tell you."

"Tell me what?"

"I don't know if I'm supposed to ..."

"Tell me what?"

"I can't believe she didn't..."

"Emma ..."

"Well, it's just, we might be moving to New York."

"When? How long has this been in the works?"

"I don't know. It's kind of new. I didn't know she didn't tell you."

Ollie sat up in the bed. "Why New York?"

"Maybe she didn't want to upset you or something. We might not even go."

"Why New York?"

"Well, Greg wants us to live there."

"Who's Greg?"

"Oh man! You don't ... This sucks."

"It's OK. I get the idea." Then more to himself he said, "Greg."

"Sorry, Dad. I thought you knew. I thought she told you."

"So it's serious with Greg?" He emphasized the name "Greg." He couldn't seem to help himself.

"I think so."

"What does he do?"

"Something in fashion, like the business end. He's some kind of hot-shot executive."

"Oh." There was a long pause. Then Ollie spoke again. "You like him?"

"I don't know. He's kind of working too hard. You know, I mean, to make me like him. This is so unfair that I'm the one telling you about this."

"Your mother and I don't communicate very well these days."

"Yeah," Emma said. "Well, I'm sorry. I know you kind of ... I don't know."

"Yeah," Ollie said. "So listen, I heard your solo was great. I'm really proud of you. You have to send me the video."

"I will."

"I'm sorry I wasn't there."

"I know. Well, have a good show tonight."

"I will," Ollie said.

"Bye, Dad."

"Bye, sweetheart. I love you."

"I love you too."

Ollie hung up the phone, set it on the end table, then curled up in a fetal position and cried.

See You Tomorrow

The night before Blast was scheduled to play San Diego, Ethan sat on his bed, chatting with Candi. The sense of anticipation was exhilarating. Ethan gave himself over completely to the steamy seductiveness. He was Blast. It would not be long before would play the song he wrote for her. Candi would be filled with unquenchable desire for him. Every fantasy, every suggestion, every dirty word was about to be enacted.

"I can't wait to see you tomorrow," Candi wrote as she logged off.

"I can't wait," Ethan replied.

His body was already responding to her promises, her threats. He put his computer aside, unzipped his jeans and started to stroke. He imagined his hand was hers as they stood in a dimly lit back stage door where anyone could stumble upon them. Her desire for him was too intense to hold back. He pinned her against the wall and ripped open the satin blouse she'd described so well. His fantasy had a frightening intensity, vivid, visceral, sweaty, and pure. There was no one to judge if his dreams were not pretty. He imagined everything she'd described to him—her skirt, her garters, her stockings. He imagined them down around her ankles, he conjured her wetness and her sighs. He saw her cheeks flush with pleasure and the way she opened her mouth and tensed her face as she came. He wanted to explode into her, not only with his release, but with everything he was.

Then he was ejected from the fantasy into his twin bed and the lonely mess in his hand. He wiped it off with a wad of tissue then turned to his side and rested his flush cheek against the cool side of his pillow. As he drifted toward sleep he imagined the scene at the theater door again. This time he tried to picture things as they would be. There was Candi in the same satin blouse and the short skirt that sometimes revealed a glimpse

139

of the top of a stocking. There she was with her glowing smile and her shy, inviting gazes but this time they were directed at his boss, Oliver Thomas. She didn't know Ethan from Adam. It only now occurred to him that disaster was looming. He had to call it off and do it now.

His heart raced as he got out of bed and paced the small room. He was composing an e-mail message in his mind.

"There is something I have to tell you. I am very sorry. The truth is, this is not Blast's personal e-mail. I work for him and ..." What could he say after that? "I work for him and I've been making a fool out of you, but I really like you?" "I work for him and I just wanted to see if I could get you to talk dirty to me and you did, ha ha!"

There were no words that he could come up with that could make it any better. He was certain he was in love with Candi, and he felt protective of her. Only he had the power to save her from a staggering disappointment. (That he was the cause of that inevitable pain was not foremost in his mind.) She was in love and he could not bear to let her be disillusioned.

After a half hour of pacing and brooding, Ethan came up with a plan. The computer said San Diego was only a couple of hours away. He could leave after work and be there in time for the concert. If he stood at the backstage door he could make sure Candi never crossed paths with Blast. In fact, he reasoned, if he was the one standing between her and the rock star, he would seem important in her eyes. She would try to persuade him and win him over, and they would get to talking. He knew so much about her, what she enjoyed, what she wished for, what she feared. He was sure that if he could just start a conversation she would be struck by how well they hit it off. He just needed to introduce her to the physical Ethan. Once she got to know him she would have to realize that he was the one she'd been talking to all along and he wouldn't do anything to hurt her. Yes, the concert in San Diego was going to be the beginning, not the end. This gave him the peace of mind he needed in order to get to sleep. Nothing had to change.

San Diego

O llie came off the stage at the end of a performance sweaty, high on adrenalin and a bit light-headed from two hours of continuous singing.

"Good audience tonight," Graham said as they returned to the backstage area.

Ollie wiped his face with a towel, and then pulled off his t-shirt. "Look at this," he said, wringing it out. He hung the sweat-soaked shirt over the back of a chair.

Joey rounded the corner to the back stage and immediately picked up his smart phone. Tweeting, or tumbling or whatever the kids do.

"The encore ritual is funny isn't it?" Graham said. "What do you reckon would happen if one night we just told the audience, 'Sorry, you didn't clap hard enough and fucked off.' "

Ollie laughed, "We should try it. I'd be willing to stop singing 'Partly Fucking Thursday.' Does me throat in."

"I keep telling you to drop 'Fucking Thursday,' " Graham said.

"Half the crowd is there for it," Ollie said. Then to the tune of his horrible hit he sang "Half full haalll. Do the Blast without me."

Ollie almost always finished a show in a great mood. Paradoxically the only time Ollie was not haunted by memories of Mandy was when he was on stage performing songs he had written for her. The songs were complete in themselves. It was as if she had existed so that he could write them, not the other way around. She may have left him, but the music never would. Not even "Fucking Thursday."

He stepped into the backstage shower. He imagined his body would steam when the water hit him. He scrubbed the stage makeup off his face. As the sweat and makeup swirled down the drain he became Ollie again. He remembered what he had been doing before he came to the theater. He had spent two hours researching someone called Greg. He hadn't wanted to do it, but he needed to know who had stepped into his life. Greg was Gregory Hampton Wight, owner of a chain of high-end boutique clothing shops. He was worth a few million dollars and drove a Bentley, judging by a photo in a feature he'd found on the web page of a business magazine. Ollie had learned all this by googling "Amanda Thomas" "fashion" and "Greg."

"The collection by Amanda Thomas, wife of 80s rock star Blast, was powerful and darkly romantic with muted colors and clean lines ..."

The show in question had been put on by Mr. Hampton Wight, who was looking for new talent to feature in his stores. The article was dated almost two years before Mandy had asked for a divorce.

Once Ollie had the full name he had no problem finding information on his wife's new lover. He was able to piece together a narrative and a timeline. The Wight boutiques were now featuring an expensive line called "Evenings by Mandy." Ollie recognized his wife's work even without his last name.

Ollie thought about the early days when he and Mandy had been in love. They dreamed together, and Mandy's dreams were always about fame. She loved Ollie because she saw his potential. He was going to be a rock star and she would start her career in fashion by making costumes for the band. The first part of the dream came true. They made Ollie into Blast. Mandy's big fashion career had gotten lost somewhere along the line. Greg Hampton Wight had given her the opportunity to come out of that big rock star shadow and make a name (if only a first name) for herself.

"Why didn't she tell me that was what she wanted?" Ollie wondered as he dried off with a rather flat towel. "I would have helped her if she told me. Why didn't she let me try?"

Ollie dressed slowly. He did not want to go back to his hotel room. He knew that once he did he would not be able to stay away from his computer. He would not be able to keep himself from looking up everything he could find on Mandy and Greg. He would probably torture himself with information all night.

Ollie walked out to the stage and watched the crew packing up.

"What are you still doing here? Can you get out of the way, the lights are coming down, and you're going to get hurt."

When he could find no more excuses to hang around, he navigated the labyrinth of the back stage corridors, through the loading dock and eventually to the way out. (His favorite scene in the movie Spinal Tap was the one where the band gets lost in the corridors of a stadium trying to find the stage. Ollie had lived out that exact scenario more times than he could count.)

Ollie stepped outside and snapped up his denim jacket. It was a cool, misty night. He had meandered in the theater so long that he did not expect any fans to be waiting for him, but before he had entirely got his bearings, a young woman spoke. She was standing beside the ramp of the loading dock in a pool of street light. She had no jacket, just a short skirt and a blouse that was a bit too thin for the weather.

"Hi," she said. She looked down and then cocked her head to the left, glancing up at him using only her eyes. Then she brushed a strand of hair away from her forehead and looked straight at him, biting her lower lip.

"Hi," Ollie answered.

"I can't believe we're finally meeting face to face," she said.

Ollie put out his hand for her to shake. "Nice to meet you," he said.

She took his hand in her right and put the left hand on top. She gave a light laugh, and then tilted her eyes again. "You don't have to be so formal."

"Would you like an autograph?" Ollie asked.

This time she laughed fully, right from the gut. "No," she said. Then with a sly glance she added, "Do you want mine?"

Ollie smiled. "This could be fun," he thought.

This girl was scrubbed and pressed and understated. She was not advertising her availability with a neon sign, but she was inviting him. There was no question in his mind. He liked her type much better than the women who appeared at stage doors dressed like porn stars, all cleavage and make up. She was a middle class girl impatient to throw off her cloak of propriety and he was more than willing to help.

There were so many lies about sex. "Men are dirty, lustful and any move they make on a woman is a kind of attack. It is unwanted and diminishes her." Rock musicians knew the truth—women want a chance to be the dirty ones, to cast a lustful gaze, to make a man a sex object. The rock 'n' roll world was a more healthy world, where the scales were put back in balance. He was grateful at that moment that he was a rock star. It was a beautiful thing to have a woman come up to him and express pure desire, to approach him seeking what, deep down, he didn't think he had the right to ask for.

Ollie was trying to think of a clever comeback to seal the deal when Ethan from the office appeared from out of nowhere. He grabbed the girl by the elbow.

"I'm sorry," he said, "Blast is very busy."

"What are you doing here?" Ollie asked him.

"I ..." Ethan stammered a bit. "I just decided to ... I wanted to get here earlier ..."

"It's OK," Ollie said to Ethan. "This isn't your job." He waved him off, but Ethan did not get the signal and kept standing there.

"It's fine," Ollie said. He emphasized this with raised eyebrows. Ethan kept standing there. Was he really going to have to spell it out for the kid?

"You can go now," Ollie said with uncharacteristic force.

"Yeah, but, fans aren't supposed to ..."Ollie glared at him. Ethan looked down at his feet, and then walked off all slumped.

"He's protective of you," the woman said.

"He works in the office," Ollie said with a little shrug. "I don't even know what he's doing here. You don't have to go."

The woman looked to be in her late 20s or early 30s. Ollie decided not to do the math to figure out if he could have fathered her. He wasn't sure if the age difference proved he was a manly stud or that he was a pathetic old lech. Somehow he managed to feel a bit of both at the same time. That conflict created an erotic charge—the sweetness of the shame.

"It was a great show tonight," she said.

She moved in closer and he caught a whiff of subtle perfume. It was flowery and spicy. It had a hint of violet, a teasing fragrance. He'd learned from Mandy that violets have a chemical that knocks out your smell sensors, so you catch just a hint then it disappears, then it comes back, over and over.

"Meet Me after Midnight," she said, twirling a strand of her hair.

"You like that one?" he asked.

"Of course," she said. She quoted a verse from the song. "Where are you?/Alone tonight/Can't put out/The fire inside/ Meet me when I close my eyes/Dreaming after midnight."

She thought the "fire" was sex, not the stress and anger of divorce. He preferred her interpretation. She touched his forearm with the tip of her finger, and then ran it over his skin, barely grazing its surface. It tickled.

"You're shy face to face," she said, letting a strand of hair fall across her eyes.

"You're not," he said.

"Not tonight," she said with a little giggle and a tilt of the head. "So, are you staying near here?"

"Yeah," he said.

She shrugged. "Where?"

"You can walk from here."

"Well?"

"Well, yes," he said with a laugh. "Why not? Follow me."

They walked without speaking. The only sound was the clicking of her heels on the damp pavement. It is a unique moment when you've agreed to have sex with someone but you haven't started yet. Ollie never quite knew what to do with his hands. He was jealous of smokers. A cigarette not only solved the hand problem, it gave you an excuse not to talk. "I'm not lost for words; I'm taking a drag on a cigarette." At the moment, it seemed almost as if it was worth the lung-cancer risk.

The woman solved his hand dilemma by latching onto his arm. He felt her body against his. The parking lot was full of puddles, and they had to separate to go around them, then come back together. The tempo of her heels and the jumps around the puddles reminded Ollie of the Gene Kelly film *Singing in the Rain.* She must have had the same idea, because she started singing the tune. "Do do do do-do, do do do-do do do …" She giggled and jumped into a small puddle and splashed them both. When she did this he caught a glimpse of the top of a stocking and the white lace garter that held it in place. The sight triggered a small surge of warmth through his body.

"I never do this," she said.

"Don't you?"

"No. I mean, I never walk outside at night and look at the stars. Do you?"

"Not usually," he looked up. "It's cloudy tonight. There are no stars." When he looked back down she was standing very close. He caught another whiff of the teasing fragrance.

"Can I kiss you?" she asked.

"If you like."

"I like," she said.

She leaned in and at first barely brushed his lips with her own. She was taking her time, increasing the intensity moment by moment. She grasped his hair. He felt the warmth of her breath and her body. As they separated she ran her tongue over the surface of his lower lip. Then she put two fingers over her own lips and let out a coy giggle.

"You're dead cute," Ollie said.

What a lovely surprise she was. There was nothing cheap or dehumanizing about this moment, quite the contrary. It was two people admitting their need to touch and be touched, to desire and be desired, living completely in the moment, consenting to abandon their vanity, if just for one night. It was perfect and complete. It didn't require any context or promises, no greater meaning, just the freedom of two children at play. This night, of all nights, it was exactly what he needed.

"Come on," he said, cocking his head in the direction of the hotel. "We're almost there."

Ollie entered the lobby first, with the young woman trailing just a bit behind. He was pleased to find the purple-haired teenager still on duty. When he saw her he slowed down, and put his arm around his female companion's waist. He gave a little wave as if to say, "Yeah, it's me. The 80s guy. You see, I am a rock star."

The woman stepped on to the elevator first. When the door closed, Ollie got his first good look at her in the light. The left leg of her stocking was shredded. Her legs were splashed with mud from the puddles and her damp white blouse clung to her body. She didn't have a perfect body, average build, he would say, but her breasts were quite nice (and almost entirely visible under the wet fabric and lace bra). Her smile was killer.

"Room 212," he said as he slid the room key through the card reader. "Wait here a second," he said. Before he invited her in, he did a quick clean up. His underwear and dirty clothes were strewn across the bed. He balled them up, threw them into the suitcase and zipped it up. Then he straightened the bed a little. He looked at himself in the mirror and ran his fingers through his hair to untangle it before he went back to the door.

"OK, you can come in," he said. "Sorry about that."

"I sort of imagined you in a fancy suite or something," she said.

"It's only me," he said. "I don't need the space."

"You're disillusioning me about your glamorous rock star life," she said. The girl was looking around the room; she walked over to the desk and ran her fingers over his closed laptop. "Look," she said. "It's your computer. I can picture you sitting there, typing your messages. That's so cool."

"Did you come here to talk about the room?" he asked.

"I love the way you ask questions—that little downturn," she said, imitating his accent. "Did you come here to talk about the room?"

"Well, did you?"

She kicked off her shoes, then walked over to him and ran her hands over his chest. "I did not," she said. She covered his mouth and neck with a flurry of kisses. "I've never wanted anyone the way I want you," she said in a half whisper. "All that anticipation. It almost killed me."

He clutched her hair, and she responded with a wild, hungry embrace. He ran his left hand down her body, hiked up her skirt, unhooked her garter, and caressed the inside of her upper thigh.

She slid off her skirt and fell back onto the bed. Her lace panties matched the bra, visible under her translucent blouse. The blouse had only one button, and she fingered it without opening it. She was making only one request of him, to surrender to her desire.

"Wait right there," he said. "Just a minute."

He rushed to the bathroom. (He had to run his hand over three different walls before he found the light switch.) Then he started digging around in his shaving kit. It took him a few moments to get to the box of condoms hidden under the tube of Preparation H. He wondered if there was anyone in the world who had figured out how to make stopping to get a condom sexy. He checked his face again in the mirror before going back to the bed. As an explanation for his absence, he held the condom up for her to see. Then he tossed it on the end table.

He stripped down and got into bed beside her. He released the single button on her blouse and let it fall open, then unhooked her bra, ran his tongue over her nipples and watched them harden.

"Oh yeah," she said.

He rolled on top of her, left her stockings on, but reached under the lace panties to massage her between her legs. He ran the fingers of his other hand over her lips and chin and she sighed and gasped. The wetness of her lips, the warmth of her breath, and the moisture on his fingers merged into one sensation.

Then she sat up.

"I want to see you," she said. "I want you to show me what you do when you think of me. Show me how you do it yourself."

He smiled. This girl knew exactly what she wanted.

"OK," he said. As he masturbated in front of her, she unhooked the second garter and removed her panties.

"Do you like this?" he asked.

"Mmhmmm. Come here."

And then she was above him and her lips were on him. He held back her hair and guided her to the depth and tempo he liked. Just when he thought he couldn't hold back any longer, she stopped, slid back, and reached for a condom from the night stand. She tried to put it on him, but she had it the wrong way round. He laughed.

"Let me help you," he said.

"I like watching you do that," she said.

"You're a little voyeur."

And then she was on top of him, and he was inside her. She was full of energy and she was a screamer. He felt the surge inside him. And then his consciousness disappeared into pure sensation. He was new baptized, washed clean of all of his worries and fears, all of his emotions. She collapsed beside him.

He lay beside her, taking deep breaths, bathed in a womb-like warmth. He felt entirely at peace, no longer a stranger on the earth. He wanted to hold onto the moment as long as he could. If only there were a way to bottle that feeling, the moment when consciousness disappeared along with all of the worry, fear, shame, confusion. There was nothing else like it, and the moment was always too short.

He glanced at his partner, the open and playful girl he'd met a half hour before. They were living in the same altered state. He hoped she would not speak.

She turned to him, smiled, and took his hand in hers. A strand of hair was stuck to her moist cheek and with his free hand he brushed it away. She squeezed his hand and didn't say a word.

"You're dead cute," he said.

She smiled, kissed his shoulder, and then rested her head on his chest. They stayed like that, warm and silent for what seemed like half an hour, but it was probably only a few minutes.

"Do you want me to stay?" she finally asked.

"You can if you like."

"I like," she said, and closed her eyes. Ollie kissed her on the forehead. He loved the feeling of her naked body in his arms.

*****

Ollie was only half conscious of his actions when he lifted the telephone receiver and put it back down again. It was his recorded wake-up call. His mind automatically started its check list: what time is check out? What city is next?

150

Then he felt a motion in the bed beside him. "Mmmm," said a female voice. "Do we have to get up?"

"That's right," he thought. "The girl."

He turned to look at her. She arched her back, raised her arms over her head and stretched. Then she rolled on her side to face him.

"I could lie here all day," she said. He caught a whiff of her morning breath. He had hoped she might have vanished in the night like the dream she had seemed to be.

"The show must go on," Ollie said. He sat up quickly and searched the floor for his underwear.

"I wish this never had to end," she said, as he scrambled over to his suitcase and grabbed a pair of fresh underwear, jeans, and a t-shirt. He gave the shirt a quick sniff.

"I'm going to take a shower," he said. "They have breakfast in the lobby if you want."

He hoped that she would take the hint and that he would come out of the bathroom to find she had gone. She didn't. She was still there, dressed in the outfit from the night before, minus the ruined stockings. She had made some coffee, which she was sipping from a hotel cup. She had opened up the curtains and was looking out the window.

"It looks like the weather's cleared up," she said. "I guess you'll be home tomorrow. I bet you're looking forward to that."

"Yes," he said. Something about that observation made him uncomfortable. It wasn't secret information, of course. Any fan could follow his schedule on line. What bothered him was that she was mentioning his life at all. The whole charm of a one-night stand was that it was self-contained, outside of normal existence. It remained beautifully uncontaminated by reality and with any luck, his reality would stay uncontaminated by it.

"I wish I didn't have to go," she said. She walked over to him and gave him a hug. He held the embrace for what seemed like a polite period and then nudged her away.

"Thank you," he said. "This was very nice." He gave her a quick kiss on the lips.

"It was amazing," she said, her eyes were wide and she bit her bottom lip.

"Well," Ollie said, gesturing to the door.

"I'm so glad we did this," she said.

"Yeah, me too," he said. He gave a little wave.

As she walked out thedoor she said, "I'll see you online."

"Sure," he said. "Bye."

Puddle Wonderful

Candi sat at her computer trying to put her thoughts into words. The night before everything had become tangible—the man in the posters, the voice in the chat room—they had come together and she was reliving every moment that made Ollie so real. There was the rough texture of the denim of his jacket, the clean smell of his freshly scrubbed skin, the lines that appeared around his eyes when he smiled, the hints of grey in his hair, the way he rushed to tidy the room and his snoring in the night. Those elements grounded the fantasy. The mixture of the mundane and the sublime told her that it had all been real, it had all happened and it was all happening. Ollie was a man like any other, and there was no reason to believe he could not fall in love with her.

She wanted to express the depth of her feeling, but even hinting at the L word terrified her. She wondered why she was so nervous. With all those hours online she must have communicated more with him than with any of her real-world boyfriends. They were not strangers.

"I had a great time last night."

Too flat. She hit the backspace key and started again.

Something personal, an inside joke. Something about dancing in the parking lot, and their first kiss. She remembered a line from a poem: "puddle-wonderful."

"Last night was puddle-wonderful."

Was that too over the top? She didn't care, it felt exactly right.

"Last night was puddle-wonderful. Everything I dreamed and more. When can I see you again?"

She struck out the last line. Too needy.

"Everything I dreamed and more ..."

Maybe that was too much too. She hit the backspace key and started again.

"Last night was puddle-wonderful, even if there were no stars."

Then she added " ... but you."

"I feel wonderful today. I hope you do, too."

She signed it "Your Little Voyeur" and giggled.

She reread the message several times. She was happy with it and she hit send. Then she put on her headphones and listened to "Meet Me After Midnight" over and over as she waited for Ollie's reply.

No Stars in the Sky

E than had not slept. He'd spent the entire drive from San Diego to Los Angeles replaying the scene he had witnessed—Blast kissing the girl he loved. He hadn't wanted to spy, but he couldn't help himself. He'd driven slowly, at a distance, with his lights off and watched as they walked and laughed and touched. Even worse than what he had seen was the notion of what he had not: Ollie Thomas, who gets the AARP magazine, undressing Candi, fondling her. It was disgusting.

Ethan didn't know which of them to hate more—the washed-up old rock star who would sleep with Candi as if she were a groupie, or Candi, who was so shallow, so blind, that she couldn't tell the difference between him and the man she spoke to online. She had betrayed him. Intellectually, Ethan understood that he had no one to blame but himself, but his emotions were screaming so loudly they drowned out all reason.

Ethan had purposely not checked his secret "Blast" e-mail before leaving for work that morning. He wanted to hear from her, but he knew he would be hurt by whatever she had to say. Going to the office was torture. There were pictures of his romantic rival everywhere: t-shirts, posters, records—that damned gold record with the spider in it. Ethan made a pot of strong coffee and sat at his desk drinking it, pretending to be focused on some important documents. It was a busy day at the office. The band was coming home for a few of weeks before flying off to Europe. They would arrive at the office that afternoon so the staff could help unload the tour bus and take the merch off the truck. Among most of the staff, the mood was light. Ethan hated them, too.

Just before lunch, something occurred to Ethan that he had not considered, distracted as he had been by the sex. Ollie and Candi had spent a lot of time together. What had they said to each other? Wouldn't she say something that would give Ethan's secret away? Could they really have spent the whole night together without figuring out that Candi had been speaking to someone, but not Blast? Ethan's heart began to race. His cheeks went red. What he felt was not guilt but shame. Guilt is a sense of self-loathing when you have done something wrong. Shame is different. It is what you feel when you are in danger of losing your sense of honor. He knew he'd done the wrong thing, but it had all been an accident. Everyone made bad choices sometimes. It didn't shake his faith that he was, deep down, a decent guy. What disturbed him was the notion that when other people found out what he had done they might not feel that way.

He logged onto the Blast account. His fears of discovery were instantly dispersed and replaced with something even worse.

> "Last night was puddle-wonderful, even if there were no stars ... but you. I feel wonderful today. I hope you do, too. Your Little Voyeur."

What was that? What had happened? He typed in a fury:

> "Is that all you care about—stars? Why do women always chase after fame?" He hit send and closed the browser.

"They're here," someone called out.

Graham was the first of the band members to come into the office. When he saw Ethan he said, "How you doing, mate? Ollie says you came to see the show. What did you think?"

"Yeah," Ethan said. "It was great." (He had not gone into the theater, and he'd hated the only show he'd seen that night.)

Joey and Max followed. "Yes! Coffee!" said Joey. He and Max made a beeline for the coffeemaker.

Over Graham's shoulder Ethan could see the rock star near the back door. He was carrying a box of t-shirts or something on his hip. He had stopped to talk to Brenda. Ethan couldn't make out what they were saying but it was probably not what Ethan imagined which was, "I banged this hot groupie last night."

"There were no stars ... but you."

Gross.

"First I'm going to stop at Home Depot," Max was saying as he and Joey walked past. "I have a list of fixtures."

Blast set down the box and approached Ethan's desk. "Just the man I wanted to see," he said. He had an open, friendly smile. Ethan wanted to punch him in the face.

"Could you post something on the blog for the fans?" Blast asked. "Write something thanking the U.S. fans for a successful tour and then put up the Europe dates."

"Yeah, sure," Ethan said. In his own mind he added, "Bastard."

"Good man," Blast said. Then he went back to Brenda's desk and started to go over finances or visas or some such thing.

Ethan kept staring at Blast's old-man hands with their freckles and prominent veins. How could she have let those hands touch her? If he wasn't famous she would never give someone like that the time of day. Sex for status. Women were all prostitutes. Ethan hated them all. Candi especially.

The staff and the band spent the afternoon unloading the buses and putting things away. They were laughing and joking and as the day wore on Ethan's bitterness started to recede. On the drive home, Ethan thought about how beautiful Candi had been the night before. She had described that little skirt to him in so much detail, and it looked even better in life than it had in his mind. She had dressed up for him, not for Blast. She just didn't know it. That wasn't her fault. By the time he got home, he had forgiven her entirely. He ran straight to his room and logged onto the secret Blast account. Candi had sent a reply.

"Why would you say something like that to me? The thing about stars was a joke. I was not chasing after fame. If that's what you think of me, why did you sleep with me in the first place? Why did you start writing to me? You were the one who said this was real. What changed between yesterday and today? I don't understand your reaction at all. I'm really hurt if that's really what you think. I thought we really had a connection; was I wrong?"

Ethan was sorry that he'd lashed out at her. He wanted to make things right, but he didn't know how. There weren't any self-help books out there that covered this particular situation: "What to Do When You've Accidentally Tricked the Girl You Love into Sleeping with Someone Else."

He couldn't just blurt out the truth. She would hate him. What he needed to do was to figure out if she was in love with him, not Blast. Had she been seduced by the e-mails or by the music videos? If he could separate that out somehow, and it seemed like she loved him, then he would figure out a way to tell her and keep her in his life.

"I'm sorry," he wrote. "Don't be upset. I was joking too."

She must have been sitting at the computer waiting for his response. An answer came within a minute.

"It wasn't very funny."

"I was busy today getting unpacked at the office," he wrote. "I didn't mean what I said."

"Can we chat?"

Ethan didn't want to chat. He wanted time to think and compose his replies, but he didn't see how he could say no. He opened a chat screen.

CANDI36: Hello.

OLLIEBLAST: Hello.

CANDI36: You really upset me. I was on Cloud 9 all morning and then, Bam!

OLLIEBLAST: I'm sorry.

CANDI36: So what's the deal? Why did you freak out over the star thing?

OLLIEBLAST: I don't want you to think of me that way.

CANDI36: What way?

OLLIEBLAST: Do you like the guy on the computer or do you like the rock star?

CANDI36: I like you. The man I know. I started as a fan, but it's different now. I told you that.

OLLIEBLAST: But what exactly is it you like?

CANDI36: I like the guy who jumps in puddles with me, who makes me laugh.

OLLIEBLAST: Which is it? The guy who jumps in puddles or the one who makes you laugh?

CANDI36: What are you talking about?

CANDI36: Hello?

CANDI36: I'm only two hours from LA I'll drive up. Let's meet for coffee and talk.

OLLIEBLAST: I can't.

CANDI36: Why not?

Ethan had no idea what to say.

CANDI36: Hello?

OLLIEBLAST: I'm still here.

CANDI36: What happened between last night and today?

OLLIEBLAST: What if I wasn't famous? What if I was just some funny looking guy who had no money and worked in an office?

CANDI36: I would feel the same.

OLLIEBLAST: Are you sure?

CANDI36: I think we should talk about this on the phone. I want to hear your voice.

OLLIEBLAST: No, this is fine.

CANDI36: It's not fine.

CANDI36: Ollie?

OLLIEBLAST: Sort of.

CANDI36: Tell me what you're thinking.

OLLIEBLAST: I don't think you're honest about what you say you want.

CANDI36: Why? I'm being very honest. I have feelings for you. I'd like to see you again.

OLLIEBLAST: I'm trying to be honest.

CANDI36: You don't feel the same way about me?

OLLIEBLAST: You say you don't care about the fame, but I don't think it's true.

CANDI36: Why are you saying this all of a sudden?

OLLIEBLAST: You don't know who I am.

CANDI36: I want to. How many hours have we talked online? I'm not saying that because we slept together now I'm your girlfriend or we should get married or anything, if that's what you're worried about.

OLLIEBLAST: I'm not.

CANDI36: Then what? Can't you say more than that?

Why couldn't you tell the difference? Why didn't you realize that wasn't me?

CANDI36: Hello?

OLLIEBLAST: Hello.

CANDI36: I had a great time last night. I thought you did too. We don't have to get serious; I'd just like to see you again.

OLLIEBLAST: I want things to stay the way they have been and I don't want your feelings about me to change.

CANDI36: Why would they?

OLLIEBLAST: I haven't been honest with you.

CANDI36: Start now.

OLLIEBLAST: I don't know how.

CANDI36: Just tell me what you want from me. Be honest about that at least. Was it just sex?

OLLIEBLAST: No.

CANDI36: Then WHAT DO YOU WANT?

OLLIEBLAST: I don't want things to change.

CANDI36: They have changed. I can't keep talking about this in a chat. Please send me your phone number.

OLLIEBLAST: I can't.

CANDI36: Why because you're a star? If you don't want me to think of you as a star, then let's have a normal conversation.

OLLIEBLAST: I can't.

CANDI36: Are you living with someone?

OLLIEBLAST: No.

CANDI36: Is it the age difference?

OLLIEBLAST: No.

CANDI36: I'm going to e-mail you my phone number. Will you please call?

OLLIEBLAST: I'm not blowing you off. I just can't talk on the phone.

CANDI36: You can't talk on the phone now or ever?

OLLIEBLAST: Do you love me?

CANDI36: What?

CANDI36: Did you really just ask me that?

OLLIEBLAST: Do you love me?

CANDI36: I can't answer that. You're confusing me.

OLLIEBLAST: I think maybe I love you, and I want you to love me.

CANDI36: Can we please speak face to face? Why are you putting up this wall?

OLLIEBLAST: I need some time to explain everything.

CANDI36: How much time?

OLLIEBLAST: I'm not sure. I'm sorry.

Ethan logged off.

The Way Forward

Candi's eyes were red and puffy when she went to work the next day. She'd spent most of the night drinking beer, pacing, and checking her e-mail, hoping that Ollie would come back online. Her emotions were completely overloaded. She felt like one of those computers in old comedies that is fed contradictory data and it goes up in flames and throws punch cards around the room. They had made love, as if that was not sensory overload enough. Now he was saying he loved her, and that alone would have blown her mind. He also didn't want to talk to her. And he kind of called her a slut. Was he breaking up with her or saying he wanted to be closer to her? Then there was the whole mystery of the big secret. Her overriding emotion was anger at herself. She had allowed Ollie to have complete control over her happiness, and he was making her crazy.

Candi did not even bother to sit down at her desk. She went straight to Lydia. "I just really need to talk," she said. She told Lydia everything from the build up and the concert, to meeting Ollie back stage, and the puddles and the sex and the craziness that came after. By the time she had finished tears were running down her cheeks. Lydia let Candi cry on her shoulder for a couple of minutes. Then Lydia said, "Honey, he's a guy."

Candi sniffed. "I know."

"I know you know," Lydia said with a laugh. "You've seen the evidence. What I mean is, each time you move to a new stage of intimacy with a guy you have to expect him to freak out a little bit. It's part of their nature."

"It is?"

"Absolutely," Lydia said. She handed Candi a tissue. "The first time my husband and I made love, he didn't call me for a week. I thought it was over. Then suddenly he had to see me. He couldn't understand why I was upset."

"So you think he's freaking out because …"

"I think it's a good sign. He wouldn't be acting crazy if he didn't care at all. He just got out of a marriage right?"

"Yeah."

"So it's got to be scary. You know what I think? I bet you pushed some kind of button with the e-mail that has nothing to do with you. It's something to do with his ex-wife; I would bet you a million dollars."

"You're probably right."

"I know I'm right," she said.

"What about all the stuff about not being honest with me?"

"Hmm," Lydia said. "Yeah, that's all strange. If he hadn't just gone through a divorce I'd say he was a married guy, but we know that's not it."

"What do you think it is?"

"Who knows. Don't even try to figure it out. You'll make yourself crazy with guessing. Believe me; you'll come up with stuff that is way worse than it really is."

"That's true."

"Have you read *Men Are From Mars, Women Are From Venus*?"

"No."

"You should. See, men—I learned this from the book—men don't want to bother you with their emotions. They want to think about them on their own and come back to you when they've figured it all out. So they have to go off into their man cave. That's what the book calls it. So you get to a new level of intimacy, they freak out, they go off into the cave,

164

and then after a while they come out and they want you to be there. If you push him before he's ready to come out, he'll stay in there longer. So you have to just wait it out."

"Does the book tell you how not to go crazy while you wait?"

"You're on your own with that."

That was the last piece of advice Lydia gave her. They were interrupted by a group of HR people who arrived with four security guards.

"Candi Travis?"

"It's Tavris," she said.

"Oh God," Lydia said. "She stood up and gave Candi a hug."

"Lydia Green?"

With that Candi and Lydia broke into spontaneous laughter. Candi laughed so hard that she became light-headed. The next thing she knew she was lying on the floor with two of the security guards looking over her. One was holding a first aid kit.

"What happened?" she said.

"You fainted," said a woman in a pin striped suit.

"Oh," Candi said. She looked around. Lydia and her firing squad were no longer in the room. "Is Lydia gone already?" She sat up and looked at her desk. Her personals were still there. So she hadn't left the building entirely.

"She's in a meeting," said the HR woman.

"Sorry I passed out in the middle of getting fired like that," Candi said. "I'm sure you have a lot more people to un-employ today."

The HR woman didn't react. She was used to this.

"Am I the first one to actually pass out?" Candi asked as the guards helped her to her feet.

"So far," HR said. "Let's go talk about your severance package and the ways we can help you in your transition."

"Transition," Candi said. "That sounds like what New-Age people say when someone dies. They're transitioning."

Candi laughed again. Throughout the brief meeting with Ms. HR, Candi couldn't stop joking and laughing. She quipped about unemployment lines and COBRA snakes. It was beyond her control. She felt as if she was drunk. By the time the HR person asked "Do you have any questions?" Candi was laughing so hard she could hardly speak. "Just one question," she said when she was able to catch her breath. "Do I get a box? You know, the box with the handles? All the people who get fired on TV get a box."

"We can probably find a box for you if you need one."

"Excellent," Candi said. "You know why I don't have a box?"

The HR woman was beginning to lose patience.

"No, why don't you have a box?"

"Because I just got laid off from packaging!" Candi doubled over with laughter.

"OK then," HR said. "These guards will see you out once you've cleared out your things."

On the way back to her desk she thought about the strangest things— The odd talents she'd honed in her years on the job—steering a wheeled office chair with her feet and unwinding the telephone cord when it got gnarled up. She thought about the futility of having spent a full week mastering the new office voice-mail system.

When she got to her desk, she looked around the room. They'd all been let go; the entire department. She'd spent the last few years seeing the same faces every day, talking about weekends and kids and birthdays. This community would never be together again. After all those motivational speeches about "teamwork" they were being disbanded without a

166

celebration or a going-away party. Each in their own space, they collected their possessions and were led out of the building under the watch of security guards. Lydia's desk had already been cleared.

As Candi left the office, she noticed a dusty potted plant in the corner. She wondered if anyone would water it. She felt sorry for it. She thought it would be lonely.

Candi threw her purse and the folder of papers HR had given her—her "Way Forward"—onto the passenger seat. As she was pulling out of the parking lot, a perfectly polished Jaguar in a deep racing green started to exit the lot across the street. The other driver did not put on his turn signal. Candi should have waited to see which way he was going, but she just wanted to get home. She started to pull out of the lot and he turned at the same moment. They nearly collided. The Jag still had ample room to make its turn, but instead, the driver slowed and stopped in order to lay on his horn and to glare at Candi through the window. He was dressed in an expensive looking suit. Probably worked in finance. "One of the 'job creators'," she thought.

She tilted her hand forward to encourage him to get over it and move on. After another long glare he finally did. She seethed about the altercation the whole way home. Why was it her mistake when he had not bothered to signal? Does the rich man always get the right of way? Do we all have to wait for him to decide which way he is going before we get to use the road? What? Not rich enough to have a chauffeur drive you? She soothed herself with fantasies of plowing into that perfect Jag and watching the green metal fly.

That evening Candi lay on the couch, absolutely spent. The woman next door was also watching America's Got Talent. The "Whoop-whoop-whoop!"'s followed the jokes on Candi's screen.

Candi would have to tell her family, her friends. Maybe she should just post something on Facebook and let everyone know at the same time. She was not up to advertising her layoff just yet. She couldn't bear the thought of everyone's sympathy. There was only one person she wanted to speak to, the one she was supposed to be giving "some space."

"I don't care what he needs," she thought. "I need him now."

She sent Ollie a one sentence message.

"I got laid off today."

She went back to the couch with her phone so she could check her e-mail while watching TV.

Ollie did not answer.

Passive-Aggressive Housing

Ollie was sitting at a card table, drinking a cup of tea as he waited for Emma to arrive. The card table and folding chair set was one of four furniture purchases Ollie had made after Mandy kicked him out of the house. (The others were a futon, a microwave, and a television—all used.) For the first few weeks he'd lived in a hotel. When Mandy told him to get his stuff out of the house, he'd moved into this place above the office. Ollie's office was in a three-story brick building on the main street of a small suburb. The office was on the ground floor in what had once been a storefront. The upper two floors had been used for various purposes over the years. Each had, at one time, been converted into apartments. The second floor was now used for overflow storage, costumes, merchandise, amps, and other equipment. The third had been completely vacant. Until he made it his home, Ollie had almost forgotten it was there.

It was a generous space with working electricity and a shower. That was all he really needed. Ollie had left it untouched. The only decorations on the beige walls were the stains and nails that previous tenants had left behind. The kitchen had an olive-green refrigerator that probably dated to the 1970s and dark brown cabinets (to store his paper plates). There was a gap in the cabinets where the oven must once have been. The linoleum had caked-in dirt. (Max told Ollie not to try to remove it because some old vinyl flooring contains asbestos.)

There was a narrow hall that ended at the bathroom on one side and a bedroom on the other. The bedroom was full of boxes. The boxes contained everything he could claim as his alone, mementos from his music career, CDs, and anything related to making music. Everything non-musical stayed with Mandy. The only exception to the music rule was his piano. Technically, he still owned the piano. It was a term of the divorce agreement. But it would be a bitch to move up three flights of stairs and, anyway, Emma liked to play it. So his piano remained in Mandy's house, with all the other things they'd bought as a couple. He would get it after Emma graduated, if he could be bothered. His real hope was that Emma would take it one day.

Ollie did not sleep in the bedroom; in fact, he rarely went in there. He lived, instead, in the spacious room that faced the street. It had large windows, which he usually kept covered by dusty black curtains. The room still had railings and a mirror-covered wall from a brief period when it had served as a dance studio. The futon was placed near the mirror wall, surrounded by his collection of guitars and unsorted stacks of books. He'd set up his record player, but had never unpacked the albums. The television sat on top of a wooden box in the middle of the floor. During the day he folded the futon up like a couch. At night he folded it down—Voila! A bedroom.

In the right hands, the space could have been transformed into a trendy artist's loft. Ollie could have made it into whatever he wanted; he owned the entire building. He preferred it as it was: blank, empty. Usually people decorated their homes as an expression of who they are. There are paintings and photographs, vacation souvenirs. The emptiness was an expression of his inner life.

Emma probably had it right, though. She had told her father in no uncertain terms that they were going house hunting today. She said his space above the office was "sad" and that he was being "passive-aggressive."

"You're like, 'If I can't have my old house I won't live anywhere.' You need a real place."

There were times when he wasn't sure which of them was doing the parenting.

Ollie's phone made the sound of a raindrop. It was his text-message sound. (It was the phone's default. He hadn't figured out how to change it.)

"Downstairs." The text said.

Emma was the only person who he had been unable to persuade that he did not text.

He pecked out: "Come up." He had not mastered the skill of typing with his thumbs.

"Too sad. Come down."

Ollie shook his head, poured the rest of his tea in the sink, and walked down to the office.

When he got there he found Emma sitting at an empty desk. She was hunched over her phone, her thumbs in motion.

"Hiya," he said.

"Hey," she said, without looking up. Her thumbs did not skip a beat.

"Did you have me come down here to watch you text?"

"Just a sec," she said. Finally she looked up. "Here," she said. "Let's get a picture."

She stood up and Ollie stood beside her with his arm over her shoulder. She extended her arm full length and snapped an image of their two faces. Then she looked down at the phone again, started waggling the thumbs and the phone made a whoosh sound.

"You posted the picture just now?" Ollie asked.

"Instagram. Going house hunting with dad."

"You shouldn't post everything you do and every place you go," he said.

"You worry too much," she said. She clicked off the phone and put it in her purse. With a sweeping gesture she flipped back her curly red hair.

"I do worry," he said. "There's no privacy any more. People used to have privacy."

"No, you've got it backwards," she said. "Privacy is what's new. In the old days people lived in villages and everyone knew everybody. In the old days there was no such thing as anonymity. Everybody was famous."

"That's a thought," he said.

Emma ran her fingers over a t-shirt lying in a stack on the desk. "Can I have one?"

"You want to go around with your old man's picture on your chest?"

"Why not?" she said. "I like the artwork."

"Yeah, go ahead."

She picked up the t-shirt and held it up to herself to get an idea of the size.

"You should like technology," she said. "The internet was, like, invented for people like you."

"Like me?"

"Introverts. You're an introvert."

"I know that," he said. "I'm also a luddite."

"You should at least be on Facebook."

"I'm on Facebook."

"I don't mean a fan page; I mean your own page so we can see each other's updates."

"Most teenagers don't want to hang out with their parents online."

"I'm not most teenagers."

"I think it would be too depressing," he said. "Blast—100,000 likes. Oliver Thomas—4 friends."

She rolled her eyes. Her eye roll was just like her mother's. Ollie wondered how long it would be before missing Mandy would stop being the central fact of his life.

"You have more than four friends," she said.

"There's an invention called the telephone," Ollie said. "I wouldn't know how to talk on Facebook. You don't speak the same way to your daughter and your band mates and your old school friends."

"Are you saying you're a different person with me?" Emma said.

"A little bit," he said. "You're my little girl."

"So let's find you a house," Emma said with a clap of her hands. "What kind of place do you think you want?"

He pulled his own phone out of his pocket and navigated to a web page he'd bookmarked. "Urban luxury apartments." "A downtown address with a classic contemporary style."

Emma laughed. "Dad, you've met yourself, right?"

"What do you mean?"

"No offense, but you're not really a 'where the action is' kind of guy."

Brenda, who had been listening in, laughed at her desk.

"Hey," Ollie said pointing at her, "Don't you gang up on me."

"I said nothing," Brenda said with a wide smile. Then the phone rang and she answered it, "Blast Productions."

"I'm thinking something out of the way with a big lot, lots of privacy," Emma said. "Maybe a fireplace and space for a studio."

"You've already found a place like that?"

"I looked up the realtor, and I programmed the GPS."

"Of course you did," Ollie said. He kissed her on the forehead. "I miss you when I'm on the road. I don't get to see you often enough."

"Hey Ollie," Brenda said. "Sorry to interrupt." She had a line on hold. "There is a woman on the phone named Candi Tavris. This is the third time she's called."

"Who is she?" Ollie asked.

"I don't know. She won't say. She just says it's personal and she doesn't leave a message."

"I don't know a Candi Tavris," he said.

Ethan, across the room, muttered something under his breath.

"Sorry?" Ollie said.

"She's the girl from San Diego," Ethan said.

"What girl from San Diego?"

"The girl from San Diego."

"Oh, right," Ollie said. Then to Brenda he said, "I don't need to talk to her. Can you diplomatically …"

"Is she someone you …" Brenda finished the sentence by nodding and raising her eyebrows.

Ollie gave an apologetic shrug.

"What do you want me to say?" Brenda said. "She's on the line now. If I tell her you're out she'll just keep calling."

Ollie tilted his head down and glanced up at her, so his eyes were big and pleading. He knew how to charm Brenda. "Can you help me, please?"

"I'll do it," Ethan said from his desk. "I'll talk to her. What line is it?"

"Number one," Brenda said.

"Thanks, mate. I owe you one," Ollie said. Then to Brenda he said, "Well, it looks like we're off to find a house with solitude. For introverts."

"Can I drive?" Emma asked, as they walked out the door.

"Yeah," Ollie said, tossing her the keys. "But I'm going to be a backseat driver."

Friend Me

What Ethan had muttered under his breath was: "You fucked her last weekend, you bastard." He gave a disgusted sigh as he answered the line.

"Hi Candi, this is Ethan," he said. "We met backstage in San Diego."

"Hi," Candi said. "Can you put me through to Ollie?"

"The thing is," Ethan said, "He doesn't want to speak to you."

"Did you ask him or is that just what you say when fans call?"

"He told me," Ethan said.

"Is he there?"

"He just left."

"Look, I really do know him. You don't realize, but I'm not just—I knew him before the concert. He asked me to be there."

"I believe you," Ethan said. He rubbed his forehead over the bridge of his nose. "I do believe you, but I can only tell you what he said. He really was here just now and he said he didn't want to talk to you."

"But why?" It was an anguished plea.

"I don't know," Ethan said. He heard muffled sniffs. It broke his heart. He continued with his voice just above a whisper, "You really have feelings for him."

"He said he had feelings for me," she said. "I know you don't believe me."

Ethan turned so Brenda couldn't see him. He put his hand in front of his face and lowered his voice. "I do believe you," he said. He wanted to make her stop crying. He started to imagine excuses he could give. Blast's daughter was here. He really does like you, but he was in the middle of a move ...

"I'm glad someone believes me," Candi said. She sniffed. "I know it's your job to protect him and it isn't your fault."

It isn't your fault. That's when it occurred to him: Candi was speaking to directly him—not to him as Blast. She was speaking to *Ethan*. If she wound up hating the rock star, it didn't mean she would hate *him*. *Ethan* could sweep in like a knight on shining armor and comfort her. This was exactly the chance he'd been waiting for.

"You seem like a nice person," Ethan said "You're too good for someone like him. He didn't give you his cell phone number, did he? Or you wouldn't be calling here. I don't think he wants a relationship with you."

"Thanks for being honest, but you don't know what he said to me."

"No, how could I?" Ethan said. He hoped he didn't sound defensive. "Anyway, there's no reason to call here again, because you're not going to be put through. I'm really sorry."

"Thank you anyway," Candi said. She hung up without saying goodbye.

"So what did she say?" Brenda asked.

"He said he has feelings for her."

"More like, 'it feels good in you.' " Brenda said.

Ethan shook his head. "I can't believe you just said that."

"They just walk up to him and say, 'I want sex,' and he says, 'Yeah, OK.' "

"Well, yeah."

"Men," she said, shaking her head.

"What would you say if a handsome man walked up to you and said, 'I want sex with you?' "

"I'm married."

"If you weren't."

"What's he look like?"

"See?"

"No, seriously, there's a reason normal people don't do that. It's scary. He's going to get himself in trouble one of these days. Some girl with legs up to her neck will turn out to be an axe murderer. He should be more careful."

The phone rang again, putting an end to the conversation. As Brenda talked about European tour logistics with the person on the phone, Ethan brought up Candi's Facebook page. He had looked at it as a lurker almost every day. He felt a little thrill when he clicked the friend request. "This is Ethan, from Blast's office," he wrote in the message.

He went and got a cup of coffee. When he got back to the computer she had already replied.

"Are we friends?"

"I'm at work," he wrote. "It was hard to talk on the phone."

"What did you want to say?"

"I know you are telling the truth about him."

"Did he tell you something?"

"I can't talk about this at work. Can I buy you a coffee and we can talk face to face?"

"I don't live in L.A."

"You live in San Diego. It's not that far. Drive up. I can buy you lunch and you can be home in time for dinner."

"I don't like driving in L.A. You can't tell me whatever it is now?"

"I'd rather meet."

"Fine. Where should we meet?"

"Come to the office at 12. You remember what I look like?"

"I think so."

"You know the address?"

"It's on the web page."

"Then I'll see you for lunch."

Everything was working out perfectly. All Ethan had to do was come up with a story, something that would make Candi want to wash her hands of Blast. Ethan would emerge as her source of compassion and moral support. Then he could romance her in his own name. They would live happily ever after.

Stalker

On the day he died, John Lennon signed an autograph for his killer. There is a photograph of the two of them together. The image was seared in Ollie's mind. Lennon is gazing down, concentrating on his signature, but his expression also has traces of serenity, a subtle inkling of a smile. The expression was familiar to Ollie. It was the small joy that comes from knowing you made someone's day just by taking a moment to sign your name.

"He was very kind to me," Mark David Chapman later told his parole board. "Very cordial and very decent man."

Chapman shot Lennon seven times with hollow-point bullets "... because they were more deadly."

Ollie was pacing back and forth, looking at his harried reflection in the dance-school mirror. He'd had two glasses of vodka, but his hands were still trembling. Two police officers were sitting on the futon. The younger one, a muscular, short-haired woman with a name badge that said Sgt. Maverick took down notes while the older one, an avuncular white-haired man with a round face and a badge reading Sgt. Cass asked most of the questions. The police department said that this pair specialized in protecting celebrities from stalkers.

"I have to t-t-tell you the t-truth," Ollie said. "I d-did sleep with this woman. After the show in San D-diego. Lots of women ... You know, I liked her. I thought; I thought she was normal. I've n-never had anything like this happen before."

"It was a one-night stand," Cass said.

"Yeah," Ollie said. He ran his hand through his hair. "P-People understand ..." Ollie took a deep breath and tried to get his stammering under control.

"Why don't you sit down," Cass said. "First of all, with these celebrity stalkers, it's not about sex. It's about power and control."

Ollie asked if the officers would mind if he got himself a bottle of beer. They did not. He went to the kitchen, popped open a beer, and then returned to the living room with one of the folding chairs so he could sit. His hands had stopped shaking, but he was having trouble keeping his legs still.

"Why don't you start from the beginning, just tell us everything you remember," Cass said.

"From San Diego?"

"No. What happened today?"

Ollie took a sip of his beer then he started to tell them the story. It was just before noon. He had left the office on his way to the bank, but before he could get into his car, he saw the woman. She had been sitting in the lot in her car waiting for him to come out. She got out of her car and called his name.

"Candi Tavris," said Sgt. Maverick.

"I didn't know her name then," Ollie said. "She never told me her name. But she called me Ollie. She looked different from the other night."

"Different how?" asked Cass.

"She looked tired," Ollie said. "Circles under her eyes. And she looked angry."

He called back the image, the woman in her faded jeans and striped top. He remembered the tightness in his chest when he spotted her.

"She was pretending she was surprised to see me," Ollie said. "Like she just happened to run into me there in the parking lot of my office. But she drove all the way from San Diego. She'd been leaving phone messages, but I didn't answer them. I had, I had this guy in my office tell her, he t-told her I didn't want to be in contact. He told her to stop calling."

"That's when she escalated," Cass said. "She decided to come to your office in person."

"If that's what you call it," Ollie said. "Yeah, she escalated."

"Did she seem threatening?" Cass asked.

"No," Ollie said. "Not at that moment. I felt bad for her. I felt embarrassed. A little guilty. I was annoyed that I had to tell her I didn't want to get to know her. I thought she was a nice girl. I didn't want to have to explain it to her."

"Sure," Cass said. Maverick looked at him. Then she glanced back down at her paper.

"I was going to tell her that I had a good time but I didn't want it to go any further, but then she started saying, she said, 'How can you tell me you love me and then disappear.' No, it was 'leave me hanging.' 'How can you tell me you love me and then leave me hanging.' "

"Did you tell her you loved her?" Maverick asked.

"No, never. I told her. She said, 'I have it in writing.' That's when she started to scare me."

"Do you know what that means?" asked Cass.

"That she's crazy? She started talking about one of my songs and how it was written for her and the lyrics speak to her. She said the lyrics to the song told her I was in love with her."

Ollie got up and started pacing again. All afternoon he'd been thinking about Charles Manson. He couldn't get the song "Helter Skelter" out of his head.

"Did she say what she wanted you to do?" asked Cass.

"She kept going on about some secret she said I had," Ollie said. "She wanted to know what my secret was. And why I was lying to her. She absolutely believed what she was saying. If you could see her eyes … My song lyrics told her that I had a secret that was keeping me from loving her the way I said I did. In writing. I told her she had to leave and she just started crying. 'How could you do this to me? I love you.' It was awful."

"That's very common," Cass said. "'How could you do this?' Stalkers usually blame their victims."

"Just for the record," Maverick jumped in. "You didn't say anything that might have given her the wrong impression."

"I didn't say I loved her," Ollie said. "I didn't even know her name. I certainly didn't tell her my songs were written for her."

"But you said you liked her," Maverick said.

"Yeah," Ollie said.

"But you only met the one time? There was nothing more to it?"

He stopped pacing and held on to the ballet studio railing for support. "She seemed fun, normal. I didn't notice anything weird about her. She did mention the song—that night in San Diego. I remember now, she said something about 'Meet Me After Midnight.' That's the song she thinks I wrote for her."

"What did she say about it?" asked Cass.

"She just said she liked it."

"Did she say anything else you remember?" asked Cass.

"There was one thing. She said something about, she was made redundant—she lost her job. She was upset that when she was fired I didn't, I don't know, comfort her, help her. We have a relationship, so I was supposed to come running to her when she got fired."

"That's actually a good sign," said Cass, sitting forward. "It means that some stressful situation may have triggered this. When a stalking episode is linked to a particular trauma it has a better chance of being temporary."

"So she might not come back?" Ollie asked.

"That's not likely," Cass said. "I don't want to give you false hope. It sounds like erotomania. She believes she's your girlfriend or your wife. I think at the very least you should take out a restraining order against her. Here's what you have to know: ordinary stalkers, the ones who go after their ex-girlfriends or -boyfriends, if they're going to become violent, they usually threaten something beforehand. Celebrity cases are different. They're more erratic. She sees you on television and in the posters. It reinforces her delusion that you're part of her life. Just the fact that she has a delusion that you're in love with her means she's potentially dangerous. She could get enraged by something you said in a YouTube video."

"If I get a restraining order, will it work?"

"It depends on the person and the strength of the delusion," Cass said.

"So it might not work."

"No, it might not. But it's the best place to start."

Life Goes On, Bra ...

Candi sat at the wheel of her Elantra, parked outside Ollie's office, sobbing. Ever since she had written that note about Ollie being a star, her world had started to unravel. She couldn't, for the life of her, figure out what that message meant to him or what she had done.

"Why do all women chase after fame?"

The night they spent together he'd seemed as happy as she was. He'd never made her feel cheap. Then overnight she'd been depersonalized, turned into just another groupie chasing after fame.

"What if I wasn't famous? You don't know who I am."

Lydia had to be right; she had triggered something, a memory of some other woman. "Why do all women ..." He was afraid that whatever had happened with this other woman was going to repeat itself. Why didn't he just say so? Then they could have a conversation like two adults. She would have a chance to convince him. It had been a poor word choice, an impulse, nothing deep.

If he'd wanted to end it right then, she would have been hurt, but she would have lived with it. She hadn't asked him to say he loved her. She hadn't pressed him. She hadn't even expected it:

"I think maybe I love you, and I want you to love me."

And then nothing. He wouldn't answer her e-mails, he wouldn't take her calls. Why had he said it? What was he hiding? What was it that he thought was so awful about himself that it would turn her against him? Was it just insecurity, or was there a serious problem there?

She imagined her brain with all of its crevices and wrinkles and pictured red liquid candle wax being poured over it, the wax seeped into every cranny and then hardened so it was impossible to remove. The red wax

185

was Ollie and there was no way to compose a thought any more that did not relate to him.

She had driven all the way to Los Angeles to meet the mop-haired kid from Ollie's office because he promised he had some answers. She spent the whole drive trying to imagine what could be so serious that the guy was afraid to tell her on the phone. Was Ollie living with someone else? Ethan would have told her that, wouldn't he? There would be no need for these spy games. It had to be something his staff would know but the rest of the world didn't. Did he have a terminal disease? An addiction? Was he mentally ill? The last one was starting to seem the most plausible.

She hadn't expected to see Ollie that day. She hadn't bothered with makeup and she was dressed in a striped shirt and old jeans. But when she pulled into the parking lot, there he was. She had never seen him like this, completely out of costume, completely off-guard. He was also dressed in jeans; his hair was pulled back in a messy ponytail. He was reading some documents through a pair of thick horn-rimmed glasses.

She opened the door and stepped out of her car. "Ollie," she shouted. He looked up. She hoped he would smile in recognition of the face he loved. He didn't. He looked exasperated and annoyed. She felt the need to explain that she had not come there looking for him. "But I'm glad I ran into you."

He just looked at his feet with a pained expression on his face.

"Look," he said. "You can't come around here."

Candi had gotten tired of groveling, waiting and of letting him use a fortress of celebrity to keep her at arm's length.

"If you don't want me to treat you like a star then talk to me like a human being," she said. She had practiced that line many times in her head.

"Yes, you're right," he said. He shuffled back and forth and didn't make eye contact. "The truth is, it was nice, but it was a one-night stand. I didn't think you expected more than that. That's all I can give you. I'm sorry."

"Fine," she said, working hard to fight back tears. "But if that's true, why did you tell me you loved me, that you wanted me to love you? What was that about?"

Ollie took two steps back. He feigned surprise, "I never said such a thing."

"You know you did," Candi said, unable to hold back the tears any longer. "If it's over, fine, but I don't know why you're playing with my head like this. Can't you just tell me what happened, what made you change your mind?"

"I didn't change my mind," he said. "Nothing is over; there was nothing to begin with."

"If you felt that way, then why did you say the things you did? You didn't need to say you loved me."

That was when he said the horrible thing:

"I never said I loved you. I'm sorry to put it so bluntly, but it was a fuck. We had a little fun, you get to go off and tell your friends you bedded a rock star. That's how it works. I thought you understood that. We never had a relationship and we're not going to have one."

Candi stood with her mouth open, absolutely stunned. She could not believe he could be so cruel. It took her a moment to find any words.

"I didn't just show up at the back stage door," she said. "You invited me. No relationship? Why because it wasn't face to face? We talked for hours. I still have all the messages you wrote. You wrote 'Meet Me After Midnight' for me. How can you say it was nothing?"

Ollie backed away from her; the papers in his hands were shaking.

"If you don't leave I'm calling the police," he said.

After that it was all a blur. She was a crying mess, telling him everything she felt, and he denied ever having known her. It ended with him dialing the police and retreating into his office, as if he was afraid of her.

Now she sat hunched over the steering wheel. She couldn't process any of it, she couldn't muster outrage, she couldn't grieve the loss, she couldn't run away, she couldn't think. She could only wail and sob. She heard a knock on her window. The mop-haired kid was staring at her. She wiped her cheeks with the back of her hand and rolled down the window.

"I heard what happened," Ethan said. "He's calling the police; we should probably go before they get here."

"We?" Candi said.

"Our lunch," Ethan said. "I know you're kind of in a state, but you still need to eat, right?"

Candi couldn't imagine eating, her stomach was clenched. Yet she felt too weak to do anything but follow along. The kid was giving her a place to go, a next step.

"There's a really good Thai place," he said.

Candi felt a twinge remembering the time she and Ollie had bonded over their mutual love of Thai food. Ollie had told her about the time he went to his favorite restaurant and decided on a whim to order his gang kea warn hot instead of medium. His face turned bright red after a single bite.

They had no relationship? Wasn't this the kind of thing relationships were made of? It wasn't the sex or the rare deep conversations about the meaning of life. A relationship grew out of the slow accumulation of stories about the quirky ways you each lived your everyday lives. She imagined it again, Ollie cleaning up the mess in his hotel room, the lines beside his eyes, the sound of his snoring.

At the restaurant Candi ordered a bowl of soup and sat stirring it. She wasn't sure she could keep even that down. Her companion was digging into an overflowing plate of pad thai with gusto. He reminded her of a hungry sheepdog. He was chatty and smiling. He seemed to be in a good mood.

Candi wondered if this was the same restaurant Ollie liked. It was near his office, so it was possible, even likely. What if he walked through the door?

"Are you listening?" Ethan asked.

Candi put down her spoon and looked up at him. "Sorry, no," she said. "I'm distracted about what happened. It's like he's two different people. Jekyll and Hyde."

"But you like the nice one? You like Hyde?"

"I think Jekyll was the good one," she said. "It's Doctor Jekyll and Mister Hyde."

"Just because he has a medical degree doesn't mean he's a good guy."

"In the story it does. Dr. Jekyll takes a potion and turns into the evil Mr. Hyde."

"If they're actually the same guy, shouldn't they both be doctors? Does Hyde just forget his medical training?" Ethan had a big smile; he was pleased by his own cleverness. Candi was not in the mood.

"You had me drive all this way. What is the big secret you wanted to tell me?"

"Oh yeah," Ethan said, scratching his head. "That's it really. He's Jekyll and Hyde."

Candi sighed. "Care to elaborate?"

"He's, you know, bipolar. He tried to kill himself one time."

"Yeah, I know."

"He has mood swings."

"That wasn't a mood swing, what I saw today. When he says he loves me one day then he calls me a slut and says he doesn't even know me. That's multiple personalities." Her stomach was starting to unclench a bit. She picked up her spoon and took a sip of the soup. "You couldn't tell me 'bipolar' on the phone?"

"He does this thing," Ethan said. "It's not just you. There are others."

"So it's not personal. That makes me feel much better."

"That was sarcastic, right?"

She glared at him.

"I didn't mean for you to run into him like that," Ethan said.

"What did you want?"

"You're nice," he said. "You're too good for a guy like that. I hoped I could convince you that's true and make you feel better."

The kid seemed sincere and well-intentioned even if his methods were clumsy. Had he taken this job on himself? Soothing the feelings of the women the rock star left in his wake? Or was this lunch part of his job description, protecting the boss?

"Good luck making me feel better," she said. "This is probably the worst week of my life. You know in the middle of all this I got laid off from my job."

"Yeah, I know," he said. "I'm sorry."

"Thanks. Wait. You know? How did you know?"

Ethan looked startled. "How did I know?"

"I haven't told anyone yet. Not even my family."

"You told Blast."

"And he told you?"

"I guess."

"He talks about me?"

"Sometimes."

Candi ran her hand over her face. "I'm so confused."

"Let's not talk about him any more," Ethan said. He went back to attacking his plate of noodles.

Candi was trying to come to grips with this new piece of information. It didn't make sense. Not only had Ollie said he loved her, he talked about her to other people. Then why would he pretend he didn't know her at all?

"How did it come up?" she asked.

"I don't remember," Ethan said, covering his half-full mouth.

"I wrote to him when I lost my job, but he never answered."

"Maybe he didn't know what to say."

"But he told you about it."

"I told you, he's not normal."

"But he was thinking about me."

Ethan seemed annoyed with her questions. "He'll mess with your head and make you crazy," he said.

Candi rubbed her temple. "This restaurant doesn't serve alcohol, does it?"

*****

The next day Candi woke up in a Motel 6. Her memories of the previous night were fragmented. The early part was clear enough. Ethan had persuaded her not to drive home.

"You're too upset, it's not safe."

He offered to get a hotel room for her. It had seemed like an act of pure kindness, and she was grateful for it, because the thought of going back to her home with no job, no money and no hope was too oppressive. Ethan called into work, she had no idea what he told them, and he took her to a bar called The Vault. It was in a converted bank. The college-aged clientele mingled where the money once had been. The music was loud. She and Ethan had to raise their voices to speak and be heard. Candi didn't recognize any of the songs. She tried to remember if there had been an exact moment when new music had started to belong to younger people.

Ethan had a punch card for the place. They had a laundry list of beers, and you could use the card to record the menu numbers of all of the beers you tried. You got a t-shirt when you'd tried them all.

191

Candi rolled over in her motel bed and glanced at the end table. There was her own brand-new punch card. She picked it up and examined it. There were five holes.

She remembered Ethan smiling and joking. She was envious of him. Candi was young enough to be accepted as his peer, but old enough to know she wasn't. Lydia had once said that the difference between a youth and an adult was "life-humbling experience." The expression stuck with her. She had probably aged a decade in the last week. She imagined herself at Ethan's age—what was he? —22, 23?—not yet crushed by debt. Not yet comparing herself to her friends and wondering how she had fallen so far behind.

She managed to keep enough focus on the young man's words to nod and say "Uh-huh" in the pauses in his sentences. Inside she was replaying the parking lot confrontation with Ollie on a continuous loop.

"It was a fuck. … You get to go off and tell your friends you bedded a rock star."

Somehow it came up that Candi did not have a change of clothes and Ethan called his friend, Ale. He said Ale's girlfriend Sasha could lend her something to wear. Sasha was a patchouli scented swirl of Indian beads and organic, rainbow-colored fabric. She handed Candi a hand-woven hemp satchel with a sun dress inside. It was made of bandanas of the same pattern in multiple colors sewn together at the tops so the bottoms flowed freely.

"You can keep this," Sasha said. "I make these. Sell them at concerts." She handed Candi a business card. "I sell them on the internet too."

"She should open a shop," her boyfriend, Ale, chimed in.

"Ah, that's too rooted," she said.

Candi wanted to be Sasha, not rooted to anything, selling just enough skirts and bags to buy tickets and a ride to the next show, a life that was all about friends and music.

"Nothing is over; there was nothing to begin with."

192

Her companions talked about bands she had never heard of. Sasha, in particular, seemed to revel in their obscurity. Then Ale said, "Let's get out of here and have a smoke."

"I don't smoke," Candi said.

"Not cigarettes," Ethan said, making a gesture for smoking a joint.

"It's not really my thing," Candi said.

"It won't make you crazy or hallucinate," Sasha said. "It just mellows you out. You really look like you need to get stoned."

Candi found it hard to argue with that. They met up at the motel. Ale had a device with speakers for his iPhone. He put on a playlist of J-pop covers of Beatles songs. Candi had a vivid memory of sitting on the bed next to Ethan, sucking in the smoke that smelled of burning leaves, and singing "Life goes on, bra ..." in a Japanese accent.

"You ever watch that Bourdain travel show?" Ale asked the group.

"Is that the one where the guy goes around the world and eats bugs?" Ethan asked.

"No, man," Ale said. "He's the tall alcoholic one, with the attitude."

"Oh yeah," Ethan said.

"I saw this one where in Tokyo they have these bars where guys go in and women fawn over them."

"Are they prostitutes?" Sasha asked.

"No," Ale said. "They just flirt with the guys and tell them what manly studs they are. They have them for women too. These young guys flirt with middle aged women."

"Sounds depressing," Sasha said.

"I don't know," Ethan said. "It might be fun."

"But you know they're not really into you," Sasha said. "What would the fun be in that?"

Candi flashed back to the beginning of her correspondence with Ollie. *"It's a nice little ego stroke."*

"It's a nice little ego stroke," Ethan said.

Candi felt a chill run down her spine. She stared at Ethan.

"Why did you say that?" she asked.

"I mean, I think it kind of feels the same when someone tells you how great you are. It feels good, even if you think maybe it's not true," Ethan held eye contact with Candi as he said this.

"Go off and tell your friends you bedded a rock star."

"I think there would be a big crash later," Candi said. "You'd feel great as long as they were talking to you, and then when you had to go back to reality, it would be a huge letdown."

"It could get addictive," Sasha said.

"Yeah but if it makes these worker guys happy," Ethan said. He seemed to be losing his train of thought but he soldiered on. "If it makes them happy, then they can go back to work, their boring, hard work. I mean, why is the boring, hard work the real life and not the one where they're happy? Can't the fantasy be, I mean, can't you make the fantasy part the real one and count the boring work one as just what you have to do, I mean, to be able to have your real life—the fantasy one?"

"Dude," Ale said. "You're totally stoned."

The conversation shifted. Sasha said there is no such thing as the self. It is only a social construct and people in power tell us how to think and feel. "We're manipulated by advertising," she said. "We organize our whole lives around the people who want us to buy things."

She talked about how art was "put in boxes" because it had to make a profit. "It's a crime against idealism!"

"A crime against idealism."

That was it, Candi thought. She idealized Blast. She idealized Ollie.

"Why do women chase after fame? … You don't know me … I love you and I want you to love me."

He didn't want to be idealized.

"It was a fuck!"

That had been a crime against idealism. He had taken violent action against her illusions of him. Disillusioned. Not having any illusions. It was a good thing if she was going to love the real man, not a false image of him. He did it on purpose. He was brilliant. It was a crime against idealism. She felt as though she were on the verge of everything making sense, his words of love followed by his denials. It was perfect. That line of thinking stopped because her synapses seemed to have gotten slogged down in molasses. She stared at Sasha.

"You are so beautiful," Candi said. "No really, you're just free and young. And young and free. I wish I was like that. What if I never went back to San Diego? What if I just ran away and took a new identity? Lived in the Haight and called myself Moonbeam?"

"I think she's had too much," Ale said.

Then Ale and Sasha were gone and Candi was alone with Ethan on the bed. "I hope you're feeling better," he said. Ethan was playing with a strand of her hair.

"Yeah," Candi said. She rested her head on his bony shoulder. "Thank you."

Then Ethan put his hand under her chin, lifted her face, and kissed her on the lips. He slipped in his tongue. She pushed him away.

"What?" was the only thing she could manage to articulate.

"I thought …"

"Do I have a sign around my neck that says 'screw with me?' " She could not remember if she had said that out loud.

"I like you," Ethan said. He looked like a wounded puppy.

"Why is he making me think right now?" she wondered. "I'm flattered," she said.

"Oh no," he said. "Flattered isn't good."

"But, Ethan, why? The only thing you know about me is that I'm in love with someone else."

"And that he doesn't deserve it."

"It was a fuck. …tell your friends you bedded a rock star."

"You're sweet," she said. "I can't."

She had a vague recollection of showing him to the door. That's the last thing she remembered.

She stayed in the bed, wide awake, staring at a water stain on the ceiling. She imagined the life she was going back to and tears filled her eyes. Only a few days before she'd had a dream come true. She couldn't imagine for the rest of her life ever having another experience that could match it. Looking forward, she saw nothing but emptiness. What did she have to look forward to? What did she have to live for?

That's when she decided she had nothing to lose. She had to confront Ollie. She had to give it one more shot. Ollie's Jekyll-and-Hyde routine had been so extreme that she had to believe it had something to do with his proximity to the office. He was acting; putting on a show for somebody.

(Had she reflected more deeply, she would have realized that even though they were at the office no one had been watching.) Her only hope was to get him entirely alone, away from the public and their prying eyes.

She got out of bed and put on the bandana dress. She could tell by its scent that it had been stored in a room with incense. Its empire waist and bohemian form did not suit her at all. Her bra straps were completely on display, so she had to go without. "Life goes on, bra!" There was something entirely incongruous about her staid black purse with its sharp angles in combination with her frock. She laughed a bit, in spite of herself, at the previous night's drug-addled idea of becoming a full-time hippie.

She sat down at the desk and used her phone to check the internet. She brought up interview after interview with Blast, trying to find clues as to places he might go. One article mentioned the name of his neighborhood in suburban L.A. She typed the name into a search engine and up popped a real estate site. It offered a 3D street view of the neighborhood in question. She used the small arrows to virtually navigate what she believed was Ollie's street. It was a typical middle class neighborhood, ranch houses with Spanish tile roofs and aloe and cactus decorating the yards. It was not nearly as upscale as Candi had imagined for a rock star's home. The street had been photographed on trash day. The bins were all out on the curb. The truck must have come already, a couple of houses showed empty recycling bins lying on their sides on their lawns. Candi had never before imagined Ollie doing something as mundane as taking out the trash. She felt a twinge to realize he had a full life she knew nothing about and that it had nothing to do with her.

She had honed in on his subdivision, but that was not much help. She had no idea which house was his. Then she remembered an article she had read a while back. It had a picture of Ollie sitting on his front porch with his dog at his feet. It took her a while to remember where she'd seen it but she eventually found a link in an old post in the Blast fan forum. Once she retrieved it, she studied what she could see of the surroundings. The yard had bushes with red flowers and a distinctive cement railing around the porch. She went back to the street view and navigated around until she saw a house with a railing like the one in the photo. The door behind it looked the same, and as she navigated around and changed her perspective she saw the floral bushes. It was his home. No question. In the left hand corner was the street address. She wrote it down.

She checked out of the hotel, got into her car, and typed Ollie's address into her GPS. Somewhere in the back of her mind she knew it was a terrible idea to go to his house uninvited. She couldn't help herself. There was nothing else for her. She needed something to hope for, something to give her life meaning. She would never forgive herself if she didn't do everything in her power to hold on to him. Ollie held the key to all her future happiness. She needed to see him. She needed answers.

Ethan's Good Date

Ethan hummed "Ob-la-di, Ob-la-da, ..." as he filled his Blast Productions coffee mug. He poured the sugar in with a flourish. Brenda looked on from her desk.

"Sounds like you're in a good mood," she said.

"I had a date last night," he said. "Well, kind of a date."

"Kind of?"

"Yeah," he said. "It's this girl, we've been chatting on line and we finally met face to face. I mean we met once before, but this was like ..."

"A date?"

"Kind of."

"So it went well?"

Ethan walked over to Brenda's desk and cradled the warm mug close to his face. "I think so. I mean, mostly."

"Mostly?"

"Well, we had a good time." He smiled as he imagined Candi trying on Sasha's hippie dress and spinning in front of the mirror while Japanese pop played in the background. "We really hit it off."

"So, why 'mostly?' "

"I tried to kiss her, and she kind of said no."

"Bummer."

"But I think, you know, over time ..."

"Sure. Well, I hope it works out for you."

That's when Ollie came charging through the back door. His pink, freckled skin looked even more pale than usual.

"That bitch keyed my car," he said. Ethan had never heard Ollie use the word "bitch" before.

"What?" Brenda said.

"The crazy stalker woman," he said. "I went out just now and there's a big scrape on the side of my car."

Ethan set his coffee mug down on Brenda's desk. "She couldn't have done it," he said.

"Who else would have done it?" Brenda said.

"Maybe someone dinged you in the parking lot," Ethan said.

"Oh come on," Brenda said.

"She's never going to let up," Ollie said. He started to pace.

"I'm calling the police again," Brenda said, picking up the phone.

"But wait," Ethan said. Brenda paused with the receiver in her hand a few inches from her ear. She and Ollie were both staring at him. He wanted to say "She couldn't have done it. She was with me all night." But he was not willing to explain why he had been on a dream date with Blast's stalker.

"We can't prove it was her, can we?" he said. "It could be just a scrape. Someone driving too fast in the lot. Random."

"That would be a pretty big coincidence, wouldn't it?" Brenda asked.

It was a big coincidence, Ethan was certain of that. He'd talked to Candi all evening. He knew how she felt about Ollie. She was confused, not angry. Ethan wanted to say all of that but he remained mum as a fever of shame formed in the pit of his stomach and then filled his entire body leaving him light-headed. He watched the activity around him as if in a dream. He saw Brenda dialing officer Maverick. (A surreal enough name in itself.) Ollie pacing, terrified of a little woman with an upturned nose.

Ethan returned to his desk and tried to stay out of it. "Why don't you man up?" he chided himself. "Are you really going to let Candi take the fall rather than admit what you've done?"

His need to think of himself as a good guy and his instinct for self-preservation were at war. The fact that Ollie and Brenda believed he was thoughtful and loyal made it all that much worse. He was trapped. He didn't want to lose their faith in him, and yet he knew he didn't deserve it. Allowing them to keep the illusion was his blessing and his curse. No, Ethan was not willing to give himself up and the price for that was intense self-loathing.

He couldn't tolerate hating himself for long, though. So his psyche went to work on healing the wound. Ethan called on his innate talent for lying. Its new form was rationalization. Hiding what he had done was not for his benefit, it was really for Candi. She loved the man she corresponded with, and he loved her. The only way to get to a happy ending was to keep the secret. He could make her forget all about Blast and Blast would forget her. Anyway, Blast deserved to have his car keyed, didn't he? He used good women and threw them away.

He was still convinced that this could all be fixed without revealing the truth. If he could hold out for just a bit longer this would all blow over.

She's Escalating

Later that day after the police had come and gone, Ollie sat at his kitchen table with an acoustic guitar on his knee and a spiral notebook on the table in front of him. It had taken him some time to calm his nerves after the keying incident. He had tried to read a book, but his eyes kept going over the same passage without comprehension. After a drink and a hot shower, he decided the only way to clear his mind was to throw himself into his work. For the moment it seemed to be working, at least as far as his nerves were concerned. The songwriting itself was stalled.

He was still struggling with "The Non-Moving Party." The idea was there but it was labored, not inspired. The muse was a demon lover—fickle. She came when she wanted, not when he called. He sometimes tried to conjure her with meditation or a random word-generating computer program. Occasionally something intrigued her enough to show up, but usually she stayed away only to whisper in his ear when he was in bed without a pen.

He had a vivid image he wanted to use. When he and Mandy were dividing their possessions, he had wanted to take the photo album with the wedding pictures. Why should she keep it? She was the one who didn't want the marriage. But she wouldn't give them to Ollie. She said she was afraid he'd tear them up or burn them. She'd packed them away somewhere.

> *The moving party*
> *shall have custody*
> *of the album where*
> *wedding photos are bound.*
> *She said that she*
> *would keep them from me*
> *in order to let me*
> *move on unbound.*

"That's great, really great," he said out loud to himself. "Rhyme bound with bound. Really clever."

> *The moving party*
> *keeps the pictures*
> *from their wedding day.*
> *He wonders in silence*
> *if she's packed them away.*
> *He doesn't need them:*
> *They're all in my head, dear.*
> *When are you moving?*
> *Well, maybe next year.*

Ollie crossed out the lyrics and then scribbled over them. His phone rang.

"What now?"

He leaned the guitar against the table and went to the other room to pick up the phone. He was surprised to see that it was Mandy. It was the first time she had called since the divorce was finalized.

"Well if it isn't my ex-wife," he said.

"Hi," she said.

"I now pronounce you man and woman."

"That's clever," she said. She didn't sound amused.

"What's up?"

"I thought I should tell you that your fans have started coming to the house again. This one was really weird. She asked strange questions. Is the address posted somewhere?"

Ollie felt his chest tighten. "Who came to the house? What did she look like?"

"Just a fan. Young."

"What did she look like, you have to tell me."

"What's wrong?"

"There's this crazy girl who's been stalking me. She keyed my car."

"You have a stalker? Why didn't you tell me?"

He thought: "Like you told me about Greg?" He said: "We haven't exactly been talking."

"If you have a stalker who might show up at the door …"

"I didn't expect … What did she look like?"

"A hippie chick. Deadhead dress. Long hair. That type."

Ollie sat down on the futon. "That doesn't sound like her. What did her face look like?"

"I'm not good at describing faces. Brown hair. You think your stalker came to our house?"

"God Mandy, I've called the police on her twice. It was terrifying. She was standing there talking about how she knew I was in love with her and 'Meet Me After Midnight' was written for her."

"'Meet Me After Midnight?' "

"It's the new single. You didn't know that?"

"I haven't been following."

"Sure. Anyway …" He was distracted for a moment by the idea that she wasn't interested in his music any more.

"This girl didn't say anything like that. She did say she was a friend of yours. She said you correspond with her in e-mail."

"I didn't."

"Obviously if she was a friend of yours she would know you don't live here. She asked if you and I were back together, as if that were her business. I just thought she was a fan trying to con her way in and get an autograph. So she just showed up saying you were soul mates?"

"She, no, she … I met her after the show in San Diego."

"You slept with her."

Ollie stood up again and started to pace. "I'm a single man," he said. "You can't give me grief about sleeping with anybody."

"I can if she's a crazy stalking woman who shows up at my door. What were you thinking?"

"I didn't know she was crazy. She seemed normal."

"I hope the sex was good."

"Don't do that."

"Is she dangerous?"

"I don't know. What did she say to you?"

"Not a lot. Something like 'Sorry; I forgot about the divorce.' She asked if I thought you had a new girlfriend. I told her it was someone else's day to watch you."

"She didn't try to come in?"

"No, she left. Oh, I remember now. Her name is Candi. She said, 'If you talk to him tell him to please call Candi.' "

"Holy shit."

"That's her isn't it?"

"I'm going to come right over."

"No, it's fine. She's gone."

"It's not fine. She's tracking down my family now. It's not fine. What if she comes back and Emma opens the door? "

"Ollie …" She gave a heavy sigh and stopped speaking.

"What?"

"This isn't your house. I'm not your family."

"Yeah. Thanks for that."

"Emma is your family. She'll always be your family, but you can't come racing over here to protect us. I'll take care of it."

"I want to send a couple of police officers over there; they're dealing with the case."

"I think that's a good idea."

"And I'm coming over."

"No. It's fine."

"I want to be there. She's my stalker."

"It's not a good idea."

"Why?"

"Look … I've been seeing someone. Greg is staying here right now. Just for the week."

"That's great," Ollie said with the forced cheerfulness he'd rehearsed. "I'm really happy for you."

"You don't sound happy."

"I'm happy," he said through clenched teeth. In spite of his best intentions, he sounded angry. He was staring at himself in the giant mirror. He looked old.

He heard a small sigh and he pictured her biting her fingernails. She always bit her nails when she was under stress. "I'm not ready for the two of you to meet," she said.

"Why? You think I'm going to be rude? Punch him in the face?"

"No, of course not. No. I think … I'm not comfortable. How can I say this? I know you think I'm bitter and heartless."

"No, I don't."

"Yeah, you do. I get it. But I don't like hurting you."

"I never thought you did."

"I don't think seeing me and him together is something you need to deal with right now. It's hard to see you pretending to be happy."

"My emotions are my problem."

"Sure, but I deal with them too. I see you and I feel guilty, and then I get angry at you for making me feel guilty. Then everything I say comes out too harsh. I just want to let some time pass. Look, I appreciate you wanting to come and help us. I should have said that. I don't think I said the right things."

"It's OK."

"I want you to be happy."

"I'm happy."

She laughed. "You've always been a terrible liar."

"Do you think some time we can get to more than amicable."

"Friends?"

"Yeah. What do you think?"

"Yeah. Sure."

"But not yet."

She changed the subject, "So, your first stalker. That's a rite of passage. Do you get a cake or something?"

"Don't joke. She's scary. I'm jumping out of my skin. I keep thinking I'm going to wake up and she's going to be standing over me with a knife. It scares me that she came to the house. I'm going to hang up and call the police right now."

"OK, I'll be here."

"She's going to be arrested. Everything's going to be fine. Don't worry."

"You don't worry either."

The Right to Remain Silent

"On the day I was arrested" was not a phrase Candi had ever thought she was going to have to use.

She was lying on her couch wearing an oversized t-shirt and slouchy sweat pants with holes in them, snacking on microwave popcorn and watching Project Runway off her DVR when there was a knock at the door. She assumed it was another person confusing her place with the trailer park rental office and she was annoyed because she hadn't intended for anyone to see her dressed as she was.

When she opened the door to see two police officers she was surprised but not terribly alarmed. There was a male officer, a handsome African-American man, and his partner, a white woman, about 5'5" and shaped like a square. The woman said her name in a serious tone and took out a pair of handcuffs.

"All this for smoking one joint?" she thought.

"Candi Tavris you're under arrest for menacing, stalking, and harassment. You have the right to remain silent ..."

Menacing, stalking, and harassment?

"You must have the wrong person," she said. She was shocked but still did not have the good sense to panic. She was sure it was a case of mistaken identity and they would figure it out as soon as they got her into the car.

"You have the right to an attorney. If you cannot afford one ..."

"How could I possibly afford an attorney?" Candi thought. She was out of work, in debt, and lawyers made $300 an hour. She didn't even know how you found a criminal attorney. What kind of people had a criminal lawyer on call? Surely anyone who was best equipped to defend himself immediately after an arrest was someone who least deserved it.

The police helped her into the back of the police car by putting a hand on her head just like they did on TV. She sat in the back of the car perplexed and dazed. Why was any of this happening? She wasn't a stalker, and she was far from being menacing.

This was not supposed to be happening to her. It was supposed to be happening to someone else. Candi knew she was broke, but she'd never thought of herself as "poor." She had certainly never thought of herself as criminal. Frightening as it was to have the police take her away, it was even more overwhelming to realize how having no money limited her options. She was no better off than anyone else who was dragged away in handcuffs. When they looked at her they no doubt saw poor, white trailer trash.

Because she had done nothing wrong, Candi did not exercise her right to remain silent. She asked many questions and it became clear that the officers had not taken her by mistake. Ollie had filed charges against her.

What kind of a man was he? He had encouraged her, led her on, slept with her, said he loved her, and then had her arrested? Jekyll and Hyde? Bipolar? That didn't even begin to cover it. Was this what Ethan had been trying to warn her about? Was this some kind of sadistic power game? She could think of no other explanation, and yet she still found it almost impossible to accept even when the evidence was all around her.

"Is this, I mean, am I charged with a misdemeanor or a felony?"

"It's a felony," the female officer replied. She seemed bored.

I'm a felon?

Candi shimmied, trying to get comfortable with her wrists still shackled together. The air smelled of disinfectant and she tried not to let herself imagine what it had been used to clean up.

"This has to be a mistake," she said. "I didn't do anything."

No one answered.

"I didn't do anything illegal," she said. "I talked to him in the parking lot and I knocked on his door and asked to see him. Those are public places. That's not illegal."

"You vandalized his car," said the officer in the passenger seat. "That is illegal."

"What? No, I didn't do anything like that," she said, and then more to herself, "I thought I knew him so well. I can't believe he would do this to me. I never said I was in love with him. He was the one who said he loved me. If he didn't want to see me any more, that's fine, he didn't have to have me arrested."

She stared at the back of the two officer's heads through the steel mesh cage and bullet proof glass. They had lost interest in her and were chatting to each other. Just another day at work. She couldn't hear what they were saying over the pounding of blood in her head. A little vein beside her ear was pulsing. She raised her cuffed hands to her face to try to make it stop.

When they got to the police station, the square woman took Candi to a plain, beige room with a couple of folding chairs, a long grey table and a video camera on a tripod while the handsome officer (Candi took him for the "good cop") went to fill out some paperwork. The square officer asked if she wished to waive her right to remain silent. Because she was innocent, Candi believed that the best way to end this all quickly was to speak.

The woman tried to develop a rapport with Candi by mentioning how much she liked music, and Blast's music in particular.

"I'm a fan too," she said. Candi didn't believe her.

"So you really know him?" she asked.

"We met online," Candi said.

"But you said you have a romantic relationship with him? He said he loves you?"

"That's what he said. I didn't say it."

"How did he tell you?"

"In writing. We chatted on line. He said he was in love with me and he wanted me to love him too. He wanted to accelerate things."

"Did you?"

"I wanted to talk to him in person first."

"So when you say he told you in writing," Square said, looking at one of the papers in her file, "You mean in his song lyrics."

"No," Candi said. "I mean in writing. In e-mail. He did write a song for me, but that's not what I meant. Look, I didn't do anything wrong. We had a relationship. We were lovers. Did he say we weren't? Do you believe him because he's famous and I'm not?"

The officer didn't answer.

"I just wanted to talk to him," Candi said. "I didn't sneak in any windows or break down doors or threaten anything. I just asked him politely if he would talk to me."

"Did you scratch his car?"

"No."

"What would you say if I said we had you on video?"

"What? No, you can't. It's not possible."

"You're denying it's you in the tape?"

"Maybe it's someone who looks like me. I didn't do anything like that. I wouldn't."

"I understand completely why you would do it. I've been mad at boyfriends too. He told you he loved you, he wrote music for you, then he won't even talk to you. Anyone would get angry."

212

Candi could not stop thinking about the video. Did they really have some sort of video of someone vandalizing Ollie's car? Did they have a reason to think it was her? She didn't think a police officer would lie to her. (She would later learn that the officer was lying to her, and that police are allowed to lie during interrogations.)

"Of course I was upset," Candi said. "I was confused, but I wasn't angry. I wasn't menacing."

"Well, let's clear this all up," Square said. "Where were you that night? Where did you go after you confronted Blast in the parking lot?"

"I didn't 'confront' him," Candi said. "I bumped into him and I talked to him."

If she'd been watching a police drama on television, Candi would have been shouting at the screen, telling the suspect to ask for a lawyer, but she didn't because it all seemed so absurd. How could she possibly have anything to fear if she'd done nothing wrong? She wanted to show she had nothing to hide. Even if she could afford one, calling a lawyer would make her look guilty.

"Where did you go after that?" Square asked.

"I went to a Thai restaurant with Ethan from the office."

"What office?"

"Blast's office. I was there to meet Ethan, not Ollie. After I talked to Ollie, Ethan took me to the restaurant and then we went to a bar called The Vault. Then we went to the Motel 6 and I stayed there all night. You can ask Ethan. He was with me most of the night."

"You went to a bar? Were you drinking?"

"Yes."

"How much did you drink?"

Candi knew that she'd had at least five beers, but it didn't seem wise to give that answer. "I don't remember."

"You don't remember because you drank a lot and you lost count?"

"Look, I know what you're getting at, but I didn't ..."

"Here's what I think happened. You went to meet Blast and you expected him to say he loved you, but he rejected you. So you got angry and you did what anyone would do, you went out and got drunk. I bet you don't remember everything that happened that night, right? There are a few fuzzy parts of your memory?"

Candi was no longer entirely sure of anything. There were parts of that evening she had forgotten. She was basing her belief that she had not damaged Ollie's car on her knowledge of herself—it wasn't the kind of thing she would do. It was nothing she'd ever imagined doing. She hated movies where characters feel entitled to seek revenge; it was just not in her nature. But did that remain true when she was full of beer and marijuana? She had never smoked marijuana before. What kind of person was she when she was stoned? Was it possible that she had worked herself up into a rage and had no memory of it? She'd had fantasies of crashing into the rich road rage driver's green Jag, hadn't she? Could she have fantasized something like that about Ollie too? Did they really have a video tape of her doing it?

When would she have done it? With Ethan and his friends before they went to hotel or after Ethan left? No, it couldn't have happened. Ethan wouldn't have gone along and attacked his boss's car and she was way too drunk and stoned to get out of bed after he left. This was not an alibi that she thought prudent to use.

"I didn't do it," she said, fighting back tears.

"You don't know everything you did that night, do you? If you don't remember, how can you be so sure you didn't do it?"

That was when it finally struck Candi that she was out of her depth. "Could I please have a lawyer?"

The Five Ws

Ethan had barely made it through the office door when Brenda said, in an excited tone, "Did you hear what happened?"

Ethan set down the bag he was carrying. "That's too general a question for me to answer. When? Where?"

Brenda laughed. "They arrested that girl."

"What girl?"

"The stalker."

"What, why?"

"Now you just need to ask 'Who? How?' " Brenda laughed again.

Ethan felt like he was being squeezed by a giant boa constrictor, a great, big boa constrictor. He could even picture it: grey-green with diamond shaped splotches; at least that's what he imagined a boa constrictor looked like. He wasn't all that sure, but some kind of giant snake represented his guilt and anxiety and it was squeezing the breath right out of him.

"She showed up at Mandy's house. She was dressed in some kind of weird hippie dress and she said she was Ollie's girlfriend and she wanted to come in and wait for him. She asked Mandy all these weird questions."

"What questions?"

"I didn't get the full story, but I think she accused Mandy of being the other woman. She wanted to know what she was doing with her man. I've heard about stuff like this, but it is weird when it happens to you."

Ethan couldn't believe what he was hearing. Could Candi really have gone to Ollie's old house and told Mandy she was his new girlfriend? He had trouble imagining her doing that, but then again, it was possible. Thanks to him she did think she was Blast's girlfriend. Ethan pumped

Brenda for information. He needed to know if she had already told the police about the e-mails. He hoped that the nervous high pitch of his voice came across as curiosity and excitement rather than panic.

"When did they arrest her? Did she tell the police anything? What did she say to Mandy about her relationship with Ollie?"

Brenda didn't have a lot of information. She only knew what Ollie had told her: that the crazy woman went to his old house.

"He looked white as a sheet when he told me about it. He said, 'I'm putting a stop to this.' "

She gave a blow by blow account of the conversation, but Ethan could not stay focused. He was trying to figure out how much time he left had before everything fell apart.

When he returned to his desk he could only pretend to work. He wanted to curl up into the fetal position and then keep on curling until he disappeared. In his mind, he started to practice his big speech—the one that would persuade Candi that he never meant for any of this to happen, that he had only done it because she was wonderful and he wanted her to keep talking to him. He hoped he could come up with something as persuasive as Jerry McGuire's "You complete me."

That night Ethan had an epiphany. He realized that even if Candi told the police about the e-mails, and even if they read them, they had no way of knowing that he had sent them—at least he assumed they didn't. They might even believe that the messages had come from Blast and that he was lying about the whole stalking thing. The detectives would detect. They would realize Candi was not delusional. It would all be over soon.

Candi knew him now as Ethan. Ethan (as himself) was her Facebook friend. They had each other's numbers. Things were going according to his plan. The arrest would make her hate Blast even more. As soon as her name was cleared, their real, honest romance could begin.

Ethan began to feel optimistic. Other less generous souls might have called it denial. The dictionary defines denial as "an unconscious defense mechanism used to reduce anxiety by ending thoughts, feelings, or facts that are consciously intolerable."

It was consciously intolerable to Ethan to let himself be aware of the damage he had wrought in Candi's life. The more out of hand the situation became, the more his defenses kicked in and the more convinced he was that he had the power to fix everything.

Sentence First

The legal aid attorney was skinny, uptight, and younger than Candi. He tried to project an air of confidence through the use of legal jargon. Candi tried to be reassured by this, but some instinct (the way a dog can sell fear) told her he didn't know what he was doing. The lawyer jumped right past any question of innocence and suggested she plead insanity. Candi wondered what was in the papers he was shuffling and why did he believe them before he had ever spoken to her?

"I'm not pleading insanity," she said. "I'm not guilty. I didn't do anything wrong."

"Pleading insanity will keep you out of jail."

"Jail?" Candi was trying not to give in to panic, but she wasn't having much luck. Her voice came out louder than she wanted and at a higher pitch. "Not being guilty will keep me out of jail, too, won't it?"

"It looks like the case is pretty strong against you."

"What case? I knocked on his door and asked to see him. What law is that?"

"You're getting pretty agitated."

"Wouldn't you? Let me ask you something, if you had to—could you prove you were sane?"

"If you just knocked on his door then we could argue you're not dangerous to him, but you did key his car."

"I didn't do that. It wasn't me."

"Can you prove you didn't do it?"

"What? How could I do that? How can I prove I didn't do something? Can you prove you didn't have sex with a donkey yesterday?"

219

"Please calm down."

"Stop telling me to calm down. It's making me crazy. I'm not crazy."

"You had an argument with him, you went to his house uninvited and between those two events his car was keyed. If you didn't do it, who else could have?"

"How should I know? I only know who didn't do it. Isn't it supposed to be the prosecution's job to prove that I did something, not mine to prove I didn't?"

"That's how it works in theory."

"In theory? But in reality?"

"In reality, you look like the most likely suspect."

"But it isn't true."

"You have to get the idea of true and not true out of your mind. In court it's about the case you can build. The most convincing story ..."

"But if something is true—if it's actually true—how can it be impossible to make it convincing? You went to law school, can't you make the truth as convincing as a bunch of lies?"

"Not if the truth is less believable."

"Great. Do you even believe me?"

"It doesn't matter what I believe."

"Well, that's an answer isn't it. Why's it so hard to believe I could actually know a famous person? He's a person."

"He claims he doesn't know you. He only met you once before you showed up at the office."

"He's lying."

"Why would he do that?"

"I don't know!" she shouted. "You're asking me to prove things I didn't

220

do, and now you want me to explain why someone else is acting the way he is. I can't do any of that."

"You're right. Let's just stick to what you can prove."

"I can prove I knew him. I have all the e-mails. If you don't believe me, you can read them yourself. They're on my computer at home."

"You think he wrote his songs to speak to you?"

She felt as though she was stuck in a science fiction worm hole. The more she defended her sanity, the crazier it made her sound. Yet admitting she was mad would not make her sound sane.

"No, you're making it sound … I think he wrote *a* song for me. It's not a delusion if it's true."

"I've asked for a competency hearing," the lawyer said.

"Can you do that without my permission? Don't you work for me?"

"Yes, but we need to determine if you should even stand trial. It's a formality."

"It doesn't sound like one."

"I want to have you speak to a psychologist, OK?"

"Will that prove I'm sane?"

"If this is all a mistake it will prove it, if it's not it could keep you out of jail."

"What would happen then?"

"You would go to a hospital for a while."

"Can I leave if I want?"

"No, you can leave when a doctor clears you."

"Then how is it different from jail?"

"It isn't jail."

Because she had no money for bail, and she was too ashamed to call her parents or sister, Candi stayed in jail for three days as she waited for her appointment with the psychologist. In the meantime her lawyer went to Candi's apartment and printed out all of her e-mail correspondence with Ollie. She was sure that when they read the messages and saw that she was telling the truth the nightmare would be over.

The court-appointed psychologist had shoulder-length brown hair with streaks of grey. She had a habit of absent-mindedly wrapping her hair around her index finger as she listened. The psychologist, Candi would later learn from her testimony in court, saw herself as an expert on delusional disorders. Her expertise was her only proverbial hammer and she immediately recognized Candi as a nail.

By now Candi had gone back to referring to Ollie as "Blast." Having to do this was dishonest and uncomfortable, but she realized that referring to him by his given name came across as some kind of paradoxical proof that she did not know him. If she used his real name it was false intimacy, proof that she was delusional.

By the time she met the psychologist she had worked herself up into a state. She was angry and frightened. She had not slept. She had sunken eyes and pale skin and she was becoming increasingly paranoid. She had never had an enemy before, and now she had a powerful one—Blast. She didn't know what his next move might be or why he would torture her.

She had to convince the therapist that she was a normal woman and not a danger to anyone. Her entire future depended on it. The more she tried to sound reasonable, the more her voice took on a hysterical edge.

"So let's talk about the confrontation in the office parking lot," the psychologist began.

"I didn't *confront* him. I wanted to talk to him."

"Why?"

"We slept together. He did admit that much, didn't he?"

"Yes."

"Yes. OK. The next day he wrote to me and said he loved me, but he also said that he had some secret. He couldn't tell me what it was. You have the e-mails, don't you?"

"Yes."

"I didn't say I was in love with him. He was the one who said it. But he was also being completely confusing. He got upset because I said he was a star and then he didn't want to talk. So I thought if we could speak face to face ... but no, I didn't even think that. I even didn't go there to meet him. A guy from his office invited me, but when I saw Oll ... Blast, I took the opportunity."

"You just happened to be there."

"Yes. You can ask Ethan at the office."

"What did you want to know from Blast?"

"I wanted to know what was going on."

"How did he react?"

"He looked guilty. He walked up to me. He told me it was a one-night stand and I was just a groupie."

"What did he say exactly?"

Candi sighed. "He said something like 'It was a fuck; you can go tell your friends you slept with a rock star.' "

"Harsh. That must have hurt your feelings."

The psychologist's conversational tone put Candi at ease for a moment. "Yeah," she said.

"Can you tell me about that?"

"Well, it wasn't like I just ... I wasn't a groupie. It wasn't true."

"So it made you angry?"

"Not angry enough to want to hurt him. More hurt than angry."

"And he wrote one of his hit songs for you?"

"He said he did. It's not a hit yet. It's one of the new ones you can download on his web page. Now that I think about it, that might not be in the e-mails. I think he told me that in a chat. I didn't keep transcripts of those. I don't know what's in the e-mail and what was in the chats. But he told me it was for me. Maybe he lied, but the lyrics fit."

"What do they fit?"

"It was called 'Meet Me After Midnight,' and we would meet after midnight online."

"So after he wrote this song for you, he ignored you?"

"No. We had sex. After that he ignored me."

"You expected that to be the beginning of something."

"Sure. That's normal isn't it?"

"Tell me some more about how that felt."

Candi shuffled in her chair. "I don't understand why he is doing all this. Why would he do this to me? If he doesn't want to see me any more, he could just say so."

"He did say so, didn't he?"

"At the office."

"Let's talk about what you were thinking when you keyed his car."

"Nothing. I didn't do that."

"After he said he didn't want to see you, you went to his house."

"Yes. I did that. I admit that was a mistake. I was upset and I wanted to clear things up. I should have just gone home. But I was there; I thought … all I did was ask to talk to him. I thought if we could talk away from the office he might be able or willing to speak freely."

"You told his wife you were his girlfriend?"

"No," Candi said. "I wouldn't have said that."

"She said you did."

"She's wrong," Candi said. "She remembers it that way maybe. I don't know what I said that she remembers that way. I think maybe I said I was a friend of his. That I knew him. Maybe I said something like that. I wouldn't have said girlfriend. I'm sure of that. He just completely blew me off."

"So you believed he still loved you, but there was something at his office standing in your way?"

"I thought maybe. I didn't want to go back home without giving it one more try if there was a chance. He was leaving for Europe soon. I just wanted to see his expressions when I talked to him. It's not the same in e-mails. I wanted to get an idea of what he was feeling. You read the e-mails didn't you?"

"I did," the psychologist said. "Can you tell me about this one you wrote and signed 'Your little voyeur'? Did you spy on Blast?"

"Oh God. That was a joke. This is embarrassing. I know it doesn't sound good, but it was an in-joke."

"Explain it to me."

"When we had sex that time, he called me that, because ..." Candi sighed. She found it humiliating to have to talk about her sex life. "I wanted to watch him. I asked him, you know, to ... pleasure himself. So he called me a little voyeur. When I wrote the next day, I wanted to remind him ... it was sexy at the time. I thought he'd like it. I know it sounds kind of ... Did he say it meant something else? You could ask him about it."

"I did speak to him," she said.

"You did? What did he say? He told you about the e-mails?"

"He says he didn't write to you."

"What?"

"The messages use words he doesn't use. They are full of American expressions. They come from an anonymous e-mail account that he knows nothing about. It was only set up after you supposedly started writing to him."

"Supposedly? No, it was his private account. He said it was the one he uses for private communication. So we could talk privately."

"It isn't."

"It was. If one of us is lying, why do you assume it's me?"

"Your e-mail is hosted by the same service isn't it?"

"I guess so."

"So you know how to set up an account with the service."

"This is crazy. Why would he do this to me?"

"You feel as though you're being persecuted by Blast?"

"I am being persecuted. It isn't a feeling."

"Did you set up this e-mail account in order to send messages to yourself?"

*****

Her memory after that was fragmented into series of moments, like a montage of film clips and still photographs.

She remembered walking past the statue of Themis, the blindfolded Greek goddess of divine justice holding the scales and sword. (In Greek times Themis was not depicted holding a sword. The weapon was added in Roman times. It represents the power held by those making legal decisions.) She remembered being overwhelmed and yet still confident that the judge would not possibly believe a preposterous story about Candi writing e-mail messages to herself.

Candi felt like the only actor who had not been given the script for a movie they were filming. The courtroom looked like the ones in legal dramas on TV. She was struck by the theatricality of it all, the costumes—the judge's black robe—and the staging—the raised platform to literally give the judge his elevated status. The only other profession she could think of that required a robe was the ministry. The costuming of the judge said that he was not a man but a symbol of the system; he was the physical incarnation of divine justice.

Justice Martin Hollow moved everything along at a pace that suggested he was paid by the unit, based on how many cases he could get off his desk. Candi wondered if he wanted to get home and watch a football game on TV. He joked with the lawyers. No one was acting as though they were making decisions that could tear another human being's life apart.

She remembered the reporters in the courtroom taking pictures and making drawings. She overheard a television reporter standing in the hall speaking to a camera. "... Blast, a rock star best known for his 1980s hit 'Half Cloudy Thursday' ... the alleged stalker, a 30-year-old unemployed office worker named Candi Tavris ... vandalized his car ... threatened his family ... claimed that his song lyrics were speaking to her. ..."

Candi had hoped this would blow over and none of her friends or family would ever know it had happened. Now it was clear that would not be possible. She had no idea how the reporters knew about her case. Had Ollie sent out a press release? Could this all be a publicity stunt?

There was the moment when a court official read out a notarized statement from Oliver Thomas stating that the e-mail messages had not come from his account, that he'd had no contact with Candi prior to their meeting in San Diego. Then she read a second notarized statement from Ollie's ex-wife saying that she and her daughter had felt threatened by Candi's visit. Her daughter? Candi had never even met her daughter.

Somehow "the state" had managed to find the HR person who had fired Candi. She testified that Candi had been "hysterical" that day and that her responses seemed "bizarre." A few encounters had been polished and scrubbed so that everything fit. Anything that didn't advance the narrative had been filed away.

She remembered the judge being handed State's Exhibit 1: a forensic competency evaluation.

There was something about the absurdity of the psychologist's theory that gave it special power. The idea that someone would write hundreds of e-mail messages in a misguided quest to delude herself was so unbelievable that it had to be true. No one could make something like that up. Once you've been painted as someone who is that deluded you have no credibility. There is no more presumption that your point of view can be trusted. "I didn't write those messages" became every bit as incriminating a statement as if she'd admitted she had.

She remembered her own lawyer questioning the psychologist: "Do you think my client knows right from wrong and can assist in her own defense?"

"In my opinion, no," she said. "She suffers from erotomania. Because of her delusion, she believes that Mr. Thomas reciprocates her feelings and that her behavior is appropriate. Her delusion makes it impossible for her to appreciate the consequences of her actions. Until she receives proper treatment for these delusions she will continue to be a danger to Mr. Thomas and his family."

Candi sat dumbfounded. It was like the scene in *Alice in Wonderland* in which the Queen, calling for Alice's head, shouts "Sentence first—verdict afterwards."

She thought back with nostalgia to the time when calls from creditors were her biggest problem, which led her to think about her magic bath spell with the bay leaves and the candles. Maybe the spirits were offended that she had not followed the instructions correctly and they were taking their revenge. It made as much sense as anything else.

Then Justice Hollow looking down from on high said, "Candi Tavris, doctors have found you not competent to proceed and therefore you will be committed to the Department of Health and Mental Hygiene until, in the opinion of the medical staff, you shall be deemed no longer a threat to yourself or others."

The Full Manti

As Ollie was preparing his affidavit for Candi's competency hearing, and during the hearing itself, Ethan had remained silent. He had even helped Ollie make some of the legal arrangements. Still he stayed mum. He rationalized his silence by his faith in the system. He knew Candi was not really a stalker or a danger to anyone and he thought it would be evident. He'd never heard of anyone writing e-mail messages to themselves. Was that even a thing? He was shocked when she was sent away.

The next day at the office, as he got his coffee Brenda said, "Isn't it amazing, the lengths people will go to rationalize things."

Ethan nearly dropped his mug. He thought she was telling him she knew his secret.

"I mean how long do you think it took her to write all of those messages out?" she said.

Ethan released his breath.

"I don't think she did that," he said. "Have you ever heard of anyone doing anything like that?"

"No, but I don't deal with crazy people every day. Not literally crazy anyway." She laughed.

"I don't think she wrote the e-mails, I think it was like a Manti Te'o thing."

"What's that?"

"You don't remember Manti Te'o? He's the football player who had a fake girlfriend."

"It's a person?"

"Yeah. It was all over the news."

"Oh, I don't watch cable news. It's terrible. Rots your brain," she said flipping a strand of jet black hair behind her ear. "If you read the news or you hear it on the radio you get an entirely different sense of what is happening in the world. Stuff that might affect your life. On cable it's all entertainment, O.J. Simpson, Michael Jackson."

"The balloon boy"

"Don't know that one."

"You don't know the balloon boy? Some guy told the news that his son had flown off on a big silver balloon, so the news followed the balloon around all day but there was no kid in it. See, that one was a hoax too."

"A hoax like what?"

"Manti Te'o."

"Oh, right, so what was the story with Monty Tae Bo. He had a fake girlfriend?"

"So he told everyone that his grandmother and his girlfriend died within one week and everyone felt sorry for him, but then someone thought it was kind of weird that no one had ever seen this dead girlfriend, so they did some digging and it turns out she didn't exist."

"He made her up, like Ollie's stalker made up the e-mails."

"No, that's the thing, he really thought he had this girlfriend because she wrote to him all the time in e-mail, but it turned out it was some gay guy who had a crush on him who wanted to flirt with him. So he made up this woman."

"That is really weird. People are strange."

Ethan couldn't understand why she was not following what he was saying: Candi did not write e-mail to herself.

"You don't know who you're talking to on line," Ethan said. "So anyone could have made a fake account and pretended to be Blast. I think Candi believed she knew him because someone was posing as him. I don't think she's crazy at all. Isn't that possible, that someone tricked her?"

"So you think this girl was conned by some kind of lesbian stalker?"

"I don't know if it's a lesbian—but it could be something like that."

"Seems farfetched to me."

"The whole Manti Te'o story is farfetched but it happened. Is it any more farfetched than the idea that she wrote a bunch of e-mails to herself? I'm going to look up some articles and send them to you."

Ethan ran to his desk and typed "Manti Te'o" into the search bar of his browser.

Brenda continued the conversation by shouting over to him from her desk. "They had an expert look at the messages," she said. "I assume the psychologist has seen stuff like this before. I trust the experts. They talked to this girl for a long time."

Ethan felt his chest tighten as he read the headline of the first article that appeared.

"Can You Go to Jail for Impersonating Someone Online?"

Jail?

The worst things that Ethan had thought could happen to him were that he could lose his job and that Candi would hate him. For the first time he began to realize that there could be much more serious consequences of his game.

"In California, online impersonation is a misdemeanor punishable by thousands of dollars in fines and up to a year in jail."

A second article's headline reduced his panic: "Masquerading as Online Lover Not Necessarily a Crime, Expert Says."

His relief was short-lived. The article explained that Te'o's hoaxer might be hard to prosecute because he had created a fictional girlfriend and California law expressly states that it is illegal to impersonate an "actual person." There was no question that Blast was an "actual person."

The type of sentence you might receive depends on the level of harm your prank did. "Emotional distress is harm," an expert said. "Damage to a person's reputation is harm."

Causing someone to be arrested, taken away in handcuffs and committed to a mental hospital as a delusional stalker? Ethan wasn't sure, but he guessed that would qualify as harm.

Brenda had gone back to talking about the vapidity of television news. Ethan found it hard to register her words. His hands were shaking above his keyboard. He thought Brenda should be able to see his wretchedness on his face, to feel his culpability like a vibration in the air, but she kept talking as if nothing had changed.

"Why did the balloon boy guy make up that story?"

"Huh?" Ethan said.

"The guy who told the news his kid flew off in a balloon. Why did he do that?"

"I don't remember." What have I done?

"See, that's the thing. They hype up a story and then no one ever hears the end of the story. Like, you remember the Atlanta Olympics?"

"What? ... No."

"Oh right, I forgot, you're a baby," she laughed. It amazed Ethan that anyone could laugh. "Some terrorist planted a bomb in a crowd at the Olympics. And this guy found the bomb, I don't remember the details, but first the news decided this guy was a hero and then the police wanted to question him because they thought he might have planted the bomb. Like 'he that smelt it dealt it.' The media couldn't resist the story of the hero who was actually the bomber, but it turned out he didn't do it. But they'd torn up this guy's life, and lots of people heard the first part and not the part that cleared him. Once you accuse someone of something, there's always doubt."

"Yeah," Ethan said. "So, what if ... what if Candi Tavris is the Olympic guy and she didn't do it."

234

"We know she did it."

"We know she believed she was Ollie's girlfriend, we don't know why," he said.

"Because she's nuts," Brenda said. Then the telephone rang and Brenda turned her focus back to her work.

Ethan waved his hands in front of him. He thought this might whip the shakes out. As he got over the initial shock, a narrow path out of this mess began to emerge. Somehow he had to get Candi out of her predicament. He couldn't let her rot in the madhouse. He also could not confess without going to jail. He had to persuade everyone that someone—but not him—had written her those e-mails. He had to remind everyone that internet fraud exists, get them talking about it, and yet somehow divert the attention from himself.

He found a bunch of articles on Manti Te'o that did not mention jail time for the person who tricked him and sent them to Brenda and also to Ollie's personal e-mail address. (His real personal e-mail address.) He planned to send articles on online impersonation to Candi's lawyer and the prosecutor, the judge, anyone who might have power over her life. First, though, he had to make sure no one could prove he was the culprit.

He went home and deleted all of the chat logs and e-mail files from his correspondence with Candi. It was painful to him to have to do it. It was like hitting the delete key on his romance. Self-preservation outweighed any sentiment, though. He consoled himself with the knowledge that now that she knew the real Ethan he could stay in touch with her and when all of this was over he could start up a new conversation based on who he really was. He wouldn't need the souvenirs.

After he'd deleted the files he closed the "ollieblast" account. He deleted his browser history and cookies. Next he downloaded a program to wipe the deleted files from his hard drive so they couldn't be recovered in a forensic investigation. He was still shaken, but he felt more safe.

He went back to the office the next day expecting everyone to be talking about the investigation and Ethan's theory that Candi had been duped. The subject never came up. When Ethan brought it up himself, it didn't go anywhere. No one cared. The case was closed in their minds. She wasn't bothering Ollie any more and the court had spoken. Justice had been done.

The next few days at the office went by as if everything were normal, as if there had been no trial and no verdict, as if he had not caused the woman he loved to be falsely accused of a crime and imprisoned in a mental ward. He was both terrified and elated to realize that he could, if he chose to, forget what he had done. In time the fear and the guilt would vanish. He could get away with it.

Erotomania

So when our mortal frame shall be disjoin'd
The lifeless Lump uncoupled from the mind
From sense of grief and pain we shall be free;
We shall not feel, because we shall not BE."

Lucretius, *Against the Fear of Death*

The mental hospital was not what Candi had come to expect from years of watching movies. It wasn't a hellish landscape full of screaming psychotics in restraints. (If there were such people they were in another section of the building.) Nor, for the most part, was it full of charming comic oddballs. It was populated with the bored, the lonely and the lethargic—whether this was from depression or the meds was not clear to her. They mulled about in an environment that was beige, institutional, disinfected, free of sharp corners, devoid of anything of interest, completely controlled with activities and timetables.

Outside they didn't have to think about whether they were sad or not. In here, people were constantly asking "how do you feel?" "Fine," was not an acceptable answer. She had never had to give so much thought to why she felt as she did, why she dressed as she did, why she chose the words she did.

"Why were you dressed the way you were when you went to Blast's house?"

Before you're defined as sick, things happen, they're random. Then suddenly everything is a symptom. It became clear that she didn't know the reasons behind any of her choices and actions. Was that madness?

Candi's roommate was a fair-skinned, wild-eyed woman with dreadlocks. She believed she was John the Baptist. When they met, "John" put her

237

hand on the side of Candi's face, stared deep into her eyes and said, "You do belong. Your father is in heaven. That's your father. That shame you have deep inside doesn't belong to you. Do you understand me? It doesn't belong to you. There are people who are beyond shame. You must go to the people who are beyond help. The ones everyone else blames. They need you. You can heal their shame. You need to let your shame go so you can release them. Do you understand?"

Candi did not understand, but thought it best not to say so. "Yes, I understand."

"You have great work to do," John said.

John had an intensity that lived somewhere on the border between scary and divinely inspired. You were never quite sure whether you should run screaming or ask her to put in a good word for you with the Lord. Just as Candi was beginning to wonder if she might actually be a prophet, John saw a cricket on the floor. She pounced, trapped it and ate it.

If Candi was destined for greatness, it was going to take her a while to manifest it. Her doctor had put her on risperidone, an antipsychotic, to "stabilize" her. It gave her a splitting headache. (She assumed it was the risperidone that did that. It could also have been caffeine withdrawal. They only served lukewarm decaf in the cafeteria.) The meds and the lack of caffeine made her sluggish during the day and unable to sleep at night. When she did sleep she remembered no dreams. This was just as well because dreaming of another world and then waking up as a prisoner in the mental ward was too horrible to contemplate.

The hospital had a library full of mindless-genre fiction (for people without minds). She steered clear of the romances, which she assumed could be taken as a symptom of her obsessional romantic disorder. She had no interest in science fiction and couldn't focus enough to keep track of the suspects in the mysteries.

She found it harder to be without her computer. She couldn't check in on Facebook, Instagram, or Twitter. Not being able to see the cat pictures her acquaintances from college were posting made her nervous, as if the world was moving on without her. ("I Can Haz Freedom?") Sometimes she wondered if the world outside existed at all or if it was a delusion too. Everything that had consumed her before she went in seemed like a distant fiction.

Candi had been diagnosed with De Clérambault's Syndrome also known as erotomania. When she read the description even Candi had to admit she sounded like a textbook case. "The patient, often a single woman, believes that a person of high status is in love with her. The victim is usually older and of higher social status, often a public figure or celebrity. Age at onset is usually middle or late adulthood—say around 30. Subjects are often unemployed and isolated. The patient often believes that the subject of her delusion is more in love with her than she is with him and that the subject of her delusion cannot make his feelings known for some reason."

Candi knew she was not mad, her situation only mimicked the disorder. Yet there was a disorienting doubt underneath her certainty. Didn't all erotomaniacs believe their delusions? Weren't they every bit as certain of what they knew? What troubled her most in the article was that it said erotomania could not be cured, only managed. Did this mean she would be locked up in an institution forever?

On this score she was thankful for the meds. They kept her from dwelling on the shock of having her life and her understanding of herself torn away. She had been feeling every emotion it was possible to feel all at once—fear, boredom, depression, anxiety, outrage, frustration, grief, bewilderment, humiliation, regret, anger, loneliness and shame—it was probably best that the drugs kept her from focusing on anything for long.

Her one connection to the world outside was the regular visits from her sister, Jackie. Yet this managed to have a surreal, other worldly quality as well. As soon as Jackie learned about the arrest, she took a leave of absence from her job (her income was just a supplement to her husband's anyway) and flew out to San Diego. She was staying in Candi's apartment, where she also paid the rent. At first Jackie was visiting every day. She claimed to believe Candi when she said she was not delusional. Candi suspected she was lying because she also said things like "You just need to focus on getting well." Candi hated the expression on her face when she said that, a mixture of pity and pride at being the responsible sister.

Candi may not have always lived up to her own expectations, but she'd never imagined she could find herself in the role of the problem child. After Jackie's visits Candi always felt diminished and embarrassed. On the other hand, she needed to know that the outside world had not forgotten her; that someone cared if she lived or died.

On her most recent visit Jackie had brought some homemade walnut bread. "Walnuts are good for cognitive function," she said.

Candi wanted to snap, "My brain functions just fine!" Instead she glanced down at the table, "Thank you."

"You're famous, you know," Jackie said as she took the bread out of its plastic wrap.

"Why am I famous now?"

"They talked about you on Entertainment Tonight." She seemed to be excited by the idea of being part of a national television story.

Candi shook her head. "Celebrity stalkers? Me and the lady who thought she was David Letterman's wife?"

"It wasn't terrible. They didn't make you sound too crazy."

"How could they do a story about a rock star stalker without making me sound crazy?"

"It was respectful," Jackie said.

"Great, me and Mark David Chapman. Two of a kind."

"Maybe you can do an interview and tell your side of the story," Jackie said.

"It won't help," Candi said. "It's like all the words somehow end up meaning the opposite of what I say. Anyway, who cares? You can't do much to hurt the reputation of someone whose already in the loony bin."

240

"We'll get you out of here," Jackie said. She took a bite of walnut bread and covered her mouth with her hand, "You just concentrate on getting better."

*****

When she had been working for the software company, Candi had felt unnoticed and unappreciated. Now, in the hospital, she was constantly observed.

"How are you feeling today? Did you eat? Did you sleep well?"

It was like returning to childhood where you were the center of everyone's attention. When she was a kid, being the focus of adult attention made her feel loved—and she was. But she realized now that a lot of the focus was not because she was so unique and special but because her parents were afraid she would hurt herself with a toy or pull the dog's tail or break the furniture. That was exactly the kind of attention she had now.

Surely there had to be some balance between being ignored and being smothered. She thought about all of the people going on reality shows, desperate for fame. They didn't know what it meant to be known and judged by strangers—people with no emotional investment in you. Was that why Ollie went crazy when she called him a star after they made love?

These were the kind of forbidden thoughts she had learned not to share with her therapist. She had to work them out for herself. If she spoke as if Ollie felt anything about her at all, it proved she was insane. Asking the doctors to consider whether Ollie might be the crazy one got her nowhere. The only path to freedom, it seemed, was to admit to her delusions and express remorse. The path to freedom was to lie.

Candi's case worker was younger than she thought a psychiatrist should be. Dr. Sofia Molina looked as if she was barely out of high school. Figuring how long it takes to get your medical degree, though, she must have been at least Candi's age. She was petite and slim with long dark hair, which she always wore up in a messy bun, probably to make her seem more grown-up. Candi suspected her glasses were a plain-glass affectation too. She was Puerto Rican-born and retained the slightest hint of a Spanish accent. Candi liked her. Dr. Molina was something consistent and calming to grasp onto. She was one of the few sane people in her environment who didn't seem to judge her, to pity her, or to treat her as a criminal. Candi believed Dr. Molina genuinely wanted to help, she just wasn't sure if she knew what she was doing: "I have a diploma, so I know more about your mind than you do."

For the first few days of her incarceration, the therapist didn't even ask her about Blast. She wanted to know how Candi was getting along, if she was frightened, and what effect the medication was having on her. Only after they'd established a rapport did Dr. Molina bring up love and romance.

"Is having a real relationship frightening for you?" she asked.

Candi was relieved that they were finally getting to the heart of the matter.

"What is a real relationship?" Candi asked.

"You tell me. What have your relationships with men been like?"

"I haven't had that many. Only one that was, what you'd call serious."

"What was that like?"

"Normal. Good. Then bad. We broke up. Nothing weird or traumatizing."

"What happened?"

"He cheated on me. He'd go off with other girls and then he'd act like I was smothering him because I didn't like it."

"Who ended it?"

"I don't know. We both did. He slept around and I did the logical thing. I ended it. But he didn't give me a lot of choice. The funny thing is, he was the one who was sleeping around, but he was also really jealous."

"Jealous of whom?"

"Whom?" Candi repeated. "Whom" was a code word that said "I am highly educated." "He was jealous of my friends," she said. "My family. Rock stars."

"Rock stars?"

"Yeah. People I didn't even know. He didn't like that I had posters with rock stars in them."

"Was Blast one of them?"

"Yeah. Sure. He was the main one."

"So he was jealous of this other man in your life."

"Blast wasn't in my life. He was just a poster. I didn't know him then." Candi trailed off. She found herself contemplating the word "then" in her sentence. She hadn't known him *then*.

"I didn't know him," she continued. "Chad just couldn't let it go, he wouldn't leave me alone, but he wouldn't be faithful either. Like, if I dared reject him, suddenly he needed me. But whenever I forgave him, he went back to the same old thing: that I was trying to control him."

"How did that make you feel?"

"That's a very psychiatrist kind of question."

Dr. Molina smiled. "Humor me."

"It made me feel like I never wanted to get involved with another man ever again. He would call me constantly. I'd come home from work and the voice mail would say I had six messages and they were all from him. I would just lie on the couch, look up at the posters and delete the messages one at a time without listening to them."

"And when this was happening and you looked at the poster of Blast, what did you think?"

"I don't know. It was just there."

"Give it some thought."

"I wanted to be free like a rock star touring the country. I wanted to run away and join the circus. I wanted to go back to high school when things made sense and all anyone cared about was getting tickets for a great concert."

"So your relationship was putting you under a lot of stress."

"You could say that."

"And Blast was an escape."

"I suppose so."

"He could be whatever you wanted. It wasn't complicated. Chad was accusing you of being unfaithful because you liked Blast, and Blast was an escape from your problems."

Candi felt her hands shaking. Was it fear or the medication? "You're saying I had some kind of psychotic break. You're saying everything I remember—I just made it up. But I remember it. I remember it. And Chad made me crazy, but he didn't make me, you know, certifiably insane. We broke up. People break up all the time."

"I know this is confusing for you. But I'd like you to just consider the possibility that what you think you remember was an illusion. People sometimes remember things, they have real memories, that are not historically accurate. You say you have a personal relationship with Blast. I know you're not lying. You believe it to be true. But he says it's not true. What reason would he have to lie about that?"

Candi could feel tears of frustration welling up inside. She did her best to force them back. "What reason am I supposed to have? You believe him because he's more famous than me."

Dr. Molina spoke with calm assurance. "You had pictures of him. You had videos. You heard his voice. It's not always easy for the mind to tell the difference between a lived experience and a vividly imagined experience. Memory isn't like a video camera that records everything we experience. We interact with our memories and re-shape them. I'm not taking sides. Right now I don't need you to think about what happened

244

next. I just want you to take some time and think about this time when you were looking at his poster and imagining a different life."

Candi thought about it for a moment. Could she have dreamed it all? "But, no," she said, half to herself. "If this was all in my head, why would I imagine such a bad relationship? Why would I imagine him rejecting me and playing with my head and getting me arrested and thrown in here? If I were in some kind of psychotic denial, wouldn't I be imagining happily ever after?"

"Is it possible that a fantasy came crashing into a reality that you couldn't control?"

"Well, yeah. That's what happened, but not in the way you are saying."

"Until you met Blast face to face you felt you had a good relationship, didn't you?"

"Yeah."

"After this session, I'd like you to give some thought to the timing of things. When did it feel good and when did it get bad and what else was happening in your life at the time. Also, think about this. If he was in love with you ..."

"I know he's not in love with me. I'm not in love with him any more either."

"If he did have the kind of relationship with you that you say he did, what would motivate him to suddenly accuse you of this kind of thing?"

"I don't know," Candi said, and in spite of her best efforts the tears began to fall. "That's what I can't understand. I can't imagine why anyone would do something like that. I can't imagine. It makes no sense."

"It makes no sense," Dr. Molina said. She pointed at Candi as though she had just answered her own question. "You're a smart woman. Which is more logical, that everyone is making up this story, that Blast and his office and the lawyers and all of us at the hospital are engaged in a conspiracy against you or that you are suffering from an illness and need treatment? There is no shame in having an illness."

"I wouldn't feel ashamed if I had an illness. I know what happened. He really did send me e-mails. We really did chat online for hours. I remember it. It's not just my mind. I have the e-mails to prove it."

"The court felt that it was probable that you wrote the messages yourself. Is it possible you did that?"

"But I didn't," Candi said. Her shaking was becoming more pronounced. "I'm not going to contact him again. That's what everyone is worried about, isn't it? It's what I do that matters. He's made it very clear he doesn't want me in his life. I understand that. Why do you want to take my memory away too? Why not let me remember it the way I do? Who does it hurt? A memory is only in your head. It's like a dream. When you get together with friends they never remember things the same way anyway. Who does it hurt if I remember that he told me he loved me? Can't we just say that he and I remember things differently and go our separate ways? Why do I have to believe his version? Your version?"

"I don't have a version. I'm not trying to take anything from you. I want to help you to be well. It's fine to have a dream or a fantasy if you know that's what it is. It's different when that becomes real and starts determining your future actions."

"I remember it the same way I remember Chad. Why are you asking me anything about my past anyway when all if it might be untrue? It's all stuff I have stored in the attic of my brain. None of it exists now, it's all just dreams and memory. How do I even know Chad was real? I don't know what to believe any more."

"That's a start."

Love's Delusion

The stewardesses in business class were less harried than those in coach. It was a position, Ollie suspected, that was given to the senior members of staff. Up here in second class (not swanky first, not the steerage behind the curtain) where the European tour's producer had placed the band, the hostesses did their best to act as though they were still in the golden era of flying. Back then getting on a plane at all was a mark of status. The air hostesses of the day competed for glamorous jobs that required them to look like fashion models and forced them remain single and to retire at 32; sexy, superficially charming and servile, the male business traveler's fantasy.

Ollie's stewardess was in her mid-forties, not overweight but not entirely slim, either. She had the same corporate-approved smile of her stewardess ancestors, but behind it lurked the weariness that came from being an under-paid first line of defense in the event of a hijacking, accident, or terrorist attack and repeated exposure to angry customers incensed about a la carte pricing, long lines at TSA checkpoints, scanners that revealed every body part, and the delays that came with over-full skies.

"Here you are, sir," she said as she handed Ollie a gin and tonic.

When she had passed Graham, who was in the seat beside Ollie said, "Nice legs."

Ollie turned to look and agreed that they were not bad.

"Did you notice they wear shorter skirts here than in economy?"

Ollie had not, and he suspected it wasn't true. He put his headphones back on and turned to look out the window at the clouds. Graham went back to working the crossword puzzle in the in-flight magazine. Occasionally he muttered things like, "Shade of blue" and "Greek letter."

Ollie was listening to the classical music channel on the plane's in-flight entertainment selections. He did not want to clutter his mind with the programming on his personal TV. Ollie liked flying. Being on an airplane forced you to sit still. You were outside your normal life, over the ocean, not connected to any particular place, it was a great way to get distance and perspective. He had even read that there was something about the quality of the air or the altitude that affected your brain and made you more creative.

Blast's stalker had given him more national press than he'd had in years. A deluded woman thinks she is the girlfriend of a has-been rock star—great copy. He was desperate to change the narrative and get them talking about his music again. Yet he had been completely unable to write.

Ever since Candi Tavris had appeared in his parking lot saying that she knew he loved her, Ollie couldn't get her out of his mind. He resented this because it was exactly what she wanted, and he had fallen right into her trap. It was human nature, though, to want to know your enemy, to try to understand her motivations. He had looked up all of her social media pages, gazed at her photographs, tried to imagine her life and what might have made her snap. When he got tired of researching his stalker, he would find himself googling Greg Wight and Amanda Thomas. He had the uncomfortable sensation that he was becoming a stalker himself.

He had read all the online articles on his legal case, and all of the comments on them. He knew he should not pay any attention to the bored gawkers and trolls who feel the need to express their opinions on the lives of the famous. Yet he couldn't seem to keep himself from poring over every hurtful word. There was a thread that ran through many of the comments. It was all his fault.

"He slept with her and threw her away. He brought it on himself. I have no sympathy for him."

Then there were the comments written by women who considered themselves to be feminists. (Ollie had always thought of himself as a feminist, too.) They used the word "privilege" and accused him of being sexist. "When a man pursues a woman he's romantic and gallant, but when a woman pursues a man she's a crazy stalker."

"Here is a powerful man with status. He wants women to serve him on his terms. He has no right to cry victim when women are the real victims of the world."

Who were these people? They could not know how it felt to look at someone and realize she is not inhabiting the same world, that no matter what you say it will have no impact on her fantasies. He had seen her eyes. He had seen the strength of her delusional belief. Who were they to say he had nothing to fear because he was a man and she was a woman?

As angry as the comments made him, he couldn't stop reading. It was a form of self-imposed mental abuse almost as bad as having a stalker in the first place. He read and he seethed and he shouted at the screen.

"Who are you, MK006, to judge me? Walk a mile in my shoes. Does 'no mean no' only when women say it? Don't I have the right to say no?"

Ollie took a deep breath and let the clouds, the jet engine's vibrations and Bach's Concerto for Two Violins and Strings in D Minor put him into a meditative state. His two obsessions danced in his head, Candi and Mandy, the one who wanted him and the one he wanted.

There was something fascinating about Candi and her delusion. Her determination to live in her own, more perfect world would be almost noble if it weren't so frightening. The more he tried to understand her mind, the more the line between normal and abnormal blurred. Her insanity seemed to be an extreme version of the quirks of everyone's brain.

Candi thought Ollie's music spoke to her. Didn't all music fans feel that? Less literally, of course, but fans were always telling him the music spoke to them. The music on the entertainment channel advanced to Chopin's Opus in E Flat Major. It soothed parts of Ollie that he could not even identify. Was he feeling what Chopin had felt? "Meet Me After Midnight" meant something different to Candi than it did to Ollie, but then again, did "Lucy in the Sky with Diamonds" mean the same thing to Ollie as it had to John Lennon? Surely not.

Ollie had believed Mandy loved him years after she had stopped. The signs that would have told him she didn't love him any more were there, but he ignored them all. Wasn't that delusion? Wasn't love itself a form of delusion? Romantic love might be the biggest mass delusion of them all. It was created out of whole cloth from novels, poems, and pop songs. He'd even played a part in reinforcing it with his music.

Ollie had seen a television program once about the changes in a person's brain when he falls in love. You meet someone attractive and your brain releases hormones, oxytocin, a trust hormone, and dopamine, a pleasure hormone. It is like being hooked on a drug; a chemical imbalance in the brain. It causes an almost insatiable craving to be with the beloved, an inflated sense of the importance of the other person in your life, an inability to see their faults: Erotomania. What if they called that a disorder and treated the first stages of love with antipyschotic drugs? Then we'd have to base our relationships on something more enduring than endorphins. That didn't seem like such a bad idea.

Ollie took a pen from his pocket and then he picked up his copy of the in-flight magazine. He found a page with a lot of whitespace and scribbled the title "Love's Delusion" and two lines: "She was in love but she saw right through me" and "I was in love but she saw right through me." Then he tore the page out of the magazine, folded it up, and put it in his pocket.

Persistence of Memory

*"Of course you had your illusions, lived in them
indeed, and through their shifting mists and coloured
veils saw all things changed."*

—Oscar Wilde, *De Profundis*

After three months in the hospital, Candi had come to accept her diagnosis. It was the only thing that made any sense. Dr. Molina had nudged and prodded her until Candi could connect her own longings and imagination to the things she believed Ollie had said. Of course it had been like a dream. It was a dream. She even believed she could remember the exact moment the fantasies became real to her—after The Meeting and after her terrible date. She had felt useless and frustrated that she could only seem to attract men who did not appeal to her. She wanted to be a different person and to escape completely into the video on her TV screen. She needed to be flattered and praised and told she was sexy, and some broken part of her mind had made it all happen.

Dr. Molina explained that memory is not so much a recording device as a creative process. You can erase parts and write over them. It worked like the blind spots in your eyes. There are places that your eyes cannot see, but you're never aware of it. Because the brain fills in the missing visual information based on what it expects to be there. You perceive a seamless image of the world but it is really full of holes. Memory is like that too.

Every experience gets filed away as a vague collection of impressions, sorted by category. They're like puffs of smoke that twist and tangle and float away. What your mind expects to find has to do with the narrative you have been creating about your life. You remember the details of a situation that make the greatest impression on you, and they make an impression on you based on who you are and what you think the event means. As you re-evaluate your life, you go back, revisit episodes and change them. Memories don't fade, they morph and expand.

All of this seemed plausible. When she thought back to her childhood, Candi had strong memories of events that showed up in family photos, but only the vaguest outlines of memories of events that had not been recorded using technology. Did the photos reinforce an actual memory or had the memory been created out of what she saw in the photos? She couldn't tell the difference.

Dr. Molina explained that Candi's firing, her sense of isolation and her vivid fantasy life were "event factors" that shaped what she experienced as memory. That is why she could actually remember sitting at her computer and chatting with a rock star. Candi was now convinced that this was indeed what had happened. There was only one problem: she hoped that once she came to her senses her true memory would be restored. Although she now accepted that her memory was false, she had no alternative reality with which to replace it.

Dr. Molina said this was normal. She told her about the Innocence Project, which has released wrongly convicted criminals from death row using DNA. She said about half of the innocent people who are put away go to jail because of an eye witness. The eye witnesses sit there on the stand and point to the bad guy absolutely certain about what they saw. They're not lying. They have vivid memories. They see the person's face. The memory has been shaped over the years through new information and suggestion. When it turns out this person could not have done the crime, the victims are often outraged because they know what they saw. The altered memory has become the only memory.

Candi desperately wanted to remember. She knew that it must have taken her a long time to compose all of those e-mail messages, but for the life of her she had no mental picture of herself doing it. She could only remember clicking the button for her inbox and watching messages download. Every once in a while she thought she might remember having done it, but she couldn't summon any details. Because she couldn't remember, she couldn't bring back the mindset of the person who did it. What had caused her to slip into that state? She knew on some level that woman had been her. Yet she felt little personal connection to that troubled soul, only mild embarrassment. Her embarrassment was precisely because of the disconnect she felt between that person and who she believed herself to be.

It was a profound relief for Candi to admit she was flawed and broken. All she had to do was surrender and leave her life in the hands of the doctors. There was nothing more to strive for, nothing to try to control. She could not be held responsible for the actions of her insane self. She could just float and let other people reshape her world. It had been a long time since she had really admitted she needed someone's help. She wondered why she had not done so before everything fell apart.

Candi was sitting on her bed looking over a set of papers that Jackie had brought over for her to sign. Once she signed she would officially be bankrupt. It was another step in the process of admitting reality. Even when she was working she'd been in debt over her head. She hadn't exactly been job searching over the past few months and she had a strong inkling that being a diagnosed criminally insane wouldn't help her job search much. It was one more bit of pride she had to let go, but when you've been arrested and locked away as deviant, admitting you can't pay your bills seems much less catastrophic. She had an excuse for everything. She was mentally ill.

John the Baptist was sitting on her bed. She was dressed in a white robe and was painting her toenails with pink nail polish.

"I have no idea how I ended up in so much debt," Candi said. "I got an education, I had a decent job. I did everything I was supposed to do."

John laughed.

"What's so funny?" Candi asked.

"Girl, you think you have some kind of contract with the world? 'I did what I was supposed to now God owes me a good life.' Please! The only covenant you have is that God gives you life and you do whatever he wants you to do. That's it, because life is a big gift and you owe him big time. So that means if you suffer or you hurt then you just say 'thank you.' Because you got a gift you didn't ask for and you didn't deserve. You got to be alive. You could be dead, then where would you be?"

"Hmmm," Candi said and looked down at her papers as if they required her full attention. She liked John, but she tried to tune her out whenever she went into her preacher mode.

Candi wondered what happened inside John the Baptist's head. Most people have a sense of self that comes from inside and they project it out into the world, at least that is how Candi had always conceived of it. John had gone looking for herself out in the world. She read the Bible and discovered John the Baptist and said, "There I am. That is me." It was like shopping for a self off the rack. Did she feel a sense of relief that she'd been reunited with her long-lost identity? Was it like Peter Pan looking for his lost shadow? How did it work? Of course, John was in no position to answer these questions.

John put the little brush back in the nail polish bottle so she could stand and give one of her full-on John the Baptist sermons. She raised her arms above her head and looked up at the ceiling.

"He that hath an ear, let him hear what the Spirit saith unto the churches; To him that overcometh will I give to eat of the tree of life, which is in the midst of the paradise of God."

"Him that overcometh," Candi repeated.

"Or her," John said. She sat back down on her bunk. "You're alive so you're going to suffer. People ain't perfect. But if you go with God you know you're not having a hard time because you're defective or unworthy. You're here. So you're good enough. You made it. You're alive. Say thank you."

"Thank you," Candi said.

"Amen, sister." John said, and put her hand up for a high five. Candi smiled and slapped it. That's when Dr. Molina appeared at the door.

"Are you coming to your session?" she asked Candi.

"Sorry, I got wrapped up in something," Candi said.

As they walked out the door John shouted after them: "I form light and create darkness. I make peace and create evil: I am the Lord!"

"What's that?" Candi asked Dr. Molina.

"I think it's Isaiah," she said. "Christine likes Isaiah." Christine was John's real name. No one but the doctors used it.

As they walked down the hall Candi asked, "Are you religious?"

"Catholic," Dr. Molina said.

"So you believe in God," Candi said. "And that Jesus was raised from the dead?"

Dr. Molina smiled, took a deep breath, and recited the Apostle's Creed as fast as she could—the same way a kid might recite the Gettysburg Address or a mathematics time table. "I believe in God, the Father Almighty, Creator of heaven and earth; and in Jesus Christ, His only Son, our Lord: Who was conceived by the Holy Spirit, born of the Virgin Mary; suffered under Pontius Pilate, was crucified, died and was buried. He descended into hell; the third day He rose again from the dead; He ascended into heaven, is seated at the right hand of God the Father Almighty; from thence He shall come to judge the living and the dead. I believe in the Holy Spirit, the Holy Catholic Church, the communion of Saints, the forgiveness of sins, the resurrection of the body, and life everlasting. Amen."

They had arrived at the office and Candi walked in and took a seat on the couch. Dr. Molina sat down across from her.

"Is this about John the Baptist?" the doctor asked.

"Well, yeah," Candi said. "I mean, you are a rational person."

"I like to think of myself that way."

255

"You believe a woman gave birth without having sex, and a man rose from the dead, but you have no real evidence for that. Just faith, right?"

"Yes."

"And Christine thinks she's John the Baptist. So ..."

"Yeah," Dr. Molina said. "That's a tough one."

"Why is one religion and OK and the other one delusion? Does it have to do with the number of people who believe it?"

"Hmm," Dr. Molina put her finger over her lips as she considered the question. "I suppose the difference is we have evidence that Christine is not John the Baptist."

"Yeah, but if they were to come out with proof tomorrow that there was no God or Jesus didn't walk on water or split loaves and fishes, it wouldn't mean you had been delusional to believe that stuff, would it?"

"These are tough questions."

"Is it just the name? Is that all it comes down to? If she used her own name and acted exactly the same way she'd be kind of weird, but she wouldn't be insane, right? She'd be Christine the religious zealot. There are a lot of people like that out there."

"I suppose there are."

"All kinds of religious quackery is protected by the First Amendment. I mean, If they were willing to give her a Social Security number under that name John the Baptist and people called her John and lined up for baptisms at a river—if they gave her a Ms. John Baptist driver's license and everything else was exactly the same—she wouldn't be here. Would she? If we agreed to let her be who she called herself then she would be John the Baptist. So maybe we have the problem."

"My degree is in psychology, not philosophy," Dr. Molina said with a little laugh. "I'd really like to talk about you."

"Yeah, OK," Candi said.

"So what is going on with you?"

"I signed those bankruptcy papers."

"How do you feel about that?"

Candi laughed. "You know if you gave me a recording of 'how do you feel about that' I could do this myself."

Dr. Molina raised her eyebrows into a scolding expression and Candi went on.

"Disappointed that it got to this point. Wondering what I did wrong. Embarrassed. But relieved mostly. Clean slate and all that."

Dr. Molina smiled. "A lot of positive things come out of disruptions. While we're on the subject, why don't you tell me about the layoff."

"Seems like another lifetime."

"Can you elaborate?"

"It was hard, but then I got dumped, arrested and put in here. Now it seems like, comparatively, it's the best thing that happened in the last few months."

"How did you feel when you got the news?"

"I couldn't stop laughing. I'm not being sarcastic. That's what happened."

Dr. Molina nodded. "That's not an unusual reaction."

"Oh. Well, I'm normal in some way, then. That's reassuring."

"Can you tell me how you felt about being laid off?"

"Useless. I know my job wasn't saving orphans or brain surgery, but I tried to be good at it. I tried to do a good job. What I did was, I kept track of inventory and I ordered shipping containers, wrap, stuff like that. So you're always trying to keep on top of it so they don't run out but you don't have a lot of cash tied up in packaging that is sitting around and no one is using. You're also comparing prices from different suppliers. It's mostly numbers on forms and spreadsheets. But I did a good job. I developed my own systems to do everything better. I was efficient. And you want to feel like what you do every day matters. Then they come in and say it doesn't. You've been sitting there for years doing something that doesn't need to be done. For people who don't care about you at all. The worst part was all the stuff they said to make themselves feel better about firing us, how it wasn't personal, it's just business. That makes it worse."

"How does it make it worse?"

"Because, isn't that the problem? That it isn't personal? Life is supposed to be personal. People are supposed to care about each other. Turning that off doesn't make you a better person or a more mature person. It's not a higher way of thinking. It's a cruel way of thinking. And you're supposed to feel better about that. It's like you've devoted your life to someone and you might as well not exist to them … Is this when you bring it back to Blast?"

"It's interesting that you made that association."

"I just figured you would. The thing about not existing to someone. How much is one person supposed to take? First they tell you that being fired isn't personal then they tell you that making love isn't personal either."

"So you think of Blast and your employers as part of the same process?"

"No, you're putting words in my mouth."

"I'm sorry. Tell me what you mean."

"I mean that it should be personal for somebody. I'm not just a body. Right now it feels like everyone is trying to tell me that I'm insane to think that anyone would care about me. 'Your life, it's not personal.' "

"No one is saying that. I'm certainly not saying that. I'd like to help you get to a place where you can accept love from someone who wants to give it to you. There are people like that out there."

"Looking for love in all the wrong places?"

"Something like that."

Candi gazed off into the distance. "Do you ever think that maybe there are just too many people in the world? Maybe it's just not possible to care about them all. And I'm one of the ones who falls through the cracks."

"I care about what you have to say."

Candi turned back to the doctor and shook her head. "You're paid to listen to me. That's different. I know you care, like I cared about packaging. You want to do a good job. But we're not friends. I may be an erotomaniac but I know that."

"I'm interested in the timing of these events. You learned that your company was downsizing and it was around this time that you started to believe that Blast was writing to you. So just when you were feeling rejected by your employer, feeling, as you say 'useless' that's when he showed up. It was exactly what you needed emotionally, and it appeared."

"I remember it," Candi said. "I remember it the same way I remember going to work or being in school. Even with all the drugs you pumped into me, I still remember it as vividly as anything else that is real. If this didn't happen, how do I know any of my life happened?"

"Does that idea frighten you?"

"Wouldn't it frighten you? If what you thought was your life was just neurons misfiring?"

"I imagine it would."

"How do you know it's not?"

"I guess I don't. But I seem to have confirmation from other people that the things I perceive are similar to what they perceive. So I assume I perceive the world pretty much as it is. The same way I know Christine isn't really John the Baptist—external evidence."

"Reminds me of reading Descartes in college; did you read that?"

"I think, therefore I am."

"Yeah. He couldn't prove that his senses were telling the truth about anything except that he existed. I've been having trouble working that out, too. What is the difference between 'thinking you are' and 'being'? But then Descartes went on to say God is good and God wouldn't deceive me and therefore everything is just the way I perceive it."

"Do you believe in God?"

"I'm an agnostic. I always thought that part was kind of a cop-out. Like 'Please, Inquisition, don't hurt me.' But I never really followed Descartes all the way through, really feeling it. It is disconcerting to come to the conclusion that none of what you perceive might be real at all. You have to come up with something to give you a sense that the world is there and it matters. If not God, then something."

"It sounds like you've been doing a lot of thinking."

"Yeah. So can I ask you something? How do you know, I mean, how do you know when I'm cured? I mean, maybe God can tell if you actually believe in the resurrection of Jesus or something, because he's God, but how do you know if I really believe what I say I do? You can't look at what I believe through a microscope."

"That's a good question."

"Thank you. It's just, I don't want to grow old in here."

"I get to know you and I get a sense of who you are. It's not an exact science. It's a relationship."

"But I'm not good at those, isn't that the point?"

She smiled. "We're trying to fix that."

"Well, then, hopefully you're not a delusion."

"I hope I'm not, too!"

Truth and Consequences

"You have to help me," Ethan said. He was sitting on the edge of his bed, hunched over, looking at Ale with a pleading expression. For the past three months he had been bringing up the e-mail hacker theory almost every day at the office. He only gave up when Brenda threatened to fire him if he didn't stop talking about it. He had sent the Manti Te'o articles to Candi's lawyer. He didn't answer. He sent a message saying that he had evidence that the Blast account was hacked. He still didn't answer. Finally, Ethan picked up the phone and called.

"He didn't care. He says the court already made a ruling and he's on to other cases. I asked him if I could get the case reopened, you know what he said?"

"What?"

"He said I don't have standing. No one cares. How do I get them to listen to me?"

Ale was sitting cross-legged on the floor with his back against the door of the mini-fridge. "You're not going to like my answer," he said.

"Tell me, what is it?"

Ale shook his head. "You know the answer."

Ethan turned his hands palms upward as if he expected God to drop a magical solution from the sky. "There has to be something,"he said. It sounded like a cry.

"There is something," Ale said. He shrugged. "Tell the truth. That's all you can do. Hinting isn't working. You've got to confess."

"If I tell the truth I could go to jail. Real jail."

"Where do you think your girlfriend is? You told me you were in love with that girl."

"I am."

"You're in love with her and you're fine with her being locked up in a mental hospital when you know she's not crazy?"

"I've been trying to get her out."

"You're my best friend in the whole world, OK. And you know you did something stupid. I'm on your side, but you have to tell the truth."

Tears welled in Ethan's eyes. "She'll hate me," he said.

Ale gave a deep, weary sigh. "You're still thinking about that? The ship's sailed on that one. You can't get to the happy ending any more. You have to shoot for the least-terrible ending. Getting this girl to fall for you is off the table. Keeping your job; not going to happen. Not going to jail—that's what you're shooting for. I'm just telling you the truth here, man. You want me to give it to you straight, don't you?"

"I didn't want any of this to happen," Ethan said. "I wanted to make her happy. I wanted everyone to have a good time, that's all." He buried his face in his hands.

Ale got up from the floor and sat beside Ethan on the bed. He patted his shoulder. "You can't control everything. Random shit happens. Random shit."

Ethan looked up and wiped his nose. "Let me, give me another day to figure something out, there has to be a way to …"

"Ethan, time's up. Look at me. It's over. Nothing new is going to happen between today and tomorrow. You have to end this right now. Today. Call Blast. Call her lawyer. Call the hospital. Tell everyone they made a mistake. Don't stop until they listen to you. And I love you, man, but if you don't I'm going to tell them because you can't leave Candi in that place. It's not right and you know it."

"At least," Ethan said. "At least let me talk to her first. I have to explain it. I have to see her and let her know I didn't mean for any of this to happen. I have to tell her I love her."

"Yeah," Ale said. He stood up and took his car keys from his pocket. "Let's go. I don't think you should drive."

"You're coming with me?"

"I'm with you all the way, OK? Whatever happens."

Ale and Ethan arrived at the hospital at 5 P.M. Ale pulled the handle, but the glass door was locked. A security guard walked up to the other side, he looked at the two visitors through the glass then scanned a plastic tag he was wearing and punched some numbers into a keypad. The door buzzed and clicked and Ale pulled again. It opened this time.

"Visiting hour isn't until 7," the guard said.

"Oh," said Ethan, "We didn't know. It's our first time."

"Come back at 7," the guard said. He looked down at Ethan's pockets. "Is that a cell phone you've got there?"

"Yeah."

"You can't bring anything like that in. When you come back, leave it in the car. Nothing but car keys."

"Yeah, OK," Ethan said.

The encounter with the guard left Ethan shaken. He had known that Candi had been locked away, but the key pad, the buzzer, the rules and regulations made it all real to him. The gravity of what he had done hit him all at once. He sat in the passenger seat of Ale's car jiggling his legs.

"That was so weird," Ethan said. "Maybe we should just go home."

"No way," Ale said. "We're coming back."

"Even the front door is creepy," Ethan said. "Maybe they won't even let us see her."

263

"Come on, man," Ale said. "Let's go find a place to smoke. Calm your nerves. Then we can get something to eat and it will be time to come back."

The pot didn't do much to improve Ethan's mood, but it did keep his hands from shaking. Ale didn't talk much at Burger King; but let Ethan do the talking. He nodded at all of Ethan's rationalizations and only popped into the conversation if Ethan suggested they drop the mission. Ale was determined that Ethan was going to see this thing through.

"Once I confess to her," Ethan said, "she'll know everything about me, the best and the worst."

"Uh-huh."

"She wants to be loved and I love her," Ethan said. "And I'll be very honest, and maybe she'll understand. I'll just throw myself at her mercy."

"Uh-huh."

"Maybe she'll admire that I'm willing to risk going to jail to get her out."

"Maybe," Ale said.

"Either way," Ethan said. "This whole nightmare will be over."

"Yep."

They arrived back in the hospital parking lot at 6:45. They put their cell phones and wallets into the glove box, locked the car, walked up to the front door and waited. There were already a few other people standing by. At five minutes to seven, the guard returned. This time he was holding a clipboard. He scanned his ID badge, keyed in the door code and let the visitors in one at a time, he wrote their names down on the clipboard then he sent them to the front desk. There, Ethan and Ale had to put their names down on a sign in sheet along with their "relationship to patient." "Friend," they each wrote.

Ethan was hoping the receptionist would say that only immediate family was allowed, but she did not. She wrote each of their names on stickers outlined in red with the word "Visitor." She told them to keep the stickers on their shirts at all times. Ethan had no intention of breaking that rule. He was afraid he'd be confused for a patient and never allowed to leave.

After they had signed in, the receptionist told them to have a seat. A few minutes later a friendly-looking Indian woman appeared. She was wearing the plastic hospital ID badge with her khakis and a black turtleneck. Ethan had expected the staff to be dressed in scrubs. The fact that she was in street clothes made everything feel a bit less alienating.

"Hi," the woman said. "Are you the ones here to see a patient in Ward 3?"

"Yes," Ale said. "Ward 3." He stood up. Ethan stayed in his seat.

"I'll take you there," she said. Ethan did not get up.

"Come on," Ale said. He yanked Ethan by the arm.

Ethan stood and the two friends followed the staff member. Each time they came to a set of double doors, she had to scan her badge and type in a code. Each threshold they crossed made Ethan more nervous. He felt trapped. Did Candi feel that way every day?

When they got to the visiting room, the woman asked Ale to put his car keys into a resealable plastic bag that she would keep at the nurse's station until the visit was over. Ethan stood, numb, as he watched Ale seal up the bag and write his name on it. *Keys could be used as a weapon.*

The visiting room had doors on each side, one for the guests and one for the patient. It had the look of an office conference room with a long table and a few sturdy chairs. One chair was away from the table against the back wall. The woman who had escorted them—was she a nurse?—sat down in that chair. Ethan realized that he would not have any privacy. Their talk would be observed and maybe recorded.

The second door opened and Candi entered. Ethan had half expected to see her with glazed eyes wearing a straight jacket, but she was dressed in her own clothes. She was a bit heavier than when he had seen her last, and she had deep dark circles under her eyes, but otherwise she looked the same. She smiled when she saw her friends. She was happy to see him, and it broke his heart.

"What are you guys doing here?" she said as she sat down.

"I had to see you," Ethan said.

"I don't get that many visitors," she said. "It was nice of you guys to come. What do you think of my new place?"

"It's …" Ethan trailed off.

"Yeah," Candi said.

"I'm going to get you out of here," Ethan said. He hoped it sounded chivalrous.

Ale nudged Ethan, "Ethan has something to tell you," he said.

"What is it?" Candi asked.

"It's … When I first saw you, I thought you were beautiful, and you're smart and funny," Ethan glanced over at the nurse to see if she was taking notes. She didn't seem to be. "I know you're way out of my league."

"I'm out of your league?" Candi laughed shook her head. "I'm in a mental hospital. Ethan, you're sweet, really, but like I told you before, this isn't a good time for me to think about that kind of relationship with anybody. Look where I am."

"You complete me," Ethan said.

"Huh?" Candi said. Ale rolled his eyes.

"Sorry," Ethan said. "I panicked. I mean, do you remember when you were writing to Ollie?"

Candi grimaced and backed away slightly. "Can we not talk about that?"

"I have to tell you this," Ethan said. "You loved him didn't you? The guy in the e-mails?"

"I really don't want to talk about that," she said. She put her hand on her forehead as if the subject were physically bruising her brain. Ethan soldiered on.

"All I wanted to do was to have a chance to talk to you and tell you how I felt. I never thought it would get so out of hand. Have you seen the movie Roxanne?"

"Ethan, you have to slow down," Candi said. "I don't know what you're talking about."

"Cyrano de Bergerac, you know that story? Cyrano had a big nose and Roxanne was in love with this other guy who was handsome and glamorous. But he wasn't good with words. The guy with the normal nose, I mean. Cyrano was. And he was in love with Roxanne, so he told the stupid guy with the normal nose what to say and he wrote letters for him, but he talked about his own love. He was really in love."

Candi was squinting at him as if he were speaking a foreign language and she had to work hard to understand it. "I should tell you, I'm on medication," she said. "Maybe that's why I can't follow you."

Ethan sighed and tried again. "You ever heard that expression 'Give a man a mask and he'll tell you the truth?' "

"Oscar Wilde," she said.

"What?"

"You're quoting Oscar Wilde."

"Oh, OK. See, you're smarter than I am. That's why I love you."

"I do like you," she said, "but your timing really stinks. I can't return your feelings. I'm really sorry."

"That's not all that stinks," Ale said. He nudged Ethan again, this time he shoved so hard Ethan nearly fell out of his chair. "Tell her," he said.

"I have to tell you something," Ethan said. "I want to be sure you know how I feel and why …why I did it. Do you remember when Ollie said you were like a rock star to him? It was all true; it's exactly how I felt about you. You were glamorous and out of reach."

"I'm flattered," she said, and then she stopped speaking. There was a long pause. Then her eyes became wide and her mouth dropped open slightly. She stared into Ethan's eyes.

She understood.

"How did you know that?" she asked.

Ethan nodded.

Her voice came out in a lower register with intense, controlled energy, "How do you know what Ollie told me?"

"I didn't mean for it to go this far. At first it was just for fun. I didn't think it could hurt anybody. But as I got to know you, I realized there was no one else like you. I wanted to keep you in my life. I fell in love with you, and I couldn't stop. I didn't know how to make it right. I wanted you to love me and that's why I kept it going."

"It was you," Candi said. "You wrote the messages. You worked in his office and you …"

"I didn't mean for any of this to happen."

"Why should I care what you meant?" Candi shouted.

The nurse stood up. "Calm down, Candi" she said. "Or I'll have to end the visit."

Candi continued in a measured voice, "Maybe I'm hallucinating because what you're saying makes no sense. I think I just heard you say that you conned me, you let me be arrested and committed, you turned my entire life upside down because you love me? Is that really what I'm hearing you say? Do you have any idea what it is like in here?"

"No," Ethan said, he glanced down at the table top.

"They spy on me every 15 minutes, day and night, to make sure I didn't commit suicide. My room is a bare brick cell kind of place and I share it with a woman who claims to be John the Baptist. You know, I had my doubts that she really was John the Baptist, but who am I to say that she's not? It's so hard to know if people are really who they say they are these days."

Ale laughed at this. Ethan glared at him.

Then Candi turned to the nurse, who was still standing ready to take action if things got out of control. She seemed too small to Ethan to be able to do that, but maybe she had a hypodermic needle in her pocket.

"I think Ethan is delusional," Candi said. She turned back to Ethan, "The doctors here can help you with that. They have good meds. They make you a little lethargic, and they give you a headache like a sledge hammer in your skull, but they tell me they do wonders for erotomania. They didn't do much for me, but then again, *I'm* not actually crazy."

"Everything I said in the e-mails and the chats was true," Ethan said.

"Oh really?" Candi said, "You get tired of being on the road all the time, do you? Being famous is a drag, isn't it? I'm the muse who allows you to write beautiful music; that was true?"

"Candi …" Ethan said.

Candi stood up and shouted, "Get out, you sick bastard! Get out!"

"OK," the nurse said, grabbing hold of Candi's arm. "This visit is finished." She led Candi to the patient door and pressed a button on the keypad. It was also an intercom device. "Code 6 in the visiting room," she said.

Ale stood up, "Sorry," he said to Candi as the door opened and a pair of staffers took her by each of her arms.

"He's going to tell the truth," Ale called after her. "We'll get you out of here."

She made eye contact with Ale and nodded as she was dragged from the room.

"I'm sorry," Ethan called after her. "I'm really sorry."

"That went well," Ale said.

Not Delusional, Deluded

Ollie was in a hotel in Paris when he learned about Ethan's confession. He could not register it all at once. Even knowing what Ethan had done, Ollie found it hard to release his image of Candi as an insane stalker.

He thought back to the moment in the parking lot when he had first become afraid of her. "You said you love me. How can you say you love me then just ignore me?"

It had triggered associations with Glen Close in Fatal Attraction. "I'm not going to be ignored, Dan."

He'd flash forwarded to the end of the film and saw Candi boiling the family pet. He'd wanted to run. He hadn't even tried to listen.

"You wrote *Meet Me After Midnight* for me."

She had not been delusional; she had been deluded—by Ethan. Ollie still had a file with Candi's e-mail messages on his computer from the stalking case. The psychologist in the case had told him they were the product of her sick mind. He'd had no reason to check them for information or clues as to who had sent them. He'd only glanced at them to confirm it was not his e-mail address and they hadn't come from him.

He sat on his bed with the computer on his lap and started reading the correspondence from beginning to end. It was horrifying. These were love letters written to a stranger in his name. There were references to two-hour online chats that were never recorded. He felt a knot in the pit of his stomach. Blast, that manufactured image, that fictional character, was supposed to be the best public version of himself. It was a persona for him alone to control. It was like seeing his worst fear realized; the damn character had gone off and had a life of his own without him.

No wonder Ethan had been so anxious to run interference with this fan. Ethan had appeared at the show in San Diego because he knew Candi would be there and what she was expecting. He had tried to keep them apart so they would never learn the truth. He spoke to her on the phone when Ollie was avoiding her call. What if Ollie had picked up the phone that day? Would he have figured it out? Would she have accepted his rejection and stayed home? Was Ollie's cowardice to blame?

Had they really spoken so little that night that there were no signs? He found it difficult to recapture a pure recollection of that night. His memory had been tainted by what came after. For a long time his night with Candi had been recorded as the first episode in a stalking nightmare. He made Candi retroactively sinister. Intellectually he knew he had felt something different at the time. It had been light and fun. He had enjoyed himself and been grateful for her company. Yet even though he knew this, he couldn't quite bring that feeling back.

The hint of voyeurism that he saw in her that night had become ominous and threatening. He had convinced himself that he'd felt just as anxious about it in the moment. He hadn't. It had been a provocative, sexy kick. Now it was something else again. He finally understood why she wanted to know what he looked like jerking off. The missing chat logs had to be full of cybersex. She wanted to connect the physical man to her virtual partner from the chats. Ollie suddenly remembered her talking about his computer and how she could picture him writing e-mail. Why hadn't that been a clue?

It hit him all at once. He had been her unwitting rapist. He'd taken her to bed under false pretenses. She'd had no idea what she was doing. Ollie had never had any respect for men who took advantage of women. Sure, he enjoyed casual sex, but the women were always more than willing. It was the consent that gave it all meaning. Candi had not given her consent, not in any meaningful way. He was overcome by a wave of nausea. It was like waking up from one of those disturbing dreams where you killed your best friend or had sex with your mother. You weren't conscious, and weren't responsible for it, but you felt dirty anyway.

What made it even worse was the memory of what happened in the parking lot. He had been so determined to get away from her, to avoid any responsibility. "It was a fuck." He must have seemed like a monster. As he wondered at his inability to pick up any clues from a woman who was right in front of him, his mind drifted back to Mandy. He had not known she was having an affair. He didn't realize he was not supporting her in her dreams. He had no idea that she was ready to leave until she was gone. He had always believed he was good to women. Now he wondered how many he had never even seen.

*****

A few days later, Ollie spoke to his lawyer about pressing charges against Ethan. His lawyer advised him not to have any contact with "the girl" because something he said might be used in an expensive lawsuit against him.

"I know you feel bad about what happened," the lawyer said, "but you're not legally responsible."

"Legally responsible?" Ollie said. "What about morally?"

"Morally isn't my department," the lawyer said. "You need to call a preacher for that."

"You don't need to be religious to know there is such a thing as sin," Ollie said. "I bet half of the evils in the world are done by people who didn't know any better, who weren't 'legally responsible.' She fell in love with an image I created. I gave Ethan all the passwords. I set it all in motion."

"It's possible," the lawyer said. "I'm just trying to protect your interests."

"Isn't it in my interest to be a human being? I wronged someone. I need to atone."

"Like I said, that's a moral question."

"And the law has nothing to do with morality?"

"Not a lot," the lawyer said. "I actually like to think of the law as the last line of defense when morality has failed. It's one step above anarchy."

"I don't want to be off the hook," Ollie said. "I need to make things right. I need you to help me."

Homecoming

Even with Ethan's confession, Candi was not released from the hospital right away. You can't just let a patient go because you made a mistake; there are forms and legal procedures. It was almost a month before Candi was able to check out of the hospital and return to "her old life." Candi didn't mind. She was relieved that she was not thrown back into the world right away. She had no idea what she was going back to.

She could remember the plans she'd made for her life when she graduated from high school. The path had seemed so clear, get an education, get a good job, fall in love and get married. That plan had fallen apart long ago. She'd kept going anyway out of pure momentum because she didn't know what else to do. Then everything blew up. It was as if she had been following a road until it ended, found herself lost, and when she turned back to look behind her the road she had followed had vanished, too.

Her therapy sessions with Dr. Molina continued without a beat. The doctor acknowledged that a bit of a mistake had been made but saw no reason to stop the sessions.

"You probably have a lot of anger to work out," Dr. Molina said, "over what we all put you through."

Candi should probably have lashed out at her doctor. Instead they both laughed. What else can you do? They were both just playing their roles in a system that was bigger than either of them.

On the day she was released. Dr. Molina gave her a card, apologized for everything she'd gone through, and offered Candi free sessions in her private practice.

"To deal with all of this."

Candi would go on to meet with Dr. Molina from time to time over the next year. She was a good doctor when she wasn't operating under false assumptions, but eventually Candi came to realize she didn't want a pro to help her keep an even keel. Friends were much better.

Jackie picked Candi up at the hospital. "I knew we'd prove you didn't do what they said!"

Candi knew this was not true, but she let Jackie think she believed her. Now that everyone knew she'd been the victim (her story was all over the news again) accepting help was much less demoralizing, and she was grateful her sister was there.

When Jackie handed Candi the key to her apartment, Candi almost burst into tears. She had never thought holding a set of keys could seem like such a sign of trust. Jackie offered to stay with Candi for a few days while she got used to things, but Candi wanted to be alone.

"I love you," Candi said.

"I love you too."

Candi stood and waved as Jackie drove off, and for the first time she could remember since the arrest she was alone.

Opening the door to her apartment, she gazed on a room that was at once comforting and familiar and entirely foreign. It was her home, her stuff, and yet it belonged to a version of her that no longer existed. The first thing she did was to pull the poster of Blast off the wall and throw it away. Then she took her prescription bottle out of her purse and set it on the table next to the computer. The medical staff had advised her not to go cold turkey on the meds. So she was reducing the dosage a bit each day. She felt light-headed and anxious and sometimes broke into fits of crying for no particular reason. She hadn't slept for days. The doctors told her that would pass and she would feel like herself again soon. She couldn't imagine such a thing. She'd gotten used to thinking of parts of her personality as symptoms. Even though she knew the truth, she had not hallucinated anything; she couldn't shake the notion that everything that had happened in her life up to that point had been some kind of weird dream.

Her furniture was real enough. It belonged to her. She could hear the Whoop-whoop-whoop! woman through the wall as she always had. She went into her room and looked at the clothes in her closet. They'd been purchased to fit into the corporate structure of a job that she would never return to. She'd put on weight in the hospital, a side effect of the medication. Her wardrobe didn't fit her literally or figuratively any more. She thought about the intensity with which she'd worked out in the month leading up to her meeting with Blast. She didn't think she could bring back that kind of motivation without a clear goal to drive her; a bigger dress size seemed more realistic.

She decided to finish watching the episode of Project Runway from the day she was arrested. She thought that maybe this would stitch the two ends of her life back together. She sat down on the couch and turned on the television. As she watched, her experience in the hospital faded into a strange nightmare, but the two ends of her life did not entirely meet.

It was three days before she had the courage to log onto her computer and check her e-mail. It took 20 minutes to download months' worth of spam, messages of concern from friends, and requests from reporters. She read a few messages, lost patience, and deleted the whole lot without responding. Then she went online and deleted all of her social networking profiles. At least for a while she didn't want to relate to the world in that way.

For a couple of weeks Candi couldn't do much more than walk like a zombie through the ashes of her old life. Then one morning she was frying up a couple of eggs and she started to think about John the Baptist. It hit her all at once. She was alive. That same life energy that she'd tried to touch by listening to Blast was still there. In fact, it was all that was left of her. I am not my credit score. I am not my job. I am not my memories. I am not my relationships. I am not my reputation. I am me. I am alive.

I AM.

Nothing that she had been up to that point had to define her any more. Her future was entirely open. Anything was possible. She felt giddy, elated and free. She hoped it was not a side effect of risperidone withdrawal.

Meet Me Before Midnight

The first moment was awkward. When Candi arrived at Ollie's house she could tell he had no idea how to greet her. How do you greet someone who was your lover, who you thought was your stalker, whose life you nearly ruined? Do you hug? Shake hands? He did nothing. Just opened the door and held it wide so she could pass.

"Hi," he said. He smiled, but not too wide. He had dressed up for the occasion, not in his rock-star garb, of course, but his glasses were off, his lenses were in, and he'd touched up his roots to cover the gray.

"Hi," Candi said. She felt awkward too. Although she knew she had never been Ollie's stalker, she could not get over the sense that she was doing something forbidden by being in the same room with him, let alone at his house. She had made a point not to dress up too much. She didn't want it to appear as though she was hoping for any kind of romance. She was wearing a pair of jeans and a black turtleneck accented by an understated necklace. Her weight, though not at the level she'd achieved for the concert, had dropped some. She looked like her old self.

Candi had never expected to hear from Ollie. She was not sure she wanted to. For a long time she had hated him. She had to get accustomed to the idea that he had not rejected her in the way that she thought; he had not been sadistic and played with her head. Still, she had blamed him for allowing his employee the latitude to do what he did and for not taking the time to learn the truth before turning to the law.

She was completely disarmed by his phone call, his regret, and the sincerity of his apology. He had actually broken down and cried. It made her feel guilty for hating him so long.

"There's nothing to forgive," she said. "You didn't know."

That's when Ollie had asked if they could meet face-to-face. She had to

279

laugh as she thought about how she might have felt a few months before if she'd been invited for a face-to-face with Blast. She would have been giddy. Now she agreed with reluctance. She had not wanted to meet at a restaurant or any public place. The case had been a media circus. It had all of the elements news producers love—sex, celebrities, stalking, con-men, the dangers of the internet. It had dominated the news for weeks. Ollie had no more interest in being spotted with her in public than she had. So here she was at the rock star's home.

"You have a nice house," Candi said. Ollie's new home was modest. Its interior design was a bit of a throwback, all earth tones. He had not been living there long, and the place was still full of packing boxes.

"Thanks," Ollie said, kicking a box to one side. "I'm just getting settled in. I'm always on the road, so I'm not here much."

"It's nice," she said. "I like the built-in bookshelves." Candi was a little bit surprised she did not see a television in the room. He must have been more intellectual than she thought. (Actually, the television was in the bedroom.) The shelf was stocked lots of thick books piled on their sides. She assumed that he had set them that way temporarily between unpacking and organizing the books vertically in alphabetical or subject order.

"I read a lot. History mostly." He pointed in the direction of the kitchen. "Would you like a beer or some wine? I have water and juice too, if you'd like."

"Some wine would be nice." This would be her first alcoholic drink since weaning herself from the meds.

"White or red?"

"Red."

In the center of the room was a sofa, which faced an elaborate brick fireplace with a curved mantel. Candi sat down on the sofa as Ollie disappeared into the kitchen.

"I love the fireplace," Candi shouted to the other room.

"Yeah," he called out from the kitchen. "Emma thought I needed a fireplace." He returned to the room with two wine glasses. "Emma's my daughter."

"Yeah, I know," Candi said. "Sorry. Is it weird or stalker-y that I know that?"

"No," he said. He handed one of the glasses to her.

"Thanks," Candi said.

Ollie took a sip from his glass. "Emma thought I needed a 'cozy' home," he said. "I let her make all the big grown up decisions. She's 16."

Ollie sat beside Candi on the sofa. For a moment they both sat in awkward silence and stared at the unlit fireplace. There was a painting balanced against the brick that seemed destined to be placed in a prominent spot above the mantel. It was an abstract work with shades of orange and blue. It reminded Candi of the place where the sea meets the sky as the sun sets.

"I like the painting," Candi said. "It's kind of contemplative. Is it a famous artist?"

"I don't really know much about that. The woman at the gallery said it had good resale value. Like a used car." He smiled. The smile reminded Candi that he was the same man whose photo she had stared at so many times.

"It's not an investment," he went on, "I just liked it. I think the valuing of art is all probably a con anyway. A way to trick people with money into paying artists. You have to promise rich people the art will make them richer. It's all rich people care about."

"You're probably right," Candi said.

There was an awkward pause.

Candi broke the silence. "I heard from Mr. Desmond." Mr. Desmond was Ollie's business attorney, the one who had advised him not to apologize to Candi because she might use it in a lawsuit against him.

"I wanted to thank you for your generous offer," she said, "your financial offer, but I feel strange about accepting it."

"I hope you don't think I'm trying to buy my way out of anything," Ollie said.

"No," Candi said. "It's just a lot of money and this situation is so strange. I don't know how I should feel about it."

"I don't either," Ollie said. "Truth be told, I wasn't sure what I could do. I know Ethan has no money, so you won't get any settlement from him … To get back on your feet. To do something."

"Like I said on the phone, I don't blame you for what happened. I really don't."

"That's one of us then," he said with a deep sigh. "I hope you'll take the money. I don't want to feel like I let all of this happen and I did nothing to try to make it better."

"If it's important to you I will," she said, "but you don't need to."

"That's settled then," he said. "Good."

There was another lull. Ollie took a sip of his wine and looked away. Candi, once again, broke the uncomfortable silence.

"I'm famous now, you know," she said. "All the talk shows are clamoring for me to come on. They offered me a book deal."

"Are you going to take it?"

"No. I don't think so. I don't like being the center of attention. I want to move on. They're persistent though," she imitated a reporter voice, "'We want to give you the chance to tell your side of the story.' "

"Is the book deal lots of money?"

"It's enough money that it's unreal to me, which is good. Because I can turn it down without knowing what I'm missing. You know what I mean?"

"Yeah, I do actually. I've signed some of those contracts. They didn't make me rich in the end. So you're not missing much."

"They don't care about me 'telling my side.' First they were all fascinated by the obsessive, crazy fan. Now that they know I'm not, they want me to come on and cry about how I was a victim. Those are my two choices—crazy slut or victim. I don't want to be either of those things. I just want them to go away."

"That's smart."

"There are worse things than being unknown."

"There are," Ollie said. "There are." He looked away.

Candi took a sip of her wine. There was another pause in the conversation, but it was briefer, and less uncomfortable.

"You know what I hate about all the news stories?" Candi said. "They make me too good. My life before—They say I had this successful job, I had great friends. Everything was great. I was happy. It's like, they need my life before the arrest to be this perfect thing so that my downfall will be more tragic. It's all wrong. My life was a mess. My job was meaningless. The trial didn't make me go bankrupt, I was broke already. The truth is, I didn't lose anything that wasn't worth losing. Ethan stole your identity, but sometimes I feel like these guys, they're stealing mine. They're taking the facts of my life and making them into someone else's story."

"I'm sorry." Ollie looked down at his feet.

Candi turned her head sideways to try to make eye contact. "I wish you'd stop apologizing. I kind of hate it."

"Sorry." He laughed, and smiled the beautiful smile that she had so admired.

"I think sometimes everything has to fall apart for things to end up right," Candi said. "Don't you think? It's a reset button. Seriously, I'd be horrified if I thought you felt sorry for me. I'm actually in a good place. It's true."

"OK." It seemed Ollie was finally feeling comfortable looking Candi straight in the eye.

"You know they actually made me believe I'd written those e-mails myself," Candi said. "I really thought I was delusional. And when I really thought I was mad, I looked in that deep pit, because I'd been told … How do I say this? It's like if I was sick, there had to be some explanation for it, right? And this fantasy, if I dreamed it all up, it had to come from some deep party of my psyche. The deepest part. I mean, it had to be my deepest driving force."

"What did?"

"My fantasy, my delusion, my rock star fantasy. And it hit me. Was that really my deepest desire? The rock star thing? I mean, was that all there was to it? When you think about it, when you really think about it, I didn't exist in my own deep-down fantasy, except in relation to … well, to you. And I thought, didn't I want to be something for myself? Didn't I have a dream for myself? What kind of TMZ, People magazine world is my subconscious? You know what I mean?"

"But you didn't invent it. It's wasn't your dream."

"Yeah but the thing is …" Candi paused, ashamed to finish the thought. "The thing is, it really was. Who told me that is what I should want? Reflected light? When you're a girl, no one tells you that you can be the handsome prince or the rock star. They tell you you can be with the prince. And you eat it up. You don't think you do. You think you're all modern and empowered or whatever, but deep down … And then just when I was starting to make a breakthrough and I was going to be cured, they tell me I was never sick." She made a gesture like an explosion. "I wasn't sick any more, but I still wanted to be cured. I actually learned this real thing about myself, so now what do I do with it? God, ignore me. I'm rambling."

"No, it's very interesting," he seemed to be in deep thought. "I don't imagine it's an appealing thing to live in a rock star's shadow."

Candi smiled. "Are you talking about your wife?"

"Ex-wife," Ollie said, taking another sip of wine. "Very ex."

284

Candi looked at Ollie as if contemplating a painting hanging in a gallery, "You're very shy in real life, aren't you?"

He nodded. "Very." He raised his left hand and ran it through his hair. It was the same simple, unconscious gesture she had watched over and over in the Youtube video. Candi shuddered a little, remembering how much she had once desired him and how her world had revolved around that desire.

Candi leaned in to Ollie. "Can I ask you something? You can tell me it's none of my business. I've been wondering. I mean …do you sleep with a lot of …" she made a circular gesture with her hand as she tried to come up with a decent word. "groupies?"

Ollie wrinkled his face into an apology. (The facial equivalent of a dog with its tail between its legs.) "Is that something you really want to know?" The question was phrased with a British downturn at the end.

Candi gave a half smile and then gazed at the wine glass in her hand. "I suppose not."

"You stand out," Ollie said with a gentle touch on her leg. "You needn't worry about that. I'll remember you."

"I'm sure you will! So while we're on the subject …"

"Oh no!" Ollie laughed and gave a small shrug.

"You're dead cute."

"Thanks." He blushed.

"No, that's what you said to me, 'you're dead cute."

"Oh." His face grew even redder.

"Is that something, I mean, is that just something you say?"

"Something I say?"

"You know, to all the girls."

"What?" He laughed. "No. I don't have a thing I say to 'all the girls.'

There's no script."

Candi turned her hand in a circle in front of her heart. "So that's something real, that was you and me; not Ethan, not fraud, not my imagination. ..."

"That was you and me," he said with a little nod, and then he glanced down at his lap for a moment, then with his head still tilted down, he turned just his eyes in Candi's direction and said, "You are dead cute."

"We should probably change the subject," Candi said gulping down the rest of her wine. Now she could feel the heat of a blush in her cheeks. "I'm glad we get along. I was worried. I thought a lot about that thing you said, about how I could go and tell my friends I slept with a rock star ..."

"I'm so sorry about that," he said. "You must have thought me very cruel."

"What did I say about apologizing!"

"Right, sorry."

"You thought I was a mad stalker."

"It's no excuse for ... I can't help but feel that I took advantage of you."

"No ..."

"Please, let me ... I really do need to say this. It's hard for me to put into words. Bear with me. The fact that I didn't know doesn't change anything. I made assumptions. If I had thought for a moment that night that you weren't consenting of your own free will ..."

"I was. Of course, I was."

"But you didn't know. You were acting under false information."

"Look, we were both operating under false information," Candi said. "If ignorance doesn't absolve you, it doesn't absolve me."

She waited a moment for Ollie to speak. He didn't, so she sighed and went on. "Ethan didn't make me do anything. He gave me an excuse to do what I wanted to do. I wanted to believe it. I mean, I've looked back at what Ethan wrote, and some of it, God, why did I believe it? It was so obvious it couldn't have been you." She did her best Liza Doolittle impression, "Pip pip cheerio, luv. I'm off to play a rock concert."

"You mean I don't really talk like that?" Ollie said with a laugh.

"Yeah. Nobody talks like that," Candi said, shaking her head. "I believed him because I needed to believe him. It seemed so exciting, so glamorous. I don't know why normal life wasn't good enough, but it wasn't."

Again, Ollie sat without speaking.

"So no," Candi continued, "you didn't take advantage of me. I'd have done it. I'd have had the one-night stand with you because you were Blast. I would. It was exactly like you said. I'd just have never had the courage to go for it without Ethan. I'm shy too."

Ollie smiled across his whole face. "Then something worked out well for both of us."

"It was good for you too?" Candi said with a laugh. Her cheeks were beginning to warm from the wine. The odd experience they had shared bound her to this man and she was beginning to feel as though they had been friends for years.

"You know what I read?" she asked. "In some cultures musicians save their best songs for one other person. There are songs for the community, the tribe, but then there are special songs that no one but the beloved gets to hear. So a man is attracted to a woman, and he writes a little tune for her on his flute or whatever and then he waits until they're alone and he plays it to her. If she likes it, she'll follow him and see where things go. But he never plays the song for anyone else. Their whole life, it's her special song. The theme song of their love. No one else can hear it."

"Wow," Ollie said.

"The seductive power of music. It's a real thing." Candi said raising her eyebrows. "Having your own private music has got to be as good as sex, I think, as intimate."

"Maybe more so."

At the very same second they had both become aware of their mutual contemplation of one another. They were both entirely present, not thinking about what to say, not looking to the future, not remembering the past. That may seem like a small thing, but being fully in the moment is exceedingly rare. When two people experience it in each other's presence the sense of connection is profound.

"Do you want some more wine?" Ollie asked. Before she had time to answer, he had picked up the two empty glasses and made a dash to the kitchen.

Candi laughed to herself. This rock star was not at all the powerful and confident presence she'd imagined.

"So, I'm curious," she asked when he returned with the wine. "What was 'Meet Me After Midnight' really about?"

"Nothing really," he said. "Word sounds. I had the music and I just made up a lyric that sounded right. I was going through the divorce, so some of it is about that."

"So it's not really a love song."

"I'm sure it is for some people. But it's not my love song. Listen," he said, "all of this Blast stuff is fake. There's nothing real about it."

"I know. Believe me, I know."

"I like making music, and all of the rock-star nonsense … It's for marketing, so they'll let you keeping making music. I don't …" Ollie trailed off, his eyes rolled upward to the left and he moved his left hand in a circle to show that he was searching for words. Finally he said, "Did you know that the word 'prestige' comes from a word meaning delusion?"

"Really?"

"You know the word 'prestidigitator' like a magician?"

"Yeah."

"It's related to that. Status is a magic trick."

"I'll remember that," Candi said. "I will. But I love Blast anyway. I'll always have a soft spot for him. Like my imaginary childhood friend. I know him. It's you I don't know. But you and I went through something weird together. So we're connected by that."

"I am glad you agreed to come and meet me," he said. "I was afraid you hated me."

"I have to tell you something," Candi said and then she leaned into him and spoke in a stage whisper, "You're dead cute."

He looked down. His expression was vulnerable and sweet and it filled her with affection.

"It's too bad about 'Meet Me After Midnight' though," Candi said. "I hoped it was really about someone. That someone made you feel like that."

"Me too," he said, still glancing down.

It occurred to Candi that Ollie was lonely, and that if she pushed it she probably could have a romance with him. In the same moment she realized, much to her surprise, that she didn't want to. She wanted someone who was there for her, not a man who was on the road most of the year. She wasn't secure enough to be paired with a man who women chased and fawned over. She had been Blast's fan. Things could never truly be equal between them. Next time around she wanted to be with someone who was working to impress her, not someone she thought was impressive.

They spoke for another hour and a half. Ollie told her about the circumstances under which he wrote "Fucking Thursday" and they laughed until their sides hurt. Candi told him about John the Baptist.

"She threw water from the drinking fountain on me when I left the hospital," Candi said. "And you know what? I did feel reborn."

"You know, I did some reading about the real John the Baptist," Ollie said. "He did eat bugs—He ate locusts with honey. And he probably had dreadlocks. So who knows?"

"Who knows?" Candi said.

As the sun was starting to go down, Ollie and Candi parted with a hug.

"I'm glad we did this," Candi said.

"Me too," Ollie said.

They never contacted each other again.

The Moving Party

After Candi had gone, Ollie felt happy and refreshed. He sat in his living room remembering what they had discussed, the idea of illusion and rebooting your life and especially the idea of private music.

He wanted to write a song that was too personal to be shared with the world. A song meant to communicate to only one person, not an invisible mass audience. He got out a pen and a notebook and the first person lyrics flowed through him with no conscious effort.

You kept the pictures
Where did they go?
In the attic somewhere?
The basement below?
Covered in mold
Warping and turning green?

When we spoke together
The royal "we"
It was always you
Talking for me
That was the one thing
The audience never could see

You weren't in my shadow
You cast the light
Out on my own
Am I getting it right?
A crowd of no one
Because you are not watching me

I'm the guy who stutters
When you're not around
The one with his heart

Kicked to the ground
I'm sorry I can't be
All that you want me to be

You go along but I'm still
the non-moving party.

Still in the trance of composition, Ollie took his acoustic guitar and put the lyrics to music. When he was satisfied that he had it down he recorded a rough demo with the microphone on his laptop. He had always thought that when he finished "Non-Moving Party" he would send it to Mandy to let her know how badly she had hurt him. It was only after he looked back at what he had written that he realized that what he'd wanted to tell her was not that he was angry but that he was sorry. He should have told her how much she meant to him back then when she'd needed to hear it. It was too late now.

Curiously, once it was written, he no longer felt the need to send the recording to her. It had become what it was meant to be, a song. For the first time since the divorce had started, he no longer wanted to keep her from moving on. Maybe he was ready to move on too.

One Year Later

"Hello, how are you today!" said the cheery young restaurant host as she held open the heavy door. It took Candi's eyes a moment to adjust to the dim light so she could make out a face to go with the voice.

"I'm just here to pick up a carry-out," Candi said.

"Certainly," said the pretty, teenaged host. "You can get that at the bar."

The restaurant was decorated with formerly utilitarian objects such as washboards, plows and sports equipment rendered useless when they were nailed to the walls. Vintage advertising signs competed for the attention with framed rock concert posters and other pop culture artifacts. It was an interior design version of multi-tasking. Candi wondered if restaurant proprietors received all of the ornaments in a big box, some kind of kit maybe labeled "Restaurant Wall Garbage."

As if the walls were not distracting enough, there were televisions in every corner playing different programs with the sound turned down. Thus the person on one side of the table was treated to a football game while his dining partner watched Jersey Shore. The bar was dimly lit, with the bottles on illuminated shelves that gave the liquor a magical blue glow. On the television in the corner behind the bar a talk show host was giving a silent opening monologue. Candi sat down at the bar without looking at the bartender.

"Hi, how can I help you?" he said.

"Hi," Candi said. "I'm here to pick up my carry out order. The name is Tavris."

"Tavris?" He said it in a strange way. Surprised. The voice was familiar. It took Candi a moment to recognize Ethan. He'd cut the mop of hair that had been his most distinctive feature but he still had the large nose; not much he could do about that, and he was still tall and gangly. They stared at each other for a moment.

"Is that you?" Candi asked.

"Well, yeah, anyone would have to say yes to that," Ethan said. Then he blushed and then he acted as though he was completely intent on wiping the counter.

That was Ethan's sense of humor, Candi thought. She had always liked his sense of humor. With his short hair, he looked more serious and grown up. More her age. "Life humbling experience," she thought.

"You don't live in San Diego any more?" Ethan asked without looking up from the counter.

"No, I got a job here in Los Angeles."

"What do you do?"

"I'm a credit counselor," Candi said.

"That must be tough, dealing with all those people in debt."

"Actually, I really like it," Candi said. "I feel like I make a real difference in people's lives. Sometimes people come in, they're up to their eyeballs in debt, and they're absolutely ready to commit suicide. The quality of their life has eroded so much. I can help them get their payments reduced, organize things so they can be paid down, declare bankruptcy if they have to. I try to put it in perspective and make it less scary. I feel like I give people their lives back."

"Maybe I should go into that. Does it pay well?"

"It's OK," Candi said. "I just really like the work. What are you doing besides working here?"

"Actually," Ethan said, "Ale and me, we started an online business with Sasha. We're selling her hippie gear. When we sell enough, we want to open a real store. Only problem is Sasha keeps running off to follow these jam bands. So she's not a great partner. Ale's back in school, but I really want to run my own business. I think that's the future."

"So you didn't go to jail?" Candi asked. "I mean, I heard they charged you."

"Criminal impersonation and identity theft," Ethan said. "Criminal impersonation, it's what they call a 'wobbler.' That means a judge can charge you with either a felony or a misdemeanor. It's his choice. I pled guilty and kissed up to the judge so he thought I was a nice boy. Suit and tie. Probation. I'm still working off the fine, though. The tips help."

"That must have been a relief," Candi said.

"Yeah."

"Not going to jail."

"Oh, yeah. That too."

"That too?"

"Well, I meant it was a relief to plead guilty."

"Really?"

"Yeah. It was. When they charge you and give you a punishment, I mean, punishments end, you know? Getting away with it; that never ends."

"Hmm," Candi said. "Funny how the world works, isn't it? I got sent to jail and you didn't. I guess being gullible is the bigger crime."

Ethan reached under the bar and picked up a glass.

"They're still making up your order," he said. "It'll be a few minutes. Do you want a drink or something? On me?"

"Water's fine."

Ethan poured the water and slid the glass over to Candi. He tapped his fingers on the counter. Candi looked up at the TV screen. At some point the pause got a bit too long and they both started to speak at once.

"Listen ..."

"You know ..."

"You first," Candi said.

"I was going to say, I'm sorry about what I did," Ethan said. "It got out of hand, but I didn't mean any harm by it. I really did like you a lot. I only wanted to play at being a rock star so you'd like me."

"You're too hard on yourself, Ethan," Candi said. "You don't need to be a rock star for people to like you. I thought you were kind of cute, actually."

"You did?"

Candi sighed. "You put me through a lot. By all rights, I should hate you for the rest of my life."

"I know. I really am sorry."

"I tried to write to you once," Candi took a sip of her water.

"You did?"

"I wrote to the ollieblast address, but it bounced back."

"Yeah," Ethan said. He was still wiping imaginary spills from the bar. "I had to close that. What were you going to say?"

"The truth is, sometimes I kind of miss talking to Blast." She put air quotes around the word Blast. "He made me laugh."

"I wrote those messages. He still exists."

"I know you wrote them," Candi said. "But Ethan, you can't think that I could fall in love with you because of that. I don't know you any more than I knew Ollie. You were playing a part. I fell in love with a fictional character, not with you. And, come on, knowing for a fact that I can't trust you, that's not a great place to start a relationship. I would have to be an idiot, don't you think? It could never happen. You have to know that."

"It all got out of hand. I wish I could undo it."

"You know, what you said about Ollie still existing, I don't think it's true. In the hospital, I had this roommate who though she was John the

296

Baptist …."

"Yeah. You said. You shouted it at me."

"Oh. That's right. Well, she was kind of like you. She chose to be someone who already existed instead of coming up with her own identity."

"I'm not like that, though. I knew I wasn't him."

"Ollieblast was real in a weird way, wasn't he?" Candi said. "But he wasn't Ollie and he wasn't you either. He was a little of both mixed with some of my own fantasy. I don't know what he was."

"I don't know."

"I was crazy about that guy. And I can't get him back. It's like I knew this person and he died. There was never a funeral. You're like the only other person who knew him. But you're not him."

Out of the corner of her eye, Candi caught a familiar face on the television screen. "Hey, look! Can you up the volume?" she asked pointing to the TV.

"Is that Blast?" Ethan said, squinting at the screen. "Man, this is a weird night."

Ollie was dressed in a deep green velvet jacket in an eighteenth-century style. Candi wondered if it was as heavy as it looked. He had thick black eyeliner and had also scrawled an X on his cheek. He'd cut his hair so it was straight and spiky. He looked healthy and confident, his 'rock 'n' roll self in top form.

"Congratulations on the new album," said the host.

"Thank you," Ollie said.

"It's been a long time since you were up at the top of the charts, and now the album is a huge hit, were you surprised by its success?"

"Yeah, I was really. I didn't think anyone was going to like it. I just wanted to do an honest record. This album was very personal and I wanted to do something I'd be proud of. I didn't care how well it sold."

"It does sound different than some of the songs you've done in the past. And now 'Non-Moving Party' is your first number-one hit."

"It's amazing. I appreciate it more this time around."

"Do you?"

"Of course. I'm older and wiser, I hope." He smiled across his entire face.

"How did the album come about?" the host asked.

"The idea for the album, it started with how I wrote 'Non-Moving Party.' A friend of mine told me that there were some cultures that have private music. It's music you only play for people you are close to. So a man will compose a song for his wife and no one else gets to hear the song but the two of them. I wanted to write music that way, with that kind of intimacy; as if the only audience was one person I cared about. So this is the result."

"Well, your audience is slightly bigger than one."

"It has been, yes. It's been a pleasant surprise."

"That's great. So the album is called 'Identity Theft,' I assume that is related to the stalker case that got a lot of media attention last year. Can you talk about that a little bit?"

"Man this is weird," Ethan muttered.

"It wasn't really a stalker case. That's the point. It was a case of mistaken identity. I had a guy who worked in my office who took it on himself to write to fans in my name and unfortunately he fooled one young woman into thinking that I was in love with her. So when she came to talk to me in person, talking about things I never said, I thought she was delusional. She'd been arrested as a stalker before I learned what had happened. It was the kind of situation … it had a real impact on me. It affected the way I think about everything—relationships, who to trust, the assumptions I make about people. So all of that runs through everything I've written in the past year. I'm still dealing with all of that."

"Sounds like it was scary."

"It was educational."

"So we're going to have you perform the title track here in a minute." The studio audience cheered. Ollie nodded to them.

"There is a line I love in this song," the host said, "'Reality was strange to me but fantasy was worse.' What does that line mean?"

"Be careful what you dream of," Ollie said, "that's what the line means. Because fantasies have a way of disillusioning."

Candi's attention was pulled back to the room by Ethan. "Here's your order," he said, setting a plastic bag down in front of her. Candi paid for her meal and thanked him, but she didn't make a move to get up.

"I'll be damned," Candi said, shaking her head. "He really did write a song for me."

"Isn't this totally weird?" Ethan said. "You and me here, and him on TV?"

"It is weird," Candi said. They stared at one another for a moment. "Be careful what you dream of, do you think that's true?"

"I don't know," Ethan said.

"No, I don't think it's true," Candi said. "I think, maybe, you should be careful of not dreaming. People don't dream enough. You have 200 channels and so many stories and they're all the same, the same story, the same ending." Candi raised an eyebrow and smiled on one side of her face. "If I was Lord High Commander of the world, I would make a law that TV shows and movies and books couldn't repeat a story that had been done to death."

Ethan smiled. He seemed to relax. "Is that before or after you outlaw paperwork?"

"Before, I think," she said. "Then people would get their imaginations and their brains back. I have a feeling the two things are related, actually. How much power do I have as Lord High Commander? Can I just wave a wand and make people more imaginative and more compassionate?"

"Sure. Why not."

"Then that's what I'd do." She stood up. "Well, I guess I should get going. I don't want my food to get cold."

She turned to walk out the door, then she stopped and turned back. "Can I ask you something? Do you really like Thai food?"

"Yeah."

"So that story about the spicy pad thai..."

"That was my story."

"And about being inspired by the Beatles?"

"That, that one was me trying to be Ollie."

"So you're not a Beatles fan?"

"I'm not a Beatles fan," Ethan said. "I like Green Day. Nirvana's cool. Me and Ale, we go to a lot of live shows. There's this one band ..."

"Well, anyway ..." Candi said. She shrugged and began to walk away again. Ethan called after her. "I'm not a Beatles fan," he said again.

Candi stopped and turned back to him. He went on, "I don't eat bangers and mash. I've never eaten bangers and mash. I'm not even sure if that's food. I also don't know what 'Bob's your uncle' means. I've never written a song. The only musical instrument I've ever played was a recorder in 4th grade, and I never could get the notes right. I melted it on a campfire and my mom almost killed me. The stuff I said about writing a song for you, it's, well, it's what I wish I could have written for you. You know, if I could write songs. And the rest of the stuff ... My favorite TV show really is CSI, the sex fantasies, those were mine, and I really do feel like a loser most of the time; that was true. I can't afford to move out of my mom's basement. I can't even keep a stupid job answering fan mail without almost ending up in jail. If you liked Ollie because he was a cool rock star, well, that wasn't me. But if what you liked about Ollie was that he was kind of a dorky loser—that's the part that was me." Ethan shook his head, let out a heavy sigh and said, "Yeah, that makes sense." He went back to wiping the immaculate counter top.

"Thanks," Candi said. "That's good to know … Well, I really should get going." But she didn't move. She stood for a moment smiling at the tile floor. Finally, just before she walked out she said, "You know, I still have the same e-mail address … if you ever wanted to write."

About the Author

Laura Lee is the author of the novel *Angel,* a children's book *A Child's Introduction to Ballet* and 15 non-fiction books with major and mid-size publishers including *The Elvis Impersonation Kit, Broke is Beautiful, Don't Screw It Up!* and *The Pocket Encyclopedia of Aggravation.* She divides her time between writing and producing coast-to-coast ballet master class tours with her partner, the artistic director of the Russian National Ballet Foundation.

www.ingramcontent.com/pod-product-compliance
Lightning Source LLC
Chambersburg PA
CBHW052021240626
47153CB00006B/1905